JONATHAN PINNOCK

A QUESTION OF TRUST

A MATHEMATICAL MYSTERY, BOOK TWO

To Gail, as always

This edition published in 2019 by Farrago,
an imprint of Prelude Books Ltd,
13 Carrington Road, Richmond, TW10 5AA, United Kingdom

www.farragobooks.com

ISBN: 978-1-78842-152-2

Chapter 1

The smell didn't just hit you when you walked in the flat: it knocked you to the floor, knelt on your chest and rained blows on your head until you begged for mercy. It was a malevolent synthesis of musty clothes, body odour, rotting food and something under the floorboards that had last drawn breath several months previously. Damp oozed lazily up the walls, leaving a feculent smear of black mould in its wake, and a fine layer of loose plaster from the bulging ceiling dusted the threadbare carpet. It was a home fit for a serial killer.

At some point in its recent past this spacious garden flat had been divided into two by a flimsy cigarette-paper-thin partition, which succeeded in muting neither the regular vituperative arguments between the young couple in the other flat, nor the rhythmic pounding of enthusiastic, vigorous and often quite experimental make-up sex that inevitably followed.

I navigated my way past the end of the bed that constituted the principal part of our flat's suite of furniture, taking care to avoid the quadrant of uneaten pizza lying on top of its box and the crusty remains of a bowl of cornflakes.

I removed my jacket and flung it on top of the rest of my clothes in the corner and sat down on the far side of the bed. Through the half of the French window on our side of the partition, I stared out at what once must have been a neat little patio and was now a communal lavatory for a gang of feral cats. A mangy ginger tom wandered over and acknowledged my presence by lifting its tail and spraying the lowest pane of glass.

I looked at my watch. It was eight o'clock in the evening. A damp, gloomy twilight was settling on North London and I had nowhere else to go. My stomach rumbled and I briefly considered eating that last wedge of pizza, but I couldn't remember how long it had been lying there. Or whether it even belonged to me.

There was a soft 'clunk' and the lights went out. Cursing under my breath, I fished around in my pocket for a coin to put in the ancient meter but found nothing apart from a small handful of lint and a rusty paperclip.

'Bollocks,' I said.

I kicked off my shoes and swung my feet onto the bed. I lay on my back in the dark thinking about what had happened a few hours earlier and what on earth it could possibly mean.

The door burst open and a figure stumbled into the room. I heard it grope around for the light switch, find it and try to flick it on.

'Fuck,' said the figure, flicking the switch back off.

There was a sound of movement, and then a dull thud as the figure stubbed its toe on the edge of the bed.

'Fucking bastard fuck,' said the figure.

There was more movement and some rustling of coins and clothing, followed by a click as the meter sprang into life and then finally the lights came back on. A stocky female figure with cropped purple hair was staring down at me from the end of the bed. It was currently standing on one leg and trying to peel a slice of pizza off the bottom of its shoe.

'Hi, Ali,' I said.

'Good to see you're working hard,' said Ali, throwing the pizza back onto the top of the box and wiping her hands.

This seemed unfair. 'At least there's something you can do,' I said, sitting up. 'There is literally nothing I can do right now.'

'Yeah, yeah, I know. I have a really fucking easy time of it right now.'

'I didn't mean that.'

'Listen, PR boy. I'm doing all the heavy lifting here. The only reason I tolerate your presence in my life at the moment is a nagging suspicion that you know something and that one day you're going to let it slip.'

'Oh, come on. We're not going over this again surely, are we?' I looked at her. It seemed we were.

'You were there on the night it happened.'

'I wasn't. I'd gone to visit Lucy.'

'Remind me again who Lucy is,' said Ali.

'My ex.'

'Oh yes. And why had you gone to visit her?'

'To pick up some papers. The ones that we thought had been blown up.' These belonged to the deceased Vavasor twins, Archie and Pye. The papers were originally in a briefcase that exploded during a hostage exchange in the middle of the Somerset Levels between myself and a gang of Belarusian mafiosi. It was also entirely possible that the papers had in fact been removed prior to the explosion and were now in the hands of the mathematical genius who had planted the bomb.

Life had seemed simpler then.

Unfortunately, however, life had moved on, which is how we'd ended up in this mess.

'Still seems fishy,' said Ali. 'You'd had an argument with Dorothy, hadn't you?'

'No. Not really.'

'Not really.'

'No.' I didn't think I had. I'd gone over our last conversation several thousand times since that night, and sifted through every last grain of nuance in search of clues, and I still couldn't work out what had gone on.

'Anyway,' said Ali, 'in answer to your unspoken question, no, I have not had a good day.'

'I was afraid to ask.'

'As you obviously know, I am what is known in software circles as a fucking wizard. There is no room for debate about this. I am a total rock star. But believe me, it is a fucking nightmare on stilts trying to do any hardcore bug-fixing in a Linux VM running via the Cloud on a clapped-out public library PC running an outdated version of – oh Jesus, I can barely bring myself to say the word – Microsoft-arsing-Windows.' She looked at her watch and paused for a moment. 'I was due to call Spokane around now. Tell them we were ready to deliver the final version. Maybe even get them to advance us some of their hard-earned dollars. But we're still a long way away from that. Going to have to cry off.'

'Have you told them about—?'

'No, and I don't fucking intend to tell them. As far as Spokane is concerned, we are still sitting in a nice, spacious top-end Hoxton office with a metric kilofucktonne of nice, spacious top-end equipment.'

'You're going to have to tell them eventually,' I said.

'I know, PR boy. But not until I've got everything restored to its former glory.'

'Yes, but how long's that going to take?'

'Just got a few more fixes to sort out.'

'Are you sure?'

'Listen, you. Who's the fucking wizard here, me or you? I know how close I am. Would have finished it tonight if my time hadn't run out and I hadn't had to give up my seat to some hairy wanker wanting to get stuck into his evening trolling and porn session. If only we hadn't missed that last backup, I wouldn't have needed to go through this shit.'

'Don't beat yourself up about it,' I said. In truth, I wasn't that bothered about how Ali felt. It was more a case of trying to reduce the level of anger in a small room.

'I'm not going to,' she said. 'It wasn't my fucking fault.'

'Move over,' said Ali, climbing into bed. I shifted my weight as best I could. The mattress responded by developing a kind of spongy gravity well in the middle that tried very hard to haul me back to where I'd come from. Our landlord had taken great care to point out to us that it

9

was a memory foam mattress, but it was clearly unable to focus on anything but the bad ones. It was a mattress with PTSD.

'I did find out something else today,' said Ali.

'Oh yes?'

'My registration for *vavasorology.com* got approved.'

'You what?' *Vavasorology.com* was the place on the internet where people obsessed with the aforementioned Vavasor twins hung out. Given Ali's past hostility to the very mention of their names, the idea that she had gone and registered herself there was utterly absurd. No wonder she hadn't mentioned it earlier.

'Yeah, don't laugh,' said Ali.

'I don't know what to say.'

'Maybe stick to saying nothing for the time being, pal. Because it didn't take me long to find out a few things there. Things that maybe you should have found out for yourself and saved me the trouble.' She paused. 'Jesus, have you seen some of the crap on that place?'

'Yeah, I know.'

'Mental. Absolutely mental. Believe me, I have seen some weird shit on gamer forums, but that lot are on a whole other level. Anyway, I have two interesting facts for you. Interesting fact number one coming right up.'

'Go on.'

'User *EulerIsGod* is no longer registered.'

'What?' I sat up. This was extraordinary news. *EulerIsGod* was Dorothy's user name on the forum.

'Dot's not on there any more, Tom.'

'But what does that mean? Is she dead?' A cold sweat was running down the back of my neck.

'No, Tom, she's not dead, however much I might want her to be. You don't just drop off a forum if you peg out. The online world's full of zombie accounts. Give it a few years and the dead bastards will outnumber the living. Bet you anything there are whole fucking teams of guys in Google and Facebook trying to work out how to make money out of the stiff demographic. No, what it means is that she's most definitely still alive. Because she's gone to the trouble of deregistering herself, right?'

'Jesus,' I said. 'You're right. But that's brilliant!' I thought about this for a moment. 'Then again,' I added, 'it does mean we've got one less way of trying to get in touch with her.'

'Exactly.'

'I can't even check to see if she actually read any of my personal messages, now, can I?' Ali was right. I'd got lazy. After the first few desperate weeks, I'd pretty much stopped checking what was going on in the forum. It was all too painful.

'No. I think we can assume she probably didn't, pal. Like she probably hasn't bothered reading any of our emails, texts or anything else. She may be still alive, but the default assumption is that for whatever reason, she has no interest in talking to us. We are currently pretty much dead to her.'

'Bugger.' There was a brief silence. Outside a couple of cats began to yowl at each other. 'You said you had *two* interesting facts,' I said.

'Yes, I did. Did you know there was a Vavasorology convention coming up very soon?'

'What?'

'A Vavasorology convention. Turns out it's a regular thing. Once every year like clockwork. Been on the horizon for months. Lots of folk on the forum pissing themselves with excitement about it, bless their loony cotton socks.'

'I must have missed all that.'

'You miss a lot, pal.'

'That's not fair.'

'Trust me, I'm right on this. As I usually am. Look, do you want to know about the convention or not?'

'Of course I do. So where and when is this thing?'

'At the Dog and Fishbone in Clerkenwell. Saturday morning, starting at eleven a.m. That's the day after tomorrow, in case you're not sure what day of the week it currently is.'

'Gosh,' I said, choosing to ignore the slight. 'That's—'

'Fucking awesome? Yeah, you're right. I'll take fucking awesome.'

'OK, OK,' I said. 'But this could unlock everything. Couldn't it?'

'It could do. Or we might end up spending a day pissing about with a bunch of fucking fruitcakes.'

'We? You're proposing to come along as well?'

'Like I said, I don't trust you, pal. One, I don't trust you not to fuck it up, and two, I don't trust you, full stop.'

'Right. Look, you don't have to. Really, I can handle it on my own.'

'No, you can't. And remember, I've got more skin in this game than you. My fucking livelihood's at stake.'

'That's not true,' I said. 'I was in a relationship with Dorothy, remember?' I paused. 'Maybe I still am,' I added.

'I don't think so, pal. Not after what Dot's done to us.'

I couldn't think of anything to say. Ali was right, of course. I was still struggling to come to terms with it, but Dorothy had betrayed everything we'd ever had. She and Ali had built up their business from nothing together, and she and I had built up... well, *something* together. Even if we hadn't been together long enough to figure out exactly what it was.

'Anyway, I've registered us both, so there's fuck all you can do about it. Look, I'm tired,' said Ali, turning the light out. 'Got a busy day ahead tomorrow, so try not to snore. Keep to your side of the bed, pal, and no snoring, no farting and no spooning.'

I turned over and tried to get to sleep. But I still couldn't stop thinking about what had happened earlier. Because Ali wasn't the only one of us who'd been using a public library computer that day. I'd grabbed a slot myself to check my emails, and one of them turned out to be an invitation to connect with an old acquaintance on LinkedIn. An acquaintance called Rufus Fairbanks. The only problem was that, last time I'd seen him, he was, beyond a shadow of a doubt, dead.

Chapter 2

Halfway through the afternoon on the day that Dorothy vanished, she and Ali were in the midst of a massive row. There had been a lot of these lately and I'd put it down to the pressure they were under to deliver the final prototype of their latest game to their investors. But as I walked into the office, there seemed to be more to it this time.

'The thing is,' said Dorothy. 'I'm not sure I even trust you any more.'

'WHAT?' said Ali. 'What do you mean, Dot, you don't trust me any more? I'm not sure I trust you, to be fucking honest, pal.'

'Hey guys,' I began, trying to adopt the position of a neutral conciliator.

'And you can fuck off, too,' said Ali, before I could say anything else. 'In fact,' she continued, stabbing a finger in my direction, 'in fact, now I come to think about it, which is something I should have done a LONG time ago, all this shit started when you rocked up. What have you been saying to her, PR boy?'

'He hasn't said anything, Ali,' said Dorothy.

'Well, I won't contradict that. He hasn't done anything, either, since you put him on the payroll. Against my wishes, I would remind you, Dot.'

'Hang on a minute,' I began again.

'Just shut the fuck up while we're arguing, will you?' said Ali. 'Jesus, there are too many people in this office right now. I can't hear myself think.'

'Look, Ali,' said Dorothy, 'this hasn't got anything to do with Tom.'

'THANK you—' I said.

'—at least, not directly,' continued Dorothy.

'WHAT?' I wasn't following this at all. Both of them turned and glared at me. I decided to go and sit at the battered second hand table that passed for my desk. Ali and Dorothy continued their heated conversation with muted voices and I struggled to pick up any of it, until Ali suddenly slammed her hand down on Dorothy's desk.

'Right, that's it,' she said. 'I'm off.'

'What?' said Dorothy. 'You can't just waltz out of here.'

'Fucking can and fucking will.'

'But what about—'

'Well, if you don't trust me, it hardly frigging matters, does it?' She paused. 'Nah, don't worry, I'll be back tomorrow. Got sent these tickets to a gig in Manchester. Friend of the bass player.' She turned and looked at me. 'And no, it's not anyone you'll have heard of, Mr Music Geek.'

I'd once made the mistake of telling Ali that my first ambition had been to be a music journalist and she took great delight in constantly reeling off the names of bands

I'd never heard of. To be honest, I'd never checked to see if any of them actually existed, so it's entirely possible that she was just very good at making up plausible names for bands. Possibly even entire genres.

'But you said you were going to finish debugging the opening this evening,' said Dorothy.

'Yeah, well,' said Ali, 'I didn't expect to get a chance to see this bunch. It's the only date on their tour in the UK and—'

'Fine, fine. I'll do it instead.'

'No, look, I can do it tomorrow.'

'I don't know if it can wait that long.'

'It fucking can and it fucking will.'

'Oh, I give up,' said Dorothy.

'You and me both,' said Ali, gathering her things together. Then she headed out of the room, giving the door a good slam on the way out.

There was a long period of silence after she left, punctuated only by occasional bangs and screams emanating from Dorothy's computer as she ran tests on various aspects of the game they were developing. I went over to her desk and sat down opposite her, waiting for the right moment to say something.

'You should put a notice up at the end of the game saying that no zombies were harmed during its development,' I said eventually.

'Hmmm,' said Dorothy. 'Sorry, what?'

'You're supposed to laugh. I made a joke.'

'Oh, right. What did you say again?'

'Never mind. It wasn't worth repeating.'

'OK.'

'Look, what's wrong?'

'There's nothing wrong, Tom.'

'Well, what was all the stuff with Ali about?' I said.

'It's nothing to do with you.'

'If it's to do with you, it's to do with me.'

'What? Are we some kind of joint organism now?' said Dorothy. 'Do I not get to have my own problems any more? Am I supposed to have given up any pretence to agency?'

'Well, we are supposed to be in a relationship.'

'Yeah, well.'

'Yeah, well what?'

'Look, this isn't a good time to be having this conversation. Odd things have been happening. I'm not sure who I can trust any more.'

'You can trust me.'

'Oh right, I'm, like, TOTALLY convinced now. No, the only thing stopping me from suspecting that you're behind whatever's going on is that I don't think you're capable of anything to do with it.'

'Jeez, thanks,' I said.

'Look, I'm just a bit stressed and very busy and you're getting a little bit annoying right now. Give me some space, OK?'

'Fine, Fine,' I said, putting both hands up and moving away. I went and stood by the window, staring down at the commuters heading home.

'Get us a coffee, will you?' she called out. 'Instant will do.'

I went into the kitchen and made a couple of strong black Nescafés. I took one over to her. She seemed to be on the verge of telling me something important, when my phone rang. It was Lucy, my ex.

'Hello?' I said, cautiously. I still hadn't managed to pay her back for the considerable damage I'd done to her car during that chase through the lanes outside Bristol that turned out not to be a chase at all. Then again, she still owed me for the emotional damage caused by her subsequently dumping me and installing a Belarusian pathologist and Zumba teacher in my stead, so I felt we were sort of even. But it's possible she didn't see it that way, given that Arkady had vanished following the incident with his compatriots in the middle of the Somerset Levels and I'd ended up in a relationship with Dorothy. Rumour had it, however, that she was now going out with a junior proctologist, so her life wasn't all bad.

'It's me,' said Lucy. 'Is that you?'

'Yes, it's me. You OK?'

'Yeah, fine. Look. Um. Just had something delivered here for you.'

'What sort of thing?'

'Just a big envelope, that's all.'

'OK, can you send it on to me? I'll pay for postage.' I wasn't expecting anything, but it was possible I'd forgotten something. Life had been a bit complicated lately.

'Well, um—'

There was a long pause. This was clearly not going to be a straightforward transaction.

'What's the problem?' I said.

'It's just… look, the writing on it's sort of a bit Cyrillic.'

'Sorry?'

'Y'know. Russian. Or Belarusian.'

'Huh?' This was getting weirder by the second.

'I know,' said Lucy. 'Look, do you mind if I open it? It might be from—'

Ah. That was it. 'I thought you were over him,' I said.

There was a long silence. Across the desk from me, Dorothy muttered 'Shit' under her breath and clattered furiously at her keyboard.

'Arkady was special,' said Lucy eventually. 'I mean, don't get me wrong, Piers is lovely, and please not a word to him about this, but—'

'OK,' I said. 'You can trust me. It's not that I'm likely to bump into him, is it?'

'No. So then. Is it OK for me to open it? I promise I won't look at anything personal.'

I considered this. Given that I had no idea who might have sent it to me, I couldn't see much harm in her opening it. 'Go on then,' I said.

There was a brief rustling on the other end of the line, then a sigh of disappointment.

'What's wrong?' I said.

'Oh, it's just a load of mathematical stuff,' said Lucy. 'Load of old gobbledygook.'

'Sorry? Say that again.'

'Load of mathsey stuff.'

'Hold on a moment,' I said. This was suddenly very exciting. 'Any idea where they've come from?'

There was a pause where I imagined Lucy turning the envelope over and over in her hand. 'Nope,' she said.

For a moment, I considered telling Dorothy straight away, but then it struck me that it would be far more impressive if I simply walked in the office and dropped the papers down on her desk in front of her. I imagined her saying to me 'What's this?' and me then giving the coolest of cool shrugs and saying, 'Oh, no biggie, just the Vavasor papers.'

For that was what they had to be. There was nothing else they could possibly be.

'Can I come and get them now?' I said to Lucy. 'I mean, right now? Tonight?'

'I suppose so,' she said. 'Are they that important?'

'To some people, yes, very much so. So, whatever you do, please make sure you hang onto them until I get there.'

'OK.' She still sounded disappointed about Arkady.

'I'll be there as soon as I can,' I said, ending the call. 'Right,' I said to Dorothy, pushing back my chair and standing up, 'I'm going to be off now.'

'Where are you off to?' said Dorothy, looking up with a slightly baffled expression on her face.

'Um… Lucy's.'

'Who's Lucy?'

'Um… my ex. You remember. You met her that time.'

'Oh. But she's in Bristol.'

'Yes.'

'And you're going now?'

'Yes. Look, I know it looks odd, but trust me—'

'No, it's fine. Fine. You go and see your ex and I'll carry on working here.'

'No, it's not like that,' I said. 'It's important.'

'I'm sure it is.'

'Don't do this.'

'Do what?'

'What you're doing now.'

'I'm not doing anything, Tom.' She paused. 'Anyway, it's not as if I'm staying in all evening myself.'

'What?'

'I said, I'm going out.'

'You didn't tell me.'

'You didn't ask.'

'Oh.'

'It's just a lecture, that's all. At Imperial. Some new perspectives on the Riemann Hypothesis.'

'Ah.' There was still something not quite right. 'Dorothy, why didn't you mention this before?'

'Good god, Tom, am I supposed to be in your pocket? It's a lecture on something I'm interested in. I didn't ask you because I assumed you wouldn't be interested. You probably wouldn't understand any of it anyway.'

'You could try to explain it to me.'

'I did. More than once.'

'Oh. You still might have told me.'

'I'm not obliged to tell you everything. It's my business, not yours. Or anyone else's for that matter.'

I put my hands up in mock self-defence. 'OK, OK,' I said. 'I didn't mean to—'

'And in any case, I only found out this morning. Got an email from the organiser. I was going to tell you, but I didn't get round to it.'

I put on my jacket and went to kiss her goodbye. She offered me her cheek.

'Dorothy,' I said. 'Don't do this.'

She shook her head and turned back to her work.

It was odd being back in my old flat. Last time I was here, the place was cluttered with Arkady's gym equipment. All that had gone now, to be replaced by piles of cardboard boxes.

'I'm moving out next week,' said Lucy.

I raised an eyebrow.

'Look, forget everything I said about Arkady,' she said. 'He's history. I'm starting a new life with Piers now.'

'Sure,' I said. I'd decided on the journey down that I had no interest in getting involved with the ramifications of Lucy's love life. After all, I was history, too.

'Have you got the papers?' I said.

'Oh, that. Yeah.'

I followed her into the kitchen. The brown envelope was sitting on the table. It was indeed addressed to me, but, as Lucy had said, there was also a load of Cyrillic writing on the back. I used to have a translation app on my old phone but that was before it got smashed up when I was wrestling in the street with a Belarusian mathematician called Maxim, just before he got killed by the Gretzky mafia family.

'Any idea what that all means?'

'Not a clue. I wasn't exactly with Arkady for very long, was I, Tom?'

The way she said it, it sounded like this was my fault. In a way, of course, she was right. If Arkady hadn't got involved with Maxim's brother Sergei's plot to use me to blow up the Gretzkys during that hostage exchange, he might not have had to disappear. Then again, when she started seeing Arkady, she was still supposed to be with me, so on reflection, she was being more than a little unreasonable.

I fished inside the envelope for the papers. As I looked through them, my heart sank. Even with my limited knowledge of mathematics, I could tell these had nothing to do with the Vavasors.

'Well, that was a waste of time,' I said, sitting down at the table. 'These are fakes.'

'How can you tell?'

'I've seen the real ones. Before Arkady's friend Sergei ran off with them before planting a bomb in that briefcase I was carrying around.'

Lucy rolled her eyes. 'Oh god, are you still going on about that?' she said. I don't think she'd ever really believed my account of the affair, mainly because in her mind I wasn't really the kind of person to get involved in bombs and hostage swaps and such like. To tell the truth, I found it quite surprising myself.

'Well, it's true,' I said.

Lucy responded by waving her hands dramatically and stalking off into the living room. I got up and followed her, bringing the envelope with me. I scanned it again for evidence of a courier's label. There didn't seem to be one.

'So, who delivered this thing anyway?' I said.

'I don't know. Some courier. He had a motorbike helmet on.'

'Oh. Did you have to sign for it?'

'No.'

'Why not?'

'I don't know. Sorry, do you want me to run out there and call him back?' She gestured towards the door to the flat.

'No, it's just—'

'Look. I'd just got in from work. The buzzer went. I let them in downstairs. They came up to the flat. They gave me the envelope and then they went off. That's it. Sorry if I didn't ask them if they belonged to the KGB or whatever.'

'OK, OK, I'm sorry. I was just trying to work out who's sent this to me. And why.'

She shrugged. 'Well, I can't help you there. You're the only one who's going to be able to work that one out. You and that whatsername—'

'Dorothy.'

'Yeah, her.' Except I probably wasn't going to mention it now. In fact, there was every chance that our relationship was back on course for the rocks, now that I would no longer be returning to London as the triumphant hero, bearing gifts from afar.

'So, then,' said Lucy, making a vague, sweeping gesture, 'I guess you can sleep on the floor.'

'Still no sofa, then?' I said. This had been something of a bone of contention between us when we were living here together.

Lucy gave a half-smile and shook her head. She didn't do or say anything more, and neither did I. For a few brief seconds, the atmosphere in the flat thickened, the world stood still and I realised that if either of us moved anything more than a couple of nanometres closer to each other, the whole evening might have taken a very different turn. In the event, neither of us did, but over the next few weeks, I wondered more than once if I'd made the right choice.

I still hadn't got through to Dorothy when I got back to the office later on the next morning. As I exited the lift on the fifth floor, the first indication that something was wrong was the fact that the door to the office was wide open. The lock looked as if it had been jemmied open with a crowbar. I stepped inside to find Ali standing in the middle of a completely empty room.

'Where the fuck have you been?' she said, her voice echoing around the bare walls.

'I went to see my ex-girlfriend,' I said. 'Is that a problem?'

'It is when you should have been here.'

'Why? And what's going on? What's happened? And where's Dorothy?'

'Good questions, pal. Well, what's happened is that some bastards have stolen all our fucking equipment.'

'What?'

'Every single computer we had has gone. Including that scuzzy laptop of yours.'

'Everything?'

'Listen, are you fucking deaf? Every. Single. Fucking. Piece. Of. Equipment. Has. Gone.'

'Shit.'

'Also,' said Ali, 'someone has siphoned off every single last penny in the company bank account.'

'What? Where's it all gone?'

'I don't know. They've changed the online password, too, so I haven't been able to find anything out. I only know because I went to try to get some money from the cashpoint just now, and there was absolutely fuck all in the account.'

'Oh my god.' My mind started to go through the implications of this and gave up in panic. 'What's happened to Dorothy?' I said, hoping to change the subject to something that I could deal with.

Ali shrugged. 'No idea. She's vanished. When did you see her last?'

'When I left here yesterday evening. She was due to go out to a lecture.'

'A lecture? A fucking lecture? Since when did Dot go out to lectures when we were up against a fucking deadline?'

An awful thought crossed my mind. 'Do you think she's OK?' I said.

Ali didn't answer straightaway. 'I hope so. Although if this really is her doing, I'll be very happy to oversee her slow, lingering death.'

'What do you mean?'

'I don't know if you've noticed yet, slow boy, but the only one of us three who isn't here is Dot.'

'What are you saying?'

'I'll try again. Look, there are three things that are currently missing from this office—' Ali enumerated on the fingers of her right hand '—one, our equipment, two, all our money, and three, Dot.' She mimed holding her head in her hand as if thinking very hard about a problem. 'Now,' she said, 'what if these three things just happened to be in the same place?'

'Oh, surely not,' I said.

'Think about the money, for one thing. This place was firewalled and VPNd to buggery, and the only other person apart from yours truly who knew the bank details was Dot, so draw your own conclusions.'

'Are you saying it's… no, that's absurd. It can't be her. Couldn't someone have installed, I dunno, a – what do you call them? – key logger?'

'Like I said, we took security VERY seriously. So no, it's not possible. Everything points to Dot.' She paused. 'Wouldn't surprise me if she's gambled the lot away on online poker.'

'What? Are you seriously suggesting that Dorothy's got some kind of addiction?'

'Wouldn't surprise me at all, pal. It's in her DNA, isn't it?'

I looked at Ali, wondering if this was some kind of joke. Whatever it was, it was a bit weird coming from her. 'That's a bit racist, isn't it?' I said.

'That's not what I meant,' said Ali.

'Well, what did you mean?'

'You mean you don't know?'

'What don't I know?'

'She's never told you about Third Uncle? The one who used to run the second-biggest casino in Macau? Our Dot knows a thing or two about the tables.'

'You're kidding.'

'Nope. Straight up. There's quite a few things about her you don't know, pal.'

In some ways, this was the most upsetting part about this, if it was true at all.

'I don't believe she'd do that, though,' I said.

Ali sighed. 'Maybe not,' she said, 'but you've got to admit she's been behaving strangely lately.'

'She's under a lot of pressure.'

'So are all of us. Well, two of us, anyway.' She paused for a moment. 'What about you, anyway?' she said. 'Where were you again last night?' There was a new edge to her voice that could have sliced a loaf of wholemeal bread in two seconds flat.

'I told you. I went to visit Lucy. My ex-girlfriend.'

'Why?'

'I went to pick up the Vavasor papers. Only they turned out not to be.'

'Oh, for fuck's sake.'

'What do you mean?' I said.

'Vavasor fucking papers. I thought that was all over.'

'So did I.'

'Yeah right. Well, it's all a bit fucking convenient, pal.'

'What? You're not suggesting I had anything to do with this, because—'

'I dunno what I'm suggesting, pal,' said Ali. 'All I know is that right now we have no money, no equipment to work on and no fucking Dot to explain what the fuck has just happened. Also, given that we have no money to pay the rent which just happens to be due tomorrow, you can add nowhere to live too.'

'But, hang on, I mean I know it's your money and all that, but don't you have some spare cash lying around we could use?'

Ali gave a sigh as deep as the Atacama Trench. 'I invested everything I had left over in the company,' she said. 'Every. Fucking. Penny.'

'Shit.' I tried to assemble the facts in front of me into some kind of logical order, but none of it fitted together in any sensible shape or form. 'So, what has just happened, Ali?'

She took a deep breath. 'Fuck knows. All I know is that we're in the deepest of deep shit. Right up to our oxters.'

'Right, we need to go to the police,' I said.

Ali frowned at me and shook her head.

'Do you really want to get involved with the police?'

'Sorry, what?' I didn't like where she was going with this.

'Think about it. First thing they'll do if they suspect a crime is break into the office and put forensics to work. Our dabs are all over the place, so they'll want to eliminate them. How do you fancy yours getting into their database?'

'I've got nothing to be afraid of.'

'Sure? No recent deaths on your hands?'

'Ah.'

'Ah bloody ah, pal. Ah bloody ah.'

Ali was referring to the incident where Dorothy and I had been involved in the food-processor-related death of the financier Rufus Fairbanks. For reasons of expediency, we'd taken a decision not to say anything to the authorities about this. Perhaps we should have done. Dorothy had erased all electronic traces of our presence there, but there was every chance that I'd left my prints on the coffee mug I'd been drinking out of, at the very least.

'But it was an accident!' I said. 'And, in any case, he was threatening to kill me.'

'In which case, I'm sure you'd be happy to prove that. Either way, you've got failure to report a crime on your charge sheet already, and that's just for starters.'

'Bugger.' I paced up and down for a while, trying to get my thoughts into some kind of order. However, my thoughts had other plans, which mainly seemed to involve a bacchanalian display of free-form interpretative dance, so I gave up and slumped down again with my back to the wall. Ali joined me. 'What are we going to do?' I wailed. 'We haven't got any money, we haven't got anywhere to live, we haven't got any equipment and… and, oh my god, have we lost all the code, too? Ali, tell me we haven't lost all the code. Ali?'

'No, we haven't lost all the code, pal. First thing a proper software developer does is set up a decent backup strategy. Everything we did was backed up to a central server every half hour.'

I breathed a sigh of relief. 'So, where's the central server?'

Ali waved her arms expansively. 'Here,' she said. 'At least it used to be.'

I must have been really tired by this point, because the penny failed to drop for a good ten seconds. 'Oh shit,' I said eventually. 'So that's gone too?'

'Yep,' said Ali. 'However, it was set to upload everything to the Cloud on a regular basis. Or at least I hope so. Dot was in charge of all that.'

'Ah, right. So that's all sorted. All we need to do is get you some new equipment and you're up and running again.'

'I like the spin you're putting on all of this, PR boy. But you're glossing over a few small details. No money means no replacement equipment. No replacement equipment means no way to earn money. But then no money means no replacement equipment. And so on and so on. And also, not wishing to put too much of a dampener on things, we have just mislaid fifty per cent – no offence, by the way – of our effective workforce. We're fucked, pal.'

I ignored her slight. Technically speaking, I was on the company payroll, but it was, I suppose, PR work and given the fact that the software still wasn't ready, it was mostly vague plans rather than anything concrete.

There was a long silence between us. 'I hope Dorothy's OK,' I said. 'You don't think she's been kidnapped again?' Last time this had happened, she'd ended up in the hands of the Belarusian mafia, which is how we'd both nearly got blown up in the middle of the Somerset Levels.

'You're not suggesting she's the kind of person who makes a habit of that kind of thing? Sounds a bit like victim-blaming to me.'

'No, but… it's just odd.'

'A lot about this is odd, pal. But before we start trying to get to the bottom of it all, we need to take some practical steps. We need to find somewhere to live, don't we?'

'Good point,' I said. 'So, what are we going to do?'

'Don't suppose there's a couple of spare berths in that shitty caravan of your Dad's?' said Ali.

'I wouldn't wish that on my worst enemy,' I said.

So, we spent the day searching and ended up with somewhere that was, in fact, considerably worse. And all the time I was wondering about how curious it was that I'd been called away to Lucy's that evening of all evenings. The other thing I wondered about was how significant it was that the only two people who knew about my connection to the Vavasors and who also had Lucy's address were

Dorothy – because she had been there – and Ali, because she had been the one who had arranged to courier the briefcase containing the real Vavasor papers there prior to handing them over to the Belarusian mafia.

Who the hell could *I* trust any more?

Chapter 3

The Dog and Fishbone was largely empty when Ali and I turned up on Saturday morning. It was an old school gin palace with a wide selection of old school gin behind the bar as well as a decent selection of ales and lagers on tap. The only other customer was a thirty-something bloke wearing a boat club blazer with a rakish top-pocket handkerchief over a crisp white shirt, red chinos and shiny brown boots, sipping at a designer lager while studying the Financial Times. The red of the trousers clashed violently with the pink of the newspaper, but I guess that was probably the point.

'Where is everyone?' I said to the barman as he pulled our pints.

'Sorry?'

'Not many people around,' I said.

He lifted his wrist with a theatrical flourish and checked his watch. 'It is only five past eleven. Bit early even for this part of town. But give it an hour or so and the place'll be heaving, if that's what you're looking for.'

'Well, no, we've come for the convention. You know. Is it not happening?'

'Convention?' he said. Then he looked at us, as if seeing us in a new light. As lights go, it wasn't a flattering one.

'Oh, you're looking for the Vavvies,' he said, chortling to himself.

'Jesus,' muttered Ali. 'I'm never going to live this down. I'm a fucking Vavvy now.'

'Upstairs,' said the barman, ignoring her and pointing to the stairs. We followed his directions and very soon became aware of a general hubbub above and around us. A table had been set up on the first floor landing and a grey-haired woman was sitting behind it with an expectant look on her face. She wore a badge that bore the legend *μ4PM*, and in front of her on the table was an array of badges with various other words or phrases printed on them.

'Name?' she said.

'Um… Tom… er—' my voice faltered as I remembered that it was important to stay as anonymous as possible here.

'No,' she said, as if speaking to a child, 'your forum name, please. Remember we have a "no outing" rule at *vavasorology.com*.'

'Ah, I see. Of course.' My relief at this was tempered by the realisation that use of my forum name would entail walking around all day wearing a badge that announced to the world that I wished to be known as *arsebiscuits89*. Sure enough, there was one with that very moniker among the selection on the table. I couldn't bring myself to say the word out loud, so I simply picked it up and showed it to the woman.

'Ah,' she said, before scanning a typed sheet of paper and then adding a tick at the end of one of the lines. She handed me a printed sheet of paper listing the order of events for the day and a flyer for Dinsdale Mazloumian's latest book, *Archie and Pye – The Riddle is FINALLY Solved with SCIENCE*. I still hadn't got round to reading his last one, *Perpetual Pye*, which explained how Pythagoras Vavasor had solved the perpetual motion problem and had been put to death on the orders of the global military industrial complex. I noticed from the schedule that he was due to be speaking after lunch, which was at least something to look forward to.

While I was pinning the badge to my chest, Ali stepped up and announced that her name was *AwesomeCoder*.

'You don't go in for modesty, do you?' I said to her as the woman was ticking her off.

'What's the fucking point? No point in having a nice, shiny brass trumpet if you're going to rely on someone else to blow it for you, is there? Mind if I just call you *Arse* by the way? For short?'

'Sod off.'

I ran my eyes over the other badges that were still lying there and I was startled to notice *EulerIsGod*. Dorothy's forum name. I nudged Ali.

'See that?' I said. 'You don't suppose—?'

Ali shook her head. 'Nah. She probably booked her place months ago. It's not like we're going to bump into her today and be all, like, "Hey, Dot, how's it going? Where've you been hiding for the last few weeks?"'

'No, I suppose not.'

I looked down at the badges again and spotted *PoorIntern*, which would have belonged to Benjamin Unsworth, who worked at Head Wind, a tiny independent publishing house. Head Wind had made the catastrophic mistake of taking on the late George Burgess's putative biography of the Vavasor twins, a move that ultimately led to the death by spline strangulation of the owner, Hilary van Beek, and the subsequent disappearance of Benjamin Unsworth, whose discarded clothes were found near the river Avon.

And somewhere among that lot was a badge destined to be used by Rufus Fairbanks himself, the killer of Hilary van Beek and at least two others, very nearly including myself. I briefly wondered which one it might be – *UltimateTruth*? *TheDaddy*? *DontCallMeVavvy*? – before Ali nudged me in the back.

'Oi you,' she said. 'Come on, Arse, we're going to miss all the fun.'

'Please don't do that.'

'Try and stop me, pal.'

The room was nearly full, but we managed to find a couple of seats near the back. I estimated that there must have been about fifty people present and it struck me as rather extraordinary that only Ali and myself (and I wasn't entirely sure to what extent Ali had been paying attention) knew the whole truth about what had happened between Archie and Pye. Frustratingly, it would have to remain that way for the time being, too.

A large middle-aged man with untidy red hair and beard was on his feet in front of the audience, droning his way through the health and safety arrangements. He wore a badge that simple said *BigGinge*. While he finished his spiel, I had a sneaky look at the other Vavasorologists, and I noticed Ali doing the same. It was quite easy to do this without drawing attention to ourselves because very few of them seemed to have any desire to meet another human being's eye. They were mostly – but not exclusively – male, but they varied in age from pimply teenagers through to white-haired pensioners. The majority of them had apparently got dressed in the dark that morning, without easy access to a mirror.

'What a bunch of fucking weirdos,' whispered Ali in my ear.

'Shh,' I whispered back. 'You're being judgmental.'

'Am I fuck. Listen, pal, it's not often I go somewhere and I'm the most normal person in the room. I'm enjoying this already.'

Meanwhile, *BigGinge* had finished the health and safety segment and was now running through the day's agenda.

'So. Anyway. In a few minutes time, we're going to start the proceedings with an open discussion on recent developments. I don't know if you guys all feel the same as me, but the last few months have been a bit confusing, to say the least, what with what happened to poor old George and so on, and I think we could all do with some guidance on what to make of it all and what its implications might be for the world of Vavasorology.

'So, I think we'll allow an hour for that and then knock off for a bite to eat. Can you hear me at the back, by the way? Good. Then, after lunch we'll have our keynote speaker, who I'm very pleased to say is none other than Dinsdale Mazloumian.' Here, he paused for some kind of reaction. There wasn't any, apart from a raised hand from a member of the audience sitting a couple of rows in front of me. 'Yes, *KnobHead*?' said *BigGinge*, barely suppressing a sigh.

'Why is it always Dinseyboy?' said *Knobhead*. I was familiar with his work on *vavasorology.com*, where his posts were a potent cocktail of five per cent wit, forty-five per cent complete ignorance and fifty per cent illiteracy. From where I was sitting, his physical presence appeared to be the result of an illegal attempt to create a humanoid–dandruff hybrid species.

'Well, we did originally have George Burgess down to speak, Knobby, but obviously he's no longer available. And Dinsdale's got a really interesting new book out. Maybe if you wrote one…?' there was general laughter at this point, punctuated by rueful mutterings of 'yeah, yeah' from *Knobhead*.

'Then we'll have a break for tea,' continued *BigGinge*, 'before wrapping up with a panel session on the Marginalia. Unfortunately, Margot can't be with us on this occasion—' here he was interrupted by a few half-hearted cheers, mostly from the direction of *Knobhead* '—but we've managed to put together a team of experts who I'm sure—'

'Who's Margot?' hissed Ali.

'Margot Evercreech,' I said. 'Big expert on the Marginalia.'

'I'm going to regret asking this, but—'

'A load of scrawls in the margins of the Vavasor mathematical papers. I've seen them myself, and—'

'It's OK, you don't have to tell me. I'm bored with them already.'

A balding man with a ruddy complexion in the row in front turned round and hissed at us to be quiet. Ali glared at him and he turned back again. Meanwhile, *BigGinge* had finished outlining the day's order of play and had moved on to the discussion of recent events.

'So,' he said. 'I know some of you are interested to hear about the recent sightings of Isaac Vavasor—'

'Who's Isaac, for fuck's sake?' whispered Ali. 'I thought there were only two of the bastards.'

'He's their younger brother,' I said. 'Bit of a recluse.'

'I can see why.'

'—but I guess we need to begin with George Burgess,' he continued. 'I imagine *TruthBomb* over there has some intelligence to share with us, so perhaps you'd like to lead off.' *BigGinge* pointed to a man with dark, greasy hair and glasses held together with Elastoplast, sitting in the third row. He wore a heavy green pullover that hadn't been washed for several years and he nursed a Tupperware container on his lap. He began to speak, but appeared to realise after a second or two that his mouth was full, so he put his hand up to indicate that he needed a moment or two. After a brief hiatus, he continued talking, although it turned out that he'd decided in the end not to wait until he'd completely finished his snack, with the result that his first few sentences sprayed crumbs onto the row in front.

'As many of you will know,' he began, in a slow, steady drone, 'I am fortunate enough to be a longtime resident of Swindon and have extensive contacts in the local constabulary. I was also an infrequent confidant of the late Mr Burgess, god rest his soul, so I am in possession of a number of significant insights into where he was heading with his thinking. With regard to the ongoing investigation, I have obviously been sworn to secrecy over certain aspects inasmuch as they pertain to national security—'

'WHAT?' hissed Ali to me.

The man in front turned around again.

'Oh, fuck OFF, pal,' said Ali. Somewhere to our right, a young woman wearing the badge *ItBeganInAfrika* sniggered.

'—but before I move onto that I'd just like to briefly discuss the implications of Burgess's death with regard to the future of the DiAngelo-Parkinson heresy. As I think you will all be aware, Burgess was a strong proponent of the neo-Evercreechian stance, particularly with regard to the later sections of the Marginalia. I personally found this a disappointing position to take, especially since much of this work had been discredited last year by the stellar work of Persiflage and Fitzgibbon, and I tried on more than one occasion to, so to speak, turn him back towards the light. However—'

While this was going on, I could tell that some in the audience were beginning to get restless. Chairs were beginning to creak and throats were being cleared. A voice behind me muttered, 'Oh Christ, he's off again.' Finally, *BigGinge* decided to intervene.

'Thank you very much, TB, but can we stick to the matter in hand? George Burgess's death?'

'Well, yes,' said *TruthBomb*, 'but the point I was about to make is that it is entirely possible that Burgess was killed by a breakaway cabal of Crypto-DiAngelites.'

There was a brief pause as the room digested this unexpected revelation.

'Who are the Crypto-diAngelites?' whispered Ali.

'Not a bloody clue,' I whispered back.

'And your proof for this is?' said the voice from behind me. I turned round and established that it belonged to a small pink-faced man in his sixties with a neat beard, called *FoShizzle*.

'Well,' said *TruthBomb*, 'it's not so much proof as an informed gut feeling. But unless you have any better suggestions—' This was met with a collective groan from the audience.

'What were you saying about national security?' said a middle-aged woman to my right in the row in front. Her badge identified her as *MeenaKnows*.

'Ah, I'm afraid I can't go into that,' said *TruthBomb*.

'Why not?' said *MeenaKnows*.

'National security, like I said.'

'So why mention it, you big twat?' interjected *Knobhead*, to laughter.

'Hey, lads,' said *BigGinge*, sensing trouble, 'let's keep it friendly.'

'What about the Crown Jewels?' came a clipped Welsh voice at the far end of our row.

'Ah, thank you, *DaiTheDeath*,' said *BigGinge*. 'That's a very important question. Does anyone have any information on this? I know there were a number of rumours going round.'

'What about that bloke who popped up on the forum and said he'd bumped into Burgess on a train, before deleting the post?' said *DaiTheDeath*. A shiver went down my spine at this point. It was all getting a bit close to home.

'Did anyone make a note of their handle?' said *BigGinge*. I held my breath and waited for someone to say something. But no one did. It seemed that the only person who had noticed my post had been Rufus Fairbanks, and he wasn't going to be spilling his secrets any time soon.

The discussion carried on in its strange, genial way for the next hour or so, with expert after expert in Vavasorology advancing ever more loopy theories, every single one of which I knew to have no basis in fact whatsoever. The temptation to stand up and tell everyone what had really happened to Archie and Pye – from their involvement with Rufus Fairbanks to help him launder money for the Belarusian mafia, via their parallel affairs with Fairbanks's wife, to Archie's murder of Pye with a set square and his subsequent suicide, to say nothing of Fairbanks's attempts to cover it all up via a sequence of copycat killings – was getting stronger with every passing minute. But if I'd succumbed, I would have been exposed to all manner of dangers, and there was a significant chance that no one would have believed me either.

During the lunch break, everyone mingled in the bar downstairs. Ali and I lurked on the edge of conversations, listening for any clues as to what might have happened to Dorothy. Every now and then, I tried to steer the topic under discussion towards her.

A man and a woman nearby were discussing the finer points of DiAngelo's lemma and its relation to Archie and Pye's alleged proof of the Riemann hypothesis. I was finding it hard breaking into a conversation about mathematics, especially when I didn't understand any of it, so I ended up completely fluffing my first attempt by mistiming it and mumbling.

'Sorry?' said one of them, a tall, thin, balding chap called *ZOMG*.

'Anyone know what's happened to *EulerIsGod*?' I repeated.

ZOMG frowned. 'Rings a bell,' he said. 'Mean anything to you?' The latter question was directed to his companion, a woman with wild hair and enthusiastic eyes who went by the name of *NiceMillicent*.

'Didn't *EulerIsGod* have some interesting ideas about Archie and Pye not being twins after all?' said *NiceMillicent*. 'Or was that *BollockBrain*?'

'Sounds more like *BollockBrain*'s type of thing, Millie,' said *ZOMG*. From the way he said this, it struck me that these two were probably in some kind of relationship. I hadn't really thought of Vavasorology as a kind of dating service – especially given the gender imbalance, although obviously that wasn't necessarily a barrier – but as I looked around, it struck me that *ZOMG* and *NiceMillicent* probably weren't the only couple present. I found this rather charming.

'No, awfully sorry,' said *NiceMillicent* to me, '*Z*'s right. Haven't heard anything from them for a while. Bit of a pity – they always posted interesting stuff.'

I wandered off and found another group of people to talk to, but no one present seemed to have had much to do with Dorothy. I wondered if Ali was having any more luck.

'Am I fuck,' she said, as we sat down for the afternoon session. 'And if one more of these numpties asks me for my opinion on Fahrenthold's dichotomy, I'll give it to them. Straight in the nuts.'

Dinsdale Mazloumian cut an imposing figure. He wore a purple velvet three-piece suit and light brown winkle-pickers. He had a shock of white hair and glasses dangling from a librarian's chain round his neck, which he raised up to his eyes from time to time when he wished to read a passage from his new book. The unconventionality of his attire was a perfect match for the lunacy of his argument, which built on his previous theory about Archie Vavasor's perpetual motion machine.

Mazloumian's new theory went something like this. According to conventional science, perpetual motion was impossible, as no engine was one hundred per cent efficient and energy would always be lost to the system somehow because of the second law of thermodynamics. This had led to significant objections to his theory both from within and from outside the Vavasorology community. His breakthrough was to realise that this obstacle could be overcome by sending the perpetual motion machine backwards in time, thus negating the effect of the second law. Even better, this meant that the machine would actually gain energy as it continued to spin. Obviously, it would also have to be configured to spin in the opposite direction to which it was required to do to be useful, but that was a minor implementation detail.

Mazloumian thus asserted that he had succeeded in proving that Archie Vavasor had in fact developed a time machine rather than a perpetual motion machine. As he pointed out, this gave the global military-industrial complex even more reason to have Archie killed, so this gave some additional credence to the theory.

I couldn't help feeling that this argument had a number of important holes in it, but the audience were, by and large, appreciative and what questions they had were largely benign. He was just answering the last of these before the teatime break when I heard the sound of an argument at the back of the room.

'You can't come in here without telling me your handle,' said the first voice. It was the woman who had been ticking off everyone as they arrived.

'But I can't do that,' came the second voice. It was plaintive, male and vaguely familiar.

'Why not?' said the woman. 'You know the rules.'

'If they find me, they'll almost certainly kill me,' wailed the man.

'Well, I'm afraid we can't bend the rules just like that. I'm very sorry, you can't come in.'

'But I need to. I have to find out about—'

He didn't get a chance to complete the sentence because *BigGinge* and another thickset type had marched down the room to the back and gently but firmly eased him out. As they did so, I caught a glimpse of his face, and I realised who it was. The beard was thicker and he was now wearing glasses, but there was no mistaking Benjamin Unsworth.

Chapter 4

'Back in a minute,' I said to Ali, standing up.

'What?' she said. 'Where are you sodding off to? You're not going to leave me alone with this lot, are you?'

'Just seen someone I need to talk to. You OK here for a while?'

'I'll have to be, won't I?' she said.

'I'm sure you can find someone interesting to talk to.'

Ali glared at me. I left her there and walked to the door. There was no sign of Benjamin Unsworth outside, so I went downstairs into the public bar. I couldn't see him there either, so I went out into the street. I caught sight of him walking disconsolately in a northerly direction.

'Benjamin!' I shouted, but he didn't hear me. I ran after him and caught up with him as he was waiting to cross the road. I tapped him on the shoulder. He jerked round and stared at me in terror as if he'd seen a ghost.

'It's you!' he said.

'Of course it's me, Benjamin,' I said.

'Are you with them?'

'With who?'

'With them.'

'Who's them?'

Benjamin gestured wildly with his hands. 'You know,' he said. 'THEM.'

'No, Benjamin,' I said. 'I'm not with them. Calm down, I want to talk to you.'

'How do I know you're not with them?'

I thought about this. 'If I were,' I said, 'you'd probably be dead by now.'

After some consideration, this seemed to satisfy him. I took his elbow and steered him towards a nearby café. We went inside and I ordered two black Americanos. The place was doing a trade in brisk afternoon teas but we managed to find a table in the corner by the window. We squeezed in between a middle-aged couple who were arguing about curtain fabric and a sullen teenager and her mother who were both occupied with their phones.

'I thought you were dead anyway,' I said, when we had sat down.

'Some days I wish I was,' said Benjamin. 'They're still after me, you know.' His hands were shaking. In fact, much of his upper body was shaking too.

'But who's after you, Benjamin?'

'THEY are. They're after all of us.'

The circularity of his argument was beginning to make me dizzy, so I switched to a different line of enquiry. 'What were you doing at the Vavvies, Benjamin?' I said.

'Matheson sent me.'

'Who's Matheson?'

'She thinks someone in the Vavvies is involved, you see, and I think I know who it is, but I just wanted to confirm that and I thought that if I came along today I'd be able to.'

'Benjamin, who's Matheson?'

'And, you see, she thought I'd be able to sneak in somehow because I'm a member, but she didn't realise I'm supposed to be dead and I didn't want to tell her that because it's all a bit confusing. I mean if I'd got in without using my handle I'd have been fine because no one there really knows what I look like, but if I was going around with a badge saying *PoorIntern* stuck on me, everyone would be saying "Oh god, Benjamin, we thought you were dead" and stuff, which is nice, but I wouldn't exactly be undercover any more, would I? Do you think I can trust Matheson? I don't know if I can really trust her. I mean, she's been really helpful to me, but I just don't know. She says she can protect me from them, but I just don't know.'

I had a bad feeling that we were just about to embark on another spin around the roundabout. 'Benjamin,' I said firmly, 'who's Matheson?'

He ignored my question. 'I had to fake my death,' he said. 'Those guys were going to kill me.'

'But which guys, Benjamin?'

The waitress arrived with our coffees. As she withdrew, there was an awkward moment when both Benjamin and myself had to lean to one side to allow a changeover of customers at the next table. The mother and daughter left, and a man in his twenties sat down on his own and began an animated one-sided discussion on his phone about where he was supposed to be going this afternoon.

Benjamin tried to drink his coffee, but he could barely control his cup, with the result that he managed to spill most of it.

'Are you all right?' I said.

He put his hand up defensively. 'I'm fine. Really I am. Just haven't had much sleep lately.'

I had a sudden thought. 'Do you have anywhere to go?' I said. Not that I was in a position to help him out at the moment.

'It's OK,' he said. 'It's OK.'

It clearly wasn't. And he was beginning to worry me. Perhaps it was just paranoia, but maybe we were still in danger. It was entirely possible that there were members of the Gretzky family out looking to avenge the death of several of their number in the explosion of which I was the unwitting instigator.

'I can probably manage the Dagenham drop,' said the man on the next table. 'But Barking's going to be tricky on a Saturday. Can't Denny do it?'

'Are you talking about the Gretzkys?' I whispered to Benjamin.

'Who?'

'The Gretzkys.' The couple had finished their argument inconclusively and were studying the menu cards with exaggerated interest. 'The Gretzkys were the ones after you,' I said. 'Weren't they? They were the ones after us, anyway.'

'I don't know what they were called,' said Benjamin. 'And it's not them now anyway.'

'Sorry?'

'I shouldn't have got involved. I was just trying to help.'

'Benjamin,' I said, taking a deep breath, 'please try and tell me what you're involved in.'

Benjamin glanced around nervously. The man on the next table had ended his conversation and was now scrolling through something on his phone. The couple behind us had now become embroiled in a heated discussion over whether it was better to have a sandwich on brown granary bread or a white baguette.

'Have they got any cake?' said Benjamin, unexpectedly.

'Um, I suppose they do, but—'

'It's just, I'm really, really hungry and I'd like some cake. Chocolate if possible.'

'Right. Cake.'

'Chocolate, if possible. Please.'

I stood up and made my way towards the serving counter. I was still surveying the range of cakes and trying to decide between a slice of chocolate fudge cake and a brownie when I heard a sound of raised voices and tables and chairs being scraped. The couple on the table next to us were gathering their things together before making their way towards the exit, weaving an awkward path through the other tables. I watched as they left the café and then turned back to where Benjamin was still sitting at our table.

There was something very wrong with his posture. He was staring straight ahead with glazed eyes and drooping lower lip, not appearing to focus on anything. I abandoned the cakes and raced over to him, bumping into several other customers as I did so.

I seized him by the shoulders. 'Benjamin,' I said. 'What happened?'

By way of response, all he managed to do was shake his head in the direction of the floor. I looked down and saw an empty syringe lying there.

'What have you done?' I said. But Benjamin shook his head again, this time towards the table where the man on his own was sitting. Or rather, had been sitting. In all the commotion, I'd failed to notice him leaving the place.

'Did he do this to you?' I said.

Benjamin nodded, before trying to speak. 'Mmmph,' he said.

'What?' I said, bending closer.

'Matheson.'

'Who's Matheson, Benjamin?'

Benjamin shook his head violently.

'F-f-find Matheson,' he said.

'Who is she?' I said.

'Mmmph.' Then Benjamin slumped forward and passed out.

I turned round to look at the customers in the café. 'Someone call an ambulance!' I shouted. 'Go on!' I said, waving my arms wildly, and eventually the waitress who had been serving us picked up her phone. Once I was happy he was being seen to, I ran out of the door in pursuit of the man who had been on the next table.

I looked from left to right but I couldn't see anyone that matched him. Then I spotted someone on the opposite side of the road running towards a bus stop, where a number nineteen had just pulled up. The bus pulled away and there was no sign of them any more. Shit. I had to act fast. There was a taxi heading in my direction with its light on. I waved my arm in its direction and it swerved towards me and screeched to a halt. I yanked the passenger door open, hurled myself in and slammed it shut.

'Where to, mate?' said the driver, turning round to look at me.

I paused.

Was I really going to do this?

Of course I bloody was. This was a chance to tick one off the bucket list.

'Follow that bus!' I said, triumphantly.

'You what?' said the driver.

'Follow that bus,' I said. 'The number nineteen over there.'

The driver looked around, as if trying to spot any hidden cameras. 'Listen, mate. We're not in a movie now.'

'I mean it. I need to catch that bus up.'

'Jesus.' He looked straight at me for a full ten seconds, and then shook his head, flicked the indicator and started to move out. It was a minute or two before there was a break in the traffic, but we eventually made it to the other side of the road. Worryingly, the bus was now out of sight.

'Do you know which way it will be going?' I said anxiously.

'Mate, I'm a taxi driver. 'Course I bleeding do. And hardly a day goes by without some nutter leaping into my cab asking me to follow someone.'

'Really?'

''Course it bleeding doesn't.'

'Oh.'

There was a pause as we drew up to some traffic lights. There was still no sign of the number nineteen. Shit. We'd lost him.

'You some kind of actor, then?' said the driver.

'What?' I was still peering into the distance, trying to conjure a number nineteen bus into existence by sheer force of will. 'Me? Good heavens, no.'

''Cos you ain't in the security services, I can tell that.'

'I might be,' I said. I rather resented the insinuation.

He laughed at this. 'Nah, mate. I've had a few of them in my cab and I know exactly what to look for. So, why all the fuss about catching that bus? I know. Bet you've got a bird on board.'

'What? Look, any chance you could go a bit faster? I still can't see them.'

'Not if I want to keep my licence. So, it is a bird. Thought so.'

'No, really it isn't. It's—'

Then I stopped to think. What in god's name was I doing? I'd abandoned poor Benjamin in the café – god, I hoped he was all right and someone was looking after him – to go off on another wild goose chase. I wasn't even sure if the goose in question was actually on the bus in front, and what was I going to do if I managed to catch up with him anyway? At least he'd left his syringe behind, so – unless he had a whole pocketful of them – he was probably now unarmed.

I shouldn't have left Benjamin behind. I really shouldn't have.

But this was my best chance of finding out who was trying to keep him quiet and that, in turn, was my best chance of finding my way to Dorothy.

'Well, I guess it is about a woman in a way,' I said.

'Thought so,' said the driver. 'Look, we've still got plenty of time to catch them up before we get to Finsbury Park. There's a mosque there, you know.'

Ah. Here we go, I thought.

'Had one of them Imams in my cab once,' he said. 'Lovely chap.' This was slightly unexpected, and I scolded myself for making unwarranted assumptions about taxi drivers.

'Really?' I said.

'Yeah. Anyway, want to stop to get some flowers or something?'

'Sorry?'

'Flowers. 'Cos you've had a row, right? You had a row, she flounced off and you're running after her to win her back, am I right? 'Course I am. Flowers, mate. That's what you need. Look, there's a stall just here. Lots of folk get their flowers there. I had that actor… whatsisname… in my cab a few weeks back. Lovely chap. Here we are—'

The driver began to turn the wheel towards the pavement. I banged on the partition between us in alarm.

'No!' I cried. 'I don't want any flowers. Really I don't. Can we just carry on with chasing that bus?'

'Ooh, OK. Fair enoughski. Just thought I'd check. No need to make such a fuss about it.' He seemed quite offended.

There was a break in the traffic ahead of us. I peered ahead and yes, there it was. The number nineteen was right up ahead, turning a corner.

'Yes!' I said. 'Look! We're almost catching up with it.'

'Told you we would, didn't I?'

Now came the tricky bit. I had to time my exit from the taxi just right so I could leap onto the bus before it moved off. There was every chance that I could end up sprawled on the pavement halfway through the procedure. Also, given that the bus had been out of sight for most of the journey, there was every chance my target had snuck off already.

I glanced up at the meter and made a rough calculation of how much I was going to have to give the driver. This only served to remind me how long it had been since I'd last been in a London taxi. This had been an expensive little escapade, but a moment's thought convinced me it was going to be worth it. I reached into my wallet and withdrew the amount.

'Here will do,' I said, as we neared the next bus stop.

The taxi pulled over to the side of the road. The driver turned towards me and I stuffed the notes through the partition into his hand. I dashed out of the cab and sprinted towards the bus, getting there just as the last passenger in the queue was getting on board. I scrambled through the door at the front after them, paid my fare and scanned the passengers on the lower deck. Inevitably, my man wasn't there.

Then, just as the bus was getting ready to move off, a figure hurtled down the stairs and launched itself through the doors in the middle of the bus, just as they were closing. Shit. It was him. It had to be. I dived forwards after him but before I could get to the doors, they had closed and the bus was beginning to move off, causing me to lurch sideways and land in the lap of a woman carrying a load of shopping.

'Sorry,' I said, extricating myself. I went over to the doors and banged on them in frustration. The man from the café turned round and looked at me as the bus moved away, tilted his head on one side and gave a kind of salute as if to acknowledge my fine but ultimately futile efforts. Then I reached up and pressed several times on the bell to alert the driver, but he ignored me. I ran back to the front of the bus and tried to speak to the driver.

'Can you stop the bus, please? I need to catch that bloke who's just got off.'

The driver responded by silently pointing to a notice that informed me that it was forbidden to speak to the driver while the bus was in motion.

'But—'

This time, the driver tapped his finger on another notice that stated that Transport for London took all attempts to harass or intimidate their staff very seriously indeed and would have no hesitation in prosecuting anyone who did so. I stomped back to the middle of the lower deck, found a seat and sat down until we came to the next stop.

I got off and began the long trek back to the café where I'd left Benjamin Unsworth. As I neared the place, I noticed an ambulance standing outside, along with a couple of police motorbikes. I was torn between my desire to rush in and find out what had happened to Benjamin and the continuing need to maintain a low profile. If I got myself caught up in this, there was every chance that I might end up being taken in for questioning about the death of Rufus Fairbanks, among others. And if that happened, I might never see Dorothy again.

I had to stay focused.

Reluctantly, I passed by the café on the opposite side of the road. If Benjamin was still alive, it was very likely that he'd be in hospital for a while, so all I had to do was find out which one and what their visiting hours were. There was no need to get involved now.

When I got back to the Dog and Fishbone, the final discussion was over and most of the Vavasorologists had gone home. Ali wasn't there, either.

'Anyone know someone called Matheson?' I said. It was a long shot, but it was worth a try.

BigGinge looked up from where he was rearranging chairs.

'Sorry, mate,' he said, shaking his head. 'No idea. What's their handle?'

'Dunno,' I said. 'That bloke who turned up at the end, he—' On reflection, there probably wasn't much mileage in telling *BigGinge* about Benjamin and it would also lead to a number of difficult questions that I wasn't ready to deal with yet.

I shook my head, thanked him and moved away. As I passed the table on the landing outside the room, I noticed that the unused badges were still laid out on it, including the one for *EulerIsGod*, still sitting there, defying me to work out what the hell was going on.

Chapter 5

When I got back to the flat, something had changed. The bed had been made for one thing. For another, that segment of pizza was no longer gracing the floor with its sticky tomato and mozzarella presence. The smell had gone – or at least it was now masked by a pleasingly synthetic overlay of pine air freshener. And in the middle of it all, there was Ali, bustling about, humming to herself and tidying things up.

Ali never bustled about. Come to think of it, she wasn't exactly known for her humming either. Or indeed tidying up.

'Find anything out at the convention?' I said.

'No,' said Ali, before resuming her humming.

'I managed to have a chat with Benjamin Unsworth. Before he got poisoned.'

'Oh.' Hum hum hum.

'He said he'd gone to the Vavvies on some sort of secret mission.'

'Is that so?' Hum hum diddly hum.

'Would you mind telling me what's up?' I said.

'Nothing,' she said, 'nothing at all.' Hum hum hum.

'No, there's something really weird happening. Who are you and what have you done with Ali?'

Ali ignored me and went on tidying and humming.

A few minutes later, the doorbell rang. Immediately, Ali started to get flustered, muttering 'Oh god,' to herself over and over again. She pushed her way past me to the door and opened it to let her guest in. It turned out to be the woman from the Vavasorologists who called herself *ItBeganInAfrika*. Suddenly, everything began to fall into place.

'Ah,' I said.

'This is Patrice,' said Ali, who had turned a vivid shade of red.

'Um, hi, Patrice,' I said, holding out my hand. Patrice shook it.

'Hi,' she said, with a gentle smile. 'And you are?'

'I'm Tom,' I said. 'I live here. So you—'

'We met at the Vavvies,' said Patrice.

'Right,' I said. I turned to Ali. 'Can I have a word, please?' I said, indicating our half of the French window leading out to the cat's latrine area. The handle had seized up with rust, but a small amount of judiciously applied brute force had the desired effect. I ushered Ali out and closed the door again behind me.

'So, what's this all about?' I said, trying to be as forceful as possible while keeping my voice down.

'Sorry?' said Ali.

'You know what I mean,' I hissed. 'Her. Your fancy woman.' I don't know why I said that. I literally have no idea where the phrase came from.

'You what? Listen, pal, if you think—'

'Don't you "Listen, pal" me,' I said. 'We went to that convention today to work. I—' here, I pointed to myself '—managed to track down a significant contact that may well lead us to Dorothy, and what did you do? You seem to have treated the occasion as some kind of speed-dating event so you can bring some floozie back to our home for the night.'

Ali stared at me. 'What the fuck are you on?' she said. 'Fancy woman? Floozie?'

'You know what I mean. What are you planning to do with her?'

Ali looked at me. 'You really want to know, straight boy? Well, we'll probably start with a bit of snogging. And then—'

'That's not what I meant,' I said, cutting her short. I glanced back at the flat, where Patrice was watching us with a worried expression on her face.

'Don't fuck this up for me, Tom,' said Ali suddenly. It was the first time she'd ever called me by my name.

'What?'

'Please.' I'd never heard her use that word before, either.

We stared at each other in silence for a while. I sniffed the air.

'I think I've trodden in something,' I said.

I offered to go and stay with my father for the night. I had a bit of an ulterior motive for this, as the amount of money I'd gone through buying coffees for Benjamin, chasing after buses and so on was panicking me slightly. As it happened, my old man had announced last time we'd been in contact that his finances had taken an unexpected turn for the better, so I thought perhaps he might be able to help me out.

The old man was sitting on the step of his static caravan sipping Tennants Extra from a can. Wally the dog was nowhere in sight, but a small, moth-eaten, black and white cat was curled up at his feet. It clearly hadn't taken μ very long to establish dominance. She used to belong to the Vavasor twins, but had come into my possession via their housekeeper, Mrs Standage, when I'd visited her shortly after she'd been murdered with a poisoned pork pie.

After much heart-searching, Dorothy and I had decided that μ was better off seeing out her dotage in the company of my father rather than in a fifth-floor office that was also occupied by Ali. Ali's view of cats was that there was nothing wrong with them that couldn't be fixed by a simple mass round-up and slaughter programme, and we weren't entirely sure she could be trusted if we ever had to leave μ alone with her for any extended period of time. In view of what had subsequently happened at the office, it was a distinctly fortuitous decision.

'Evening,' said my father, not getting up. μ opened an eye and gave me a look that roughly translated as 'Oh, it's you.' Having established that I wasn't a threat, she closed the one eye again and resumed her dozing.

'Evening,' I said. 'You OK?'

'Fair to middling. Can't complain, 'cos no one takes any notice.' He put his can of beer down, took out a pouch of tobacco and began to roll a cigarette. 'So, what brings you to these parts, old son? If you've brought your washing to be done, the twin-tub's knackered, so I might struggle to help you.'

This was an old gag that he trotted out on a fairly regular basis, but I laughed politely anyway. 'No,' I said. 'Had to vacate the flat for the night and I was wondering if you had a spare bed.'

'Had an argument with the missus, have we?'

'No, no, it's just—'

'If you don't mind me saying, you don't seem to be having much luck in that department lately, son.'

'No, really. Everything's fine with Dorothy.' Apart from the fact that I had absolutely no idea about where she was or what she was doing. But I wasn't going to let my father root around in that can of worms. He hadn't exactly set a good parental example with his own relationships.

'Fine, fine,' he said, putting both hands up defensively. 'I won't pry any further. As it happens, Ludmilla decided to seek her fortune elsewhere last week, so there's currently plenty of free space in Winscombe Towers.' He gestured with his head towards the caravan behind him.

Who was Ludmilla? Had I met her? It was entirely possible that I hadn't.

'I'll be back in the game soon, mind,' he said. 'Been on this Tinder thing. Amazing.' He waved a shiny new phone at me.

'You have a smartphone?' I said. When did this happen? How did it come to pass that my dissolute father had a better phone than my crappy Gold Star 3000 from the Happy Wednesday Corporation of Chongqing?

'Yeah. Amazed I managed to get this far in life without it. Turns out I can order my Viagra online with it, too. 'Course I really got it to check my portfolio.'

'Sorry?' I said. This was getting weirder and weirder. 'Look, before we go any further, have you got a spare can of beer? Think I might need it.'

My father handed me a beer and a rickety camping chair to sit on. μ adjusted her position slightly and settled down again. I looked at her hard in the eye. 'Is this your doing?', I mouthed at her. But she wasn't giving anything away.

'Tell me about this portfolio, then,' I said, trying to sound enthusiastic, despite the sinking feeling that was developing in my stomach.

'Well, see, I've been wondering about investing properly for my future for a while.'

'But I thought you were broke,' I said.

'Well, I still had a small amount left in savings. But it wasn't exactly doing much in the building society, was it?'

The sinking feeling was spreading over my entire body now. I tried to remain upbeat. 'So, what did you do with it? Apart from buying a smartphone, that is.'

He ignored my remark about the phone. 'Well,' he said, 'it was one-eyed Kev who put me onto this. Ever met him?'

'No, Dad.'

'Smart guy. Lives a few rows over. Y'see, he's been investing in crypto from day one.'

'Crypto?' I said.

'Yeah. Y'know. Bitcoins and stuff.' He tapped his nose significantly. 'That's what you and that whatsername should be getting into, y'know. That's where the smart money is. Your crypto and your blockchains.'

'Dad,' I said, 'what have you done?'

'Y'see, cryptocurrencies are the future, son,' he said. 'Decentralised money. Freedom from the fat cat banksters.'

'Please, Dad. Tell me what you've done.'

'Look.' He tapped away at his phone for a moment and then passed it to me. 'There,' he said.

'What am I looking at?' I said, staring at a screen which showed a number underneath a graph. The graph wiggled about a bit, but was heading upwards at a vertiginous rate. The number was surprisingly substantial.

'You're looking at the value of my portfolio, son.' The pride in his voice was a joy to hear, even if the sinking feeling hadn't gone away at all. There was still quicksand all around me, just waiting for me to step in.

'Really?' It really was a very large figure.

'Yup. Twenty-fold increase since the ICO.'

'ICO?'

'Initial Coin Offering. I've been in this from the start, son.'

'So, are these bitcoins then?' I'd heard about them, but I didn't have a clue what they were all about.

'Nah,' said my father, with a laugh. 'I was way too late for that.' He stopped to roll himself another cigarette. 'This is third gen altcoin stuff.'

'Sorry?'

'We're into micro-cryptocurrencies now, son. Boutique stuff. Tulpencoins.'

'Tulpencoins?'

'Yep. That's what this one's called. Thought it seemed a fun name. That's why I picked it to invest in. One-eyed Kev says there's good sentiment behind it.'

'What does the name mean?'

'Didn't they teach you anything at school? Tulpen is Dutch for tulips.'

'I don't think Dutch was on the syllabus, Dad. Why tulips?'

My father shook his head sadly. 'Dunno about Dutch, but you obviously weren't paying attention in history, son. Tulip fever! The time when everyone went nuts for buying tulips! Just like crypto, son. Just like crypto.'

'But why name a cryptocurrency thing after a financial bubble?'

My father gave a loud, rasping combination cough and laugh at this point. 'Son,' he said, 'it's supposed to be ironic. Thought your lot were all into that. You really disappoint me sometimes, you know.'

This wasn't getting any better. 'So, these Tulpencoins,' I said. 'How do you go about getting your money out when you need to?'

My father spread his arms wide. 'Why would I ever want to?' he said.

'Maybe if you needed to buy something?'

He took a long drag of his cigarette at this point and then pointed at me with it. 'The problem with you,' he said, 'is that you are still tied to physical property.' He waved his arms around himself. 'I have all I need already.'

'What about food? Beer? Tobacco?'

My father just shrugged by way of reply.

'But still, how do you get your money out?' I said.

'Well, there's a bit of a liquidity issue at the moment, but—'

'It's not going to happen, is it?'

'Oh, ye of little faith,' he said, rolling his eyes. 'You, son, are a classic no-coiner.'

'What?'

'You're a no-coiner. You're tied to antiquated notions of fiat currencies. You're a thousand years behind the curve. You're nothing but a Luddite. Whereas I—' he pulled himself up to his full height '—am a man of the future.' He stubbed out his cigarette, drained his can and waggled it at me. 'Another one?'

'Yes, please.' I needed another beer more than almost anything in the world right now. My girlfriend had vanished, I had been booted out of my own squalid flat, I had virtually no money and the funds I thought I might have had temporary access to were all currently invested in a cryptocurrency scam.

My father returned with the beers.

'Y'see,' he said, 'the thing is, your generation are too attached to their possessions and gadgets and stuff. It's folk like me, who have grown up making do and mending, that'll survive when society breaks down. We don't rely on handouts and we don't need to rely on banks now we've got crypto. I'm thinking of taking up beekeeping again.'

'Oh god, no. Please, Dad.' My father had tried beekeeping when we were last all together as a family. He'd been attracted to it as a hobby mainly because you got to wear a special suit. His first harvest produced two tiny jars of rancid, evil-smelling honey and he lost interest after that, resulting in a series of swarms that alienated each of our neighbours in turn.

'Oh, ye of little faith,' he said again. 'Y'know, son, I wonder where you get your genes from sometimes.'

I wondered too, to be honest.

When I got back to the flat the next morning, Ali had left and there was no sign of Patrice. I genuinely hoped it had all gone well. Disturbing as Ali 2.0 was, it was a massive improvement on the previous version, and the thought of having to revert to that if her relationship goals weren't met filled me with horror.

I was actually quite disappointed that Ali wasn't there, because I'd wanted to ask her about cryptocurrencies. It was bound to be the kind of thing she'd know about, even if she would probably struggle to bring her explanation down to my level of understanding. Then I remembered Narendra. I'd worked with him for a while at $mKG.Q^*$, my last place of full-time employment, before he left to go to work at Ur, a City-based company specialising in applications of blue-sky sunrise technology. I still had his number, so I gave him a call. He answered straight away.

'Tom, hi!' he said. 'To what do I owe this unexpected pleasure on a bright Sunday morning?'

'Oh god, is it Sunday?' I said. This was happening more often than I liked these days. 'Sorry.'

'No worries. Always nice to hear from you. How is the fair Lucy?'

'Ah,' I said. 'The fair Lucy is no longer with me.'

'That's sad. I liked her. So how are things at the old place?'

'Ah,' I said. 'I'm no longer there either. Long story.'

'Right,' said Narendra. 'Any other changes in your life I need to know about?'

I thought hard about this. 'Not for now,' I said. 'Look, I was wondering if I could ask you a favour. I need to know about these cryptocurrency things.'

There was a deep sigh from the other end. 'Oh, mate,' he said, 'you're not wanting to get involved in all that bullshit, are you?'

'No, no, no, good Lord, no. It's actually my father. He's gone and invested all his life savings in one.'

There was a long silence. 'Oh, mate. I think you may have failed in your filial duty of care there.'

'I didn't know he was going to do it! He thinks he's going to be loaded.'

'So do lots of people. Look, I'm not an expert on this, but I've learnt enough to know that if anyone comes knocking on your door offering you anything to do with cryptocurrencies or blockchains or any of that stuff, shout abuse at them through the letterbox until they give up and go away.'

'Really? Is it that bad?'

'Trust me.'

'I'd still like to know more about it, though. So I can at least have a decent argument with the old man.'

'He won't listen to you. They never do. Then again—' Narendra paused for a moment '—I actually bumped into a chap the other day who works with some of these people.'

'Who does he work for?'

'He's an indie. Seems to be doing very nicely. I could put you in touch if you want. He's putting together something for one of the top cryptos in the UK right now. Told me they were the flakiest bunch he'd ever encountered in his career. Now what was their name?'

I knew straightaway exactly what the name was going to be. 'It's Tulpencoin, isn't it?' I said.

'Yes! That's right! How did you… oh shit. Sweet Jesus and baby Buddha, that's what your Dad's gone and invested in, isn't it?'

'Yup.'

'You definitely need to talk to him.'

A few emails later and I was all set up for a meeting on Monday evening with Matt Blank, Tulpencoin's PR whizz.

Chapter 6

Monday dawned, and with it another new week without Dorothy. But I set off from the flat with a spring in my step. Ali had been absent all night and this had given me the opportunity to get the first decent night's sleep I'd had for some time. Even the couple in the flat next door had kept their issues to themselves for once. I had a slot booked at the local library to use one of their computers at ten o'clock and I was determined to make the best use of it. I was sure that in my present state, with my eyes bright as a pair of polished silver buttons and my tail primped to full bushiness, I would crack the whole thing open in a matter of minutes.

Over the last few weeks, I'd come to know the regulars at the library by sight, if not to talk to, in much the same way as you come to know the commuters who catch the train at the same time as you. There was even the same sense of territorial ownership, although it wasn't so much a question of possession of a particular segment of the platform as the fact that everyone had their favourite computer. Woe betide anyone who snuck in unannounced and stole one they had no right to use.

I nodded to the boring, grey-haired family-tree man and the intense, wild-haired autodidact whom I'd mentally christened Wikipedia Wally, and they both acknowledged me back with a shy wave. Email Emilia, who seemed to spend her time composing interminable missives to her boyfriend back in Spain, wasn't there yet, but Ramona the Romantic Novelist was, although she ignored me completely as she was deep into an intensely emotional scene, judging from the way her eyes were welling up as she hammered away at her keyboard.

My primary goal this morning was to try to work out where Benjamin Unsworth might have been taken to, assuming he was still alive. If I could somehow get to see him, he might be able to tell me more about the mysterious Matheson and maybe this would then lead me to Dorothy. However, this did assume that he wasn't being held in some kind of isolation or under police protection. If this were the case, I might have to use some kind of subterfuge to get to him. Some kind of disguise, perhaps. I'd picked up sufficient medical jargon from living with Lucy that I was sure I could pass off as a doctor for a short period of time.

But before I started searching for news on Benjamin's whereabouts, I had a quick look at my emails. There was nothing particularly exciting there, apart from a couple of spam invitations to take part in a new cryptocurrency venture. I realised then that I'd been getting these for some time, but I hadn't paid any attention to them until now. Having read through them, however, I was still no closer to understanding what they were all about. I was looking forward to finding out more from Matt Blank tonight.

And then there was Rufus Fairbanks's posthumous LinkedIn invitation, still sitting there, taunting me, daring me to respond. Oh, the hell with it. It wasn't as if I used LinkedIn much anyway – it always used to strike me as basically Facebook without the cat videos. The only reason I'd gone there in the first place was that I was wondering if I might need to start looking for a proper job again soon and perhaps I ought to buff up my CV a little.

I clicked on the button to accept and a second or two later I was in. I was vaguely familiar with Fairbanks's CV, having researched it over the short time of my involvement with him, but there were still one or two things I hadn't been aware of. For example, he was evidently a significant investor in life extension technologies and seemed to have served as a non-executive director of at least two of them, not that it had done him much good when faced with a rogue mixer blade heading for his jugular.

Curiously, there were several additions that had clearly been made in the months since his death, although none of these seemed to me to have any particular significance. It was all a bit of a let down. I'd been half-expecting some kind of acrostic in his education history or something like that. It's the sort of thing Dorothy would have done, anyway. Because deep down inside, a small, desperate part of me was hoping against hope that she had, for whatever reason, hacked into Rufus Fairbanks's LinkedIn account and was using it to communicate with me.

After a quick scan of the public parts of Matt Blank's profile in preparation for our meeting, I abandoned LinkedIn and instead went to the BBC News website and found that an as yet unidentified person had been found unconscious as a result of a suspected poisoning with an unknown substance in a Clerkenwell café and had been rushed to St Jude's Hospital. The phrase 'as yet unidentified' set off some alarm bells. It was, now I thought about it, only a matter of time before the authorities made the connection with this stranger and the still missing person Benjamin Unsworth, prime suspect in the murder of George Burgess's publisher Hilary van Beek. And that could lead to all manner of complications for Dorothy and myself.

The good news, however, was that he was still alive, at least for the time being. In the back of my mind, I began to formulate a plan which might enable me to obtain access to him. It would be risky, but it would be worth it if it took me closer to finding Dorothy again.

By now, my hour of computer time was nearly up, and I could see Common Sense Colin, the Twitter troll, hovering in the doorway and looking at his watch pointedly. Before I left, I checked my emails once again and noticed there was one telling me I had a message from Rufus Fairbanks. I clicked on the link to get back into LinkedIn, and this is what it said:

Hello, Tom, it said. *Nice to speak with you again.*

I sat back in my seat as a cold sweat broke out all over my body. My immediate instinct was to shut everything down and run away very fast. Who was this? Obviously, OBVIOUSLY, this wasn't Rufus Fairbanks, because that would be absurd. He was definitely dead. I thought back to that ghastly scene in his kitchen a few months previously. There was no way anyone could have survived losing that amount of blood. Or indeed losing that much of his head.

So, what was going on? Who could it be? Who would have had access to his account? And what did they mean by contacting me like this? I began to hyperventilate and Wikipedia Wally looked up at me with concern.

'You all right, mate?' he said.

I waved him away. 'Fine,' I said. 'I'm fine.' After a while my breathing calmed down, and I wrote a reply, with shaking fingers:

Who is this?

Within seconds, a reply came back:

OK, first of all, we need to take this away from LinkedIn. Could be all sorts of people listening in.

This seemed all too plausible, given the way things were going. At the end of the message, there was a bland Gmail address, which gave away nothing about the owner. I opened up a new email and put this address in the addressee box.

So, who are you and what do you want to talk about? I wrote, and then hit the send button.

The email that came back in response wasn't remotely helpful. It simply said:

The first number is 1.

What? I replied. But this time there was no reply, so after a few minutes I got up and left the library.

Matt Blank was already nursing a pint when I arrived at the pub that night. I recognised him from his profile, although when he stood up to greet me he was considerably taller than I'd expected. I hadn't anticipated the power of his handshake, either, with the result that several of my fingers were numb for the first few minutes of our meeting.

He was wearing a stylish combination of distressed jacket, T-shirt and jeans that probably cost the same as a decent condition second hand hatchback.

'Narendra tells me you're in meat,' he said, after he'd set me up with a beer. The accent was London metropolitan, but with a vague Geordie residue.

'Not any more,' I said. 'Not since I left *mKG.Q**.'

'Who?'

'*mKG.Q**. You must have heard of them. Biggest firm in the South West.'

'Nah, sorry, mate. I haven't ventured down that way for a while.'

This was odd, but it did at least save me from having to go into any of the embarrassing details concerning my departure from my previous employers. The way that the PR grapevine worked, if I had given this guy the slightest hint as to the circumstances of my departure from my old company, it would be all round the world before noon the next day. Given that my current employer was now missing in action, there was still an outside chance that I might need to call on my old boss Claudette's offer of a scintillating reference should I subsequently need one.

'No,' I said. 'I'm finished with meat for the time being.'

'That's a shame,' he said. 'Old school chum of mine's putting together a new start-up in the hipster roadkill space – could have used your expertise.'

I shook my head. 'Sorry, mate.'

'Anyway, you're well out of it, if you ask me. Tech is where the real action is.'

'So I hear,' I said. 'So, what is all this cryptocurrency stuff about?'

Blank tilted his head on one side and frowned at me. 'First of all, tell me why you want to know.'

'It's my father. He seems to have invested his life savings in one of them.'

'Ah, yes' he said. 'Narendra told me about that. Well, that was a bit silly.'

'I was hoping that was just him being cautious.'

He shrugged. 'No, he's absolutely right,' he said.

'But I thought you'd been involved with launching some of them?'

Blank grimaced. 'That's business,' he said. I didn't feel I could argue with this. If I were to tell the truth, my own moral compass had wobbled a fair bit over the years, even if it had eventually lurched back towards the vague direction of magnetic north, at the cost of my career with $mKG.Q*$.

'So, you still want to know all about crypto, eh?'

'I guess so. Be gentle, though.'

'OK.' Blank drained his pint.

'Another one?' I said. He nodded.

I went to the bar for two more pints and set them down on the table between us. He picked his up, took a long swig and then put it down again.

'Right then,' he said, rapping the table with his knuckles. 'Let's approach this from a sociological angle. What do you think is the most urgent issue facing us as we face the twenty-first century, Tom?'

'I dunno. Global warming? Antibiotic resistance? Nuclear terrorism?'

His expression told me I'd misunderstood the question. I was always rubbish at this kind of thing.

'No, Tom, that wasn't the kind of thing I was thinking about. I was thinking about societal issues.'

'Oh, right,' I said, trying to look intelligent. Lucy used to say she could always tell when I was doing this because I tended to go cross-eyed.

'I'm actually talking about trust, Tom.' Blank gave me an expectant look.

'Ah,' I said, slowly. 'Of course.'

'Trust is the key issue in the internet age. Institutions are perceived to be failing all around us. The banks have had to be bailed out. Governments are corrupt. The churches are full of child abusers. Who can we turn to?' He spread his arms in a dramatic gesture. 'The answer is that we can trust no one any more. Any system that mandates a central authority is no longer deemed worthy of our attention.'

'But that's a recipe for chaos, isn't it?'

'Precisely. Enter the blockchain, the solution to all our problems.'

'Ah. I was wondering where that came in.'

'We begin with a fellow called Satoshi Nakamoto. Or rather claiming to be called that, because no one has ever actually seen him in public. He may be Japanese as his name suggests, or – more likely – he's some white dude pretending to be Japanese to give himself a veneer of exoticism. Cultural appropriation obviously being a totally twenty-first century thing. He may even be several white dudes, for all we know. The point is, "he" wrote the paper that set out how bitcoin could work in October 2008. Remember 2008?'

I thought hard. 'Banking crash?'

'Bingo. World ripe for new paradigms. Disinter-mediation! Disruption! Get rid of the fat cats on Wall

Street, replace them with a decentralised digital currency! Very libertarian.'

'I can see how it would appeal to my father. He's an ageing hippy.'

'Well, scratch a hippy and you'll find a libertarian lurking underneath. Then again, scratch a libertarian and you'll find a fascist, so be careful what you wish for. But we'll come onto that later.'

'Interesting idea, though,' I said. 'The bitcoin thing, I mean.'

'Ooh yes. No doubt about that.'

'But how does it work? How do I keep my money safe and how do I use it to buy stuff?'

'Well, this is where the fun starts. Your bitcoins, or rather the transactions you make, are held on a thing called a blockchain.'

'Ah yes. My Dad mentioned that.'

'Basically, it's a ledger containing details of every single transaction. To make sure it's completely public and decentralised, everyone gets an up to date copy of it, too. And every time a new transaction gets added to it, it's done in such a way that it's impossible to hack without destroying the chain completely. So once a transaction's in the blockchain ledger, it's in there forever. It's all done by performing recursive cryptographic hashes, but you don't want me to go through that, do you?'

'I don't think so.'

'Very wise. So go on, ask me. How do the transactions get added safely without a central authority?'

'How do they?' I said.

'Proof-of-work.'

'What's that?'

'Basically,' said Blank, 'if you want to set up as a bit-coin miner – and believe me, you don't want to do that any more, because there's no money in it any more, and we'll come on to why in a minute – this is what you have to do. You grab a load of unprocessed transactions, perform a hash, incorporate the hash from the last block on the ledger, chuck in a random number that you've come up with yourself, perform another hash and check to see if it matches a magic number. Chances are it won't, so you change the random number you added to something else and try again. And so on, until you crack the code and you win the chance to add your block of unprocessed transactions to the ledger and collect your fee. Your fee comes in bitcoin, with its concomitant liquidity and vol-atility issues, but never mind, you've won. You basically beat everyone else by proving that you can work harder than them.'

My head was spinning. 'OK,' I said, slowly. 'I think I've got that. So, hang on—'

'Now,' said Blank. 'Here's the problem. Proof-of-work is humongously inefficient BY DESIGN. It is literally intended to use as much computing power as possible in order to slow the rate of block addition to one every ten minutes. If it looks like the blocks are added any faster than this, they make it more difficult to crack the hash. Which means one, an increasingly insane amount of computer power – and hence actual electrical power – worldwide is being devoted to bitcoin mining, possibly to the extent that global warming is being accelerated as a result, and two, it's no longer feasible for small-scale operators to be involved any more, with the result that bitcoin mining is now incorporated into a small, select coterie of high-powered units, mostly in China. So forget all that stuff about decentralisation, folks.'

The last time I'd had a conversation like this, it was the first time I'd met Rufus Fairbanks and I was listening to him describing how the City of London had set up a market in order to trade grandmothers and, in many ways, this seemed no less preposterous.

'Is this really true?' I said.

'Oh yes. There's a theory I've seen which states that Satoshi Nakamoto is actually a visitor from the distant future, come back in time in order to fool everyone into diverting every single computer resource on the planet into cryptocurrencies so that research on everything else stops, thus averting the impending Singularity. It's about as plausible an explanation as anything else, to be honest.'

I laughed at this. Then I noticed that Matt Blank wasn't joining in.

'Right,' I said. 'So where do the other cryptocurrencies come in?'

'Well, the thing is, as I've said, cryptocurrencies appeal to a certain type of mindset. And people who share that view of the world like to think they're massively clued-up individuals. The sort of people who think they can spot a sure-fire investment before anyone else on the planet. So a well-marketed ICO is like catnip. All you need to do is sprinkle it with loads of technobollocks to make it look like it's loaded with zappy new features, add some insanely optimistic and heavily qualified profit projections, get some celeb or other to buy in and Bob's your uncle.'

'What was an ICO again?'

'Initial currency offering.'

'I take it you've been involved with some of these?'

Blank cocked his head on one side and squinted ceiling-wards, as if performing some kind of calculation. 'I've done a few.' He paused. 'Yeah, I've done a few. I've sailed a hundred-metre superyacht full of techies and hookers halfway round the Mediterranean. I've flown a blimp to Abu Dhabi and back with a cargo of coked-up journalists – lost a few on the way, but no one seemed too bothered. I've bought up an entire village in Kazakhstan just so the punters could raze it to the ground with artillery fire. So, yeah, I've done a few ICOs.'

I looked at him, wondering how much of this to believe.

'What about Tulpencoins?'

'Ha, yes. That was one of the flakiest. I—' He must have caught sight of my expression. 'Oh, I remember now. Your Dad invested in them, didn't he?'

'All his life savings.'

'Ah,' he said. 'Another one?' he added, waving his empty glass at me.

'Guess so,' I said.

This wasn't getting any better.

'Been thinking,' he said as he sat down again with our beers. 'The bunch behind Tulpencoins are at it again. The Tulpencoin Super Plus. Launch coming up soon – one of the less dramatic ones, although it's sold out, with a long waiting list. But—' he paused to sip at his beer '—I could get you in if you want.'

'Why? I don't have any money to invest, and given what I now know, I really don't think I'd want to—'

'That's not what I'm saying, Tom. The only way your dad will ever get his money back is if you can shame that bunch into doing something about it. Tackle them at the launch for the Super Plus and you might just get somewhere. Just don't mention that it was me who got you in there.'

'That's... brilliant,' I said. 'Really appreciate that. So, when is this?'

'Thursday evening, at the Old Rococo Theatre in Drury Lane. I just happen to have a spare ticket.' He reached into the inside pocket of his jacket, pulled out a ticket and handed it to me. 'I also have a spare backstage pass,' he added, passing that to me as well. I studied the description of the event on the ticket.

'Who's Kevin Wilberts?' I said.

Blank rolled his eyes. 'Some alt-right tosser philosopher they've hired to pull in the crowds. He's the one who says you can use mathematics to prove the innate superiority of white heterosexual males. It'll go down a storm with the crypto crowd – they love that sort of thing.'

'How do you cope with these people?' I said.

'Like I said, it's business. But let's just say I wouldn't be totally unhappy if someone embarrassed them at the launch. I've worked with more likeable people. I'm actually trying to get out of this business altogether. It all gets a bit exhausting after a while.'

Matt Blank put his pint down and gave a deep sigh. Now I looked at him closer, he seemed tired. There were deep bags under his eyes and a general air of weariness about him.

'What are they like?' I said.

He shrugged. 'They're like the kind of people who'd hire someone like Kevin Wilberts to speak at their launch. Enthusiastic, totally dedicated to their cause and one hundred per cent focused on disrupting anything that gets in their line of sight, without any thought to the social consequences. Chief techie is a guy called Tiger de Montfort. Aussie extraction. Seems harmless enough, but I'm not sure I trust him or his software.'

'Who's in charge, though?'

'Well, that's the weird thing. They're privately owned, but no one seems to know who by. There's a rumour that the owner's coming on Thursday, but I'm not holding my breath.'

Matt Blank drained his pint and stood up.

'Gotta go,' he said, standing up and holding his hand out again. This time I was prepared and I made a pre-emptive strike. We had a brief tussle before we simultaneously released each other. 'See you Thursday?'

'Sure,' I said. 'See you then. Really appreciate this, by the way.'

'It's nothing. To be honest, I'd quite like to have someone else friendly backstage with me when Mr Big shows up.' For a moment, he almost looked frightened.

Chapter 7

Ali was back at the flat when I returned. She was lying on the bed eating a pepperoni pizza straight from the box.

'Go well?' she said, holding the box out to me. Evidently, her relationship with Patrice was continuing to prosper. I took a slice, if nothing else to encourage her in her new-found spirit of generosity.

'I don't know. I've got a ticket to some kind of cryptocurrency launch on Thursday.'

'Oh, for fuck's sake.'

'Yeah.'

'Jesus. Well, I'm assuming you're not foolish enough to be investing all your remaining pennies in it, so I'm assuming it must have something to do with finding Dot.'

'Not directly, but—'

'I'm not even going to ask why crypto. No, actually, I really am going to ask why crypto?'

'Turns out my Dad invested in one.'

'I can believe that.'

'Hey! That's not fair.'

'Remember. I've met your Dad. He would totally fall for a crypto scam.'

'Yeah, you're right. He would. And he did.' My attention was suddenly caught by a large tank sitting on the chest of drawers. 'What's that?' I said.

'It's a vivarium.'

'OK, but what's in it?'

'Bertrand.'

'Bertrand,' I repeated. 'I'm going to regret asking this, but what kind of thing is Bertrand?'

'Ball python,' said Ali. 'Just a small one.'

'What's it doing in our flat?' I wasn't entirely happy about this.

'Oh, Patrice keeps reptiles.'

As an explanation, I felt that this fell short by some distance. 'But what's Bertrand doing here?' I said.

'Ah, right. He's been feeling a bit jealous of Maryam, so we thought, well, she thought—'

'Maryam?'

'Some kind of lizard.'

'Some kind?'

'Oh, I've no idea what kind of fucking lizard Maryam is, so don't ask. Look, I'm new to all this, for fuck's sake.'

'Can we put it outside for the night?' I said. I was pretty sure what the answer would be.

'Fuck, no. Patrice'd kill me. Needs to stay at a constant temperature.'

'Great. So, um… what do you have to feed him on?'

'Mice. She's going to drop one in tomorrow.'

'Fine. And what's going to happen when our landlord finds out?'

'Details.'

I peered into the glass tank. Something was slithering purposefully inside.

'Not very cuddly, is it?'

Ali didn't bother answering me.

When I got up on Tuesday morning, I was beginning to feel I was now in a good position to make some real progress, if only I could somehow stitch all the various disparate strands together into a serviceable garment. Unfortunately, all I had right now to work with was some kind of mutant five-armed pullover with no opening for a head.

Ali and I headed back to the library, Ali to work and me to find out more about the Tulpencoin gang. I wanted to work out if it would be worth making use of my ticket for the launch. But first, I had a quick check of my emails. The very first one was another message from whoever it was who was pretending to be Rufus Fairbanks.

The email simply said, *The second number is also 1.*

Which was, obviously, massively helpful. It was exactly the sort of thing that Dorothy would do, so I opened up a reply.

Is it you, Dorothy? I began, and then thought better of it. I changed it to simply *Who is this?* and pressed the Send button.

There was an immediate reply.

After that, we have 2.

I couldn't be bothered to engage with this crap, so I decided to put the internet on one side for the rest of the day. There was other stuff to be getting on with. I needed to work out how I was going to break into a hospital.

The main building of St Jude's was located in an imposing Victorian gothic building close to the City of London. I took a stroll around the perimeter and established where all the entrances and exits were. My plan was to locate the laundry and find myself a comfy set of scrubs that would enable me to pass myself off as a junior doctor. If I did my research now, there was a good chance that there would be a different shift on when I executed the plan in the evening, which would make it less likely that anyone would notice that the chap who had been enquiring as to the whereabouts of Benjamin Unsworth and that nice new locum doctor were one and the same.

I walked up to the main reception and established that Benjamin was on the fifth floor, on Pratchett Ward, although he wasn't able to receive any visitors at the moment. Apparently, they'd closed Pratchett Ward last year, but they'd dumped him up there in case he was infectious or something. I thanked the receptionist and made to go out again. After I'd checked that no one was watching, I took a quick detour down a side corridor and found the service lift that went down into the basement. I slipped inside and pressed the button to go down. When I reached the bottom, I snuck a quick glance to left and right, then stepped out.

On the wall in front of me, a sign informed me that the laundry was to my right, so I headed that way, taking care not to catch the eye of any of the orderlies pushing trolleys back and forth along the corridor. No one seemed particularly bothered by my presence. I was in the world of the underlings here, a world where people just wanted to get on with stuff without wasting time on strangers.

The laundry was at the end of the corridor. One side of it was entirely taken up with washing machines whose drums were roughly the size and power of the engine turbines on a jumbo jet. Every now and then one of the orderlies would turn up with a new trolley full of untidy blue garments, chuck them all into one of the machines and set it going. Meanwhile, one of their colleagues would empty a completed load from one of the other machines and begin to fold them all into neat piles on another trolley ready to be wheeled back into the land of work.

'Can I help you?' said a voice behind me.

Shit.

'N-no, I was just on my way,' I said, turning round and trying to avoid catching the eye of this new arrival. Like me, it was male and wearing a jacket and trousers. Unlike me, it was also wearing an official badge, which said 'Paul Milledge, Administrative Supervisor.' I could do with one of those badges, I thought.

'I... I've just started a locum shift,' I said, 'and I managed to get lost. It's so easy to take a wrong turning, isn't it?'

'Tell me about it,' said Paul Milledge. I hoped he didn't notice my massive sigh of relief. 'This place is a bloody rabbit warren. Did they sort you out with a badge?'

'Er, no. I wasn't sure who to see about that. I haven't worked here before, and the agency weren't terribly helpful.'

Milledge rolled his eyes. 'You're not the first I've heard say that. Let me guess. MediTemp?'

'Bang on,' I said. I took a risk at this point and attempted a high five. Milledge responded perfectly and I knew that everything was going to be all right. We were mates now, me and Paul.

'Fucking muppets, they are, 'scuse my French. Word of advice. Get yourself signed up with Locums4Us – that's with a number 4, right? – 'cos they're the tits, believe me. Get paid on time, too. Look, come with me and I'll fix you up with Aysha. She can do all the paperwork. She knows all about MediTemp, oh yes.'

He turned round and headed for the lift. I had no choice but to follow him. I was in way too deep now.

Aysha's office was the place where the massed allied army of filing cabinets had decided to muster before their final assault on humanity. The surface of her desk looked as if it had last seen daylight several decades previously and her computer screen was plastered with post-it notes reminding her to pay the vet's bill, call Geoff and buy spinach.

'Aysha, my love,' said Milledge. 'Fresh meat for you.'

Aysha swivelled round in her chair and eyed me up suspiciously. She wore a floral print dress and a pair of glasses with outsize lenses. She was probably in her midfifties.

'And you would be?' she said.

Shit. I'd forgotten to have a name ready. 'Jim Beam,' I said. It wasn't the first time I'd used the name of my father's favourite tipple as a pseudonym, although I had a strong suspicion that no one had really believed me that time. 'Er, Dr Jim Beam,' I added. I was fairly sure that by this point I had probably committed some kind of criminal act. Possibly several.

'He's with MediTemp,' said Milledge, helpful as ever.

'Oh god,' said Aysha. She rummaged through the debris on her desk and located a computer keyboard and mouse. She hit return a few times and waggled the mouse, and the computer screen burst into life, displaying a request for her to type in her password to unlock it. She typed something in the box. Nothing happened. She tried again. Again, nothing happened. After the third time, she reached for her phone and tapped an extension number. She held the phone in her hand for a minute while it rang at the other end and then put it down again.

'Bloody IT,' she said. 'And you can bet that all they'll suggest is turn the bloody thing off and on again and then it'll spend the rest of the week applying updates.'

'I'll have a word,' said Milledge.

'If you could, love,' said Aysha. 'I'd appreciate that.' She opened a drawer in the cabinet on her left and pulled out a file. She scanned the first page and tutted. 'No mention of a Jim Beam here,' she said.

'Maybe they haven't sent it through yet,' I said.

'More likely they've sent it to the wrong place,' said Milledge.

'Ha, yes,' I said. 'Wouldn't be the first time they've done that to me.' We all laughed, including Aysha. Excellent. She was on team Beam now.

'Look,' she said 'I shouldn't really do this, but I'll set you up with a badge anyway.' She reached into her desk drawer and pulled out a blank badge proforma. She scribbled 'Dr Jim Beam' on it, then looked up at me. 'Department?'

I paused. It was still entirely possible that I could cock this up. 'Upper GI,' I said, remembering a phrase that Lucy occasionally used to mutter.

'With old slasher Kumar?' she said, adding 'Upper GI' to my job description. 'Best of luck with that.' We were definitely best mates now.

'I'd heard he was highly thought of,' I said, before bursting out laughing. Aysha and Milledge joined in. I was actually quite disappointed that I wasn't going to be working for Mr Kumar now. It sounded like it could be fun. I turned to go. Then I remembered.

'Where can I get some scrubs?' I said.

Aysha was about to say something, but Milledge butted in, 'It's OK, I'm going that way myself.' He beckoned to me to follow and we headed out of Aysha's office. In order to get where we were going, we had to walk past reception, but fortunately everyone there was occupied with other people, so no one spotted me. I was still expecting Milledge to put a hand on my shoulder and tell me that the game was up, sonny, but instead he led me to a storeroom full of blue scrubs.

'Here we are,' he said. Then he gave me a quizzical look. Oh god, I thought. Here it comes. But all he said was, 'Medium, I think? Am I right? 'Course I am.' Then he slapped me on the back and left me to choose whatever I wanted. So I picked out a set that looked like they'd fit me and snuck into the nearest toilet. I stripped right down, put my new scrubs on and then put my ordinary clothes back on top. Then I waddled out of the hospital, Michelin-man style, without anyone saying another word to me.

I checked my watch. It was ten o'clock in the evening. I was standing in the underground car park of St Jude's Hospital, admiring the consultants' expensive cars and trying to calm my breathing. I took a plastic bag out of my pocket and started to take off my outer clothing. Once I was down to my scrubs, I stuffed everything into the bag and looked around for somewhere to stash it. There were probably lockers in the actual building, but I'd already decided that I didn't want to do anything that might draw attention to myself. Better to stay lurking in the shadows.

I eventually found a place behind a bulkhead that looked a suitable place to dump a bag full of clothing for an hour or so, and having shed my outer skin I was now ready to face the world as Junior Doctor James Beam. Perhaps tonight I would, at last, begin to find out what had happened to Dorothy. I slung my pass around my neck and stepped out into the light, sauntered around to the front of the building and prepared to walk back into the hospital as if having just stubbed out a sly ciggie.

No one challenged me as I strode past reception and on to the lifts. Another junior doctor hopped in as the doors were closing, talking into his mobile. 'Five mil? What about Pentadoxin? No, no. Twenty-nine over twelve. Sure, but she's nil by mouth.' He looked at me as if to ask my opinion. I shrugged. The lift stopped at the fourth floor. 'Flamacor?' he said as he exited. At the precise point at which the doors were fully open, something in the departing junior doctor's pocket began to emit a screeching sound. He froze, pulled it out and examined it, before muttering 'Shit!' Then he turned round and looked at me.

'Crash call on Townsend,' he said. 'Can you give us a hand?'

'I—' I was torn between a natural desire to help and the knowledge that there was very little contribution that

I could make. Moreover, there was a very good chance that whatever contribution I did make could actually kill someone. Fortunately, the doors were now well on their way to closing again.

'Sorry,' I mouthed at him, as I left for the next floor up.

The fifth floor was eerily silent, but it was easy to tell which room Benjamin Unsworth was in, because that was the one with the uniformed police officer sitting outside, engrossed in a word search problem. It looked as if the officer was guarding him from unwanted visitors and not keeping him in custody, which was promising. Evidently, they still hadn't worked out that he was a suspect in the unsolved murder of Hilary van Beek.

'Evening,' I said, hoping that a confident demeanour would continue to serve me well. 'Come to see the mystery man,' I added.

'Evening,' said the officer, putting down his puzzle magazine. 'Second opinion, then?' he added.

'Sorry?'

He jerked a thumb towards the door. 'Your colleague's already in there.'

'Oh, yes. Right.' Who was he talking about? This was going to be more complicated than I'd imagined.

He got to his feet with some effort. 'Well, seeing as there's two of you now, think I'll grab some fresh air. Supposed to be relieved half an hour ago, but Bob's off sick and Danny got reassigned and there's no one else available.'

'Right,' I said. 'Sure. Go ahead.'

He wandered off down the corridor, back towards the lifts. I opened the door and went into the room.

There was indeed a doctor already in the room, leaning over an unconscious Benjamin Unsworth. She was wearing a white coat and seemed to be checking him over with a stethoscope. As I closed the door behind me, she looked back at me with a startled expression.

'Who the hell are you?' she said.

'I… I've come to check up on Mr Unsworth,' I said. Bugger. I shouldn't have said his name. Even so, her reaction was somewhat unexpected, because she straightened up and launched herself at me. I was completely taken by surprise and I failed to defend myself in any way as she kneed me in the balls, causing me to double over in agony.

'What did you do that for?' I gasped.

But she wasn't finished yet. As I struggled for breath and raised my head she knocked me back against the wall and put one hand on my throat, waving a scalpel in my face with the other.

'How do you know his name?' she hissed.

I was about to answer when I was distracted by the sight of the name badge attached to her blouse. The badge identified her as Dr Helen Matheson.

Chapter 8

'How do you know he's called Unsworth?' said Dr Matheson again.

'I was with him when he was attacked,' I said. There didn't seem any point in giving a full explanation for the time being.

'Who are you, for Christ's sake?'

'Dr Jim Beam,' I said. 'It says so on my pass, see? Look, would you mind not waving that thing in my face?'

'What are you doing here?'

'Like I said, I've come to check on Benjamin Unsworth. I wanted to see if he was conscious enough to finish telling me what he was trying to tell me when he was attacked. Sorry, I'm gibbering. Really, can you take that thing out of my face?'

Dr Matheson put the scalpel into her breast pocket, relaxed her grip and began patting me down. I could have told her that scrubs are pretty useless for hiding weaponry, but I didn't think that would have helped. She stood back from me and I pulled myself away from the wall, still in some considerable pain.

'I'm guessing you're not a real doctor, then,' she said.

'No. I'm guessing that you're not one either,' I said.

Matheson ignored me. 'We need to get him out of here. Despite the presence of PC Plod out there, he's still in danger.'

'Your PC Plod has just buggered off for a breath of fresh air.'

'In which case, we definitely need to get him out of here.'

'Doesn't he still need treatment?'

'My people can deal with it.'

'Your people?'

Once again, she ignored my question. She fetched a wheelchair from the corner of the room and unfolded it ready for use. She gestured to me to join her at Benjamin's bedside as she rolled the covers down and prepared to lift him out. For a weedy lad, Benjamin was surprisingly heavy and it took both of us to manoeuvre him into a satisfactory position in the wheelchair. The fact that one of us was recovering from a severe groin injury probably didn't help.

'Bet you're pleased I turned up,' I said.

'No,' said Matheson, with some feeling.

She grabbed a blanket and folded it over Benjamin, tucking it under his legs to stop it sliding off. During the whole time, he remained unconscious. Matheson arranged the drip stand behind the wheelchair and gestured to it.

'Can I trust you to look after that?' she said.

'Of course,' I said.

'Right,' she said. 'Let's go.'

Matheson pulled the door open and nudged Benjamin's wheelchair out into the corridor. I followed in their wake, one eye anxiously monitoring the drip as it wobbled along behind them.

'OK, we'll take the service lift down to the basement,' she said, turning to me. She began to speed up and I found myself having to do an ungainly half-walk, half-jog to keep pace with her. We had to stop halfway along to rearrange Benjamin, whose upper body had decided to adopt a more relaxed posture and was now dangling halfway out of the chair, with the fingers of his left hand about to jam under one of the wheels. We turned a corner and noticed another figure walking towards us at the far end of the corridor. He looked familiar, although I couldn't, at first, work out where I'd seen him before. Then I realised.

'We've got company,' I said.

'Someone you know?' said Matheson.

'It's the guy from the café. The one who attacked Benjamin.'

'You sure?'

'Positive.' Oh shit. The figure was reaching into his pocket. 'Shall I call for help?' I said.

'Too late.' The man now had something in his hand, which he was raising to point at Benjamin. Instinctively I ducked behind the chair. Matheson reached down, grabbed me by the scruff of the neck and pulled me back up again.

'Sorry,' I said, feeling embarrassed. Matheson ignored me and just spun the wheelchair around and headed back to the end of the corridor. As we rounded the corner, there was a soft thud and something embedded itself into the wall opposite. We flattened ourselves against the wall, Matheson nearest the corner, then myself and then finally Benjamin in his wheelchair.

'He's using a silencer,' she remarked. 'Well, two can play at that game.' Unexpectedly, she reached into her inside pocket and took out a gun of her own. Then she withdrew a short tube from another pocket and proceeded to screw it onto the end of the barrel. 'OK, I've got this,' she said as she poked her head round the corner, 'stay there.' This seemed to me to be an eminently sensible instruction and I decided to obey it to the letter.

Another bullet thudded into the wall opposite, and Matheson brought her head back quickly. Then she took her gun in both hands and launched herself into the corridor before taking a shot at our assailant. Then she swung back against the wall, muttering 'Shit' to herself.

'Did you get him?' I said.

She risked another glance down the corridor, then shook her head. 'He's gone.'

'Gone?'

'Yeah. Guess I scared him off.'

'Right.' I hoped she was right. I really, really hoped she was right. We edged out into the corridor again and began to make our way back towards the lift. When we got there, she pressed the button to summon it, and at this point we became aware of a clattering in the distance. Something was approaching. Matheson glanced at me and stabbed at the button again.

'Come on, come on,' she was muttering under her breath. There was a gentle 'ping' as the lift arrived, just as a trolley emerged from the end of the corridor with the gunman crouched down behind it. A bullet ricocheted off the wheelchair and lodged itself in the ceiling. 'Christ,' said Matheson, pulling her own gun out again. She appeared to aim at the rapidly advancing trolley, before changing her mind and redirecting the gun at an antiseptic gel dispenser on the wall just ahead of it.

The dispenser exploded, spraying gel all over the floor and causing the gunman to slip over, falling flat on his face and releasing his grip on the trolley. As I backed into the lift, pulling Benjamin and the drip stand after me, I saw the gunman raise himself for one last time to aim at Matheson. But before he could take his shot, she fired first, before stepping into the lift herself.

There was a moment's silence between us as we descended.

'You left him there,' I said. 'You left him there to die.'

'He's in a hospital, sweetheart,' said Matheson. 'He'll be fine.'

'But—'

'I mean, if you like, we can go back up there, pick up his unconscious body, take him down to A&E and say "Hey, guys, we just shot this chap, can you patch him up?" And they'd probably just go, "Sure, sure. Happens all the time."'

'I didn't mean—'

'Well, I guess you're right, that would be the humane thing to do. But no. Not this time.'

'Who are you, anyway?' I said, frowning.

Before she could answer, we arrived at the basement. Matheson led the way as we left the lift and headed towards the laundry for the second time that day. This time, we walked straight past it to the door that led out into the car park. I suddenly felt cold in my scrubs.

'Look, do you mind? I left my clothes in a bag over there. Can I just go and pick them up?'

'No time for that, sweetheart. Need to get moving.' Matheson pushed off towards the ramp that led up into the street, then she power-walked away from St Jude's, with me in her wake trying to keep Benjamin's drip stand from tipping over. Every now and then we had to pause to reposition him.

'Have you got any rope or something?' I shouted to her. 'There's a good chance he's going to end up on the pavement if we carry on like this.'

'No time,' she replied.

'You sure he's going to be all right?'

'Yeah. He's a survivor.'

'I hope you're right.'

'I'm always right, sweetheart.'

We came to a juddering halt on the corner a couple of blocks away and Matheson turned round to face the oncoming traffic. It was quite sparse at this time of night, but eventually a taxi turned up. There was a certain amount of fumbling to get all three of us in, especially as neither Matheson nor myself had a clue as to how to collapse the drip stand. We eventually gave up and detached the bag from it, before pushing Benjamin inside. Matheson then got involved in a heated exchange with the driver. I assumed this was about our destination, because I caught snatches about 'going south of the river at this time of night' and 'that's in bloody Kent!' At the end of it, she reached into her pocket and for one awful moment I thought she was going to threaten him with her gun. Instead, she took out a wad of cash and waved it in his face. We moved off, heading south of the river towards Kent.

As soon as we were settled in, Matheson took out her phone.

'Yeah,' she said. 'I've reclaimed the asset... yes, yes, he's fine... needed to take action... no, he won't talk... picked up a stray... claims he was there when the asset was mugged... could be useful... no, OK, OK, take your point... ciao.'

'So, who are you?' I said again. 'Who are you working for?'

Matheson put her finger to her lips and inclined her head towards the driver in the front of the taxi.

'OK,' I said, lowering my voice. 'It's just I'd like to have some idea of what I'm caught up in.'

'Sweetheart, you haven't the faintest ghost of an idea of what you're caught up in,' said Matheson. Then without any warning, she took a compact spray out of her pocket and blasted it in my face.

'So sorry about all this,' was the last thing I heard before I lost consciousness.

According to my watch, it was a little after three o'clock in the morning when I woke up again to find myself lying face down on a picnic bench in a lay-by. I could see the outline of an oast house in the distance, so I assumed I must be somewhere in the middle of Kent. The rapid shivering over my body formed an unpleasant counterpoint to the pounding jackhammer in my head and I cursed Matheson, or whoever she really was, for not letting me pick up my outer clothes.

My mouth tasted like the bottom of a cage occupied by a squabbling family of incontinent budgies that had repelled all attempts by their owner to clean up for the past year. Every muscle in my body ached as if I'd accidentally spent the last few hours taking part in some kind of moonlit triathlon. It struck me that this was almost certainly how it felt to be a zombie, which went some way towards explaining why they always seemed so mindlessly angry in movies.

I hauled myself upright and rubbed my arms and legs to get my circulation going again. The sky was clear, which at least meant that there wasn't likely to be any rain soon, but it felt cold enough to make me a hypothermia risk. I needed to find shelter for the rest of the night, so I swung my legs off the picnic bench and tried to stand up. After I'd fallen over once, I tried again. My legs went into spasm, but this time I managed a couple of steps. Then I felt a wave of nausea sweep over me and I threw up. I felt considerably better after this.

I paused, wondering which way to go. The oast house in the distance looked inviting. Perhaps it would be one of those conversions that rich people went in for around these parts, in which case there was every chance there would be outbuildings. An outbuilding was just what I needed right now – preferably one with a nice warm bed in it.

The road was unnervingly dark, and every now and then there was a scuffling in the undergrowth as some nocturnal animal took exception to my intrusion into their territory.

'Sorry, guys,' I said, more for my own benefit than theirs, the sound of my own voice being a reassuring reminder that not everything had gone to shit quite yet. I wasn't a massive fan of the countryside at the best of times, and this was one of the worst. Every now and then my vision was temporarily blinded by the undipped headlights of an oncoming car and it took several minutes to readjust afterwards. None of the drivers seemed to find it remotely unusual that a doctor in full scrubs was wandering along an unlit road at this time of the morning, which made me wonder what went on in the hospitals in this corner of Kent.

After twenty minutes or so I arrived at the oast house. It was a conversion job as I'd predicted, with a large silver BMW and the cleanest red Range Rover I've ever seen in the driveway. I tentatively nudged the gate open to let myself through and immediately a security light blazed at me. I tiptoed down the drive past the house itself, hoping that my footsteps on the gravel didn't seem as earsplittingly deafening to the residents of the house as they did to me.

A light went on in an upstairs window and I crouched down in the shadows. Someone pulled a curtain aside and opened the window.

'Can't see anything,' I heard. 'Probably those shagging badgers again.'

I thought briefly about making a noise like a shagging badger to reinforce this opinion, but I wasn't a hundred per cent sure what this might involve, so I held my breath instead. After some discussion, the window closed again and the light went off. I continued on my way towards the back of the house, where, glory be, there were outbuildings. Stables. These people had horses. Of course they had horses.

The stable block was arranged in an L shape, with two loose boxes on one side, one on the other and what looked like a general store room in the middle. All three were occupied by large wild-eyed beasts who were regarding me with some interest. Maybe they thought I was bringing food. Or perhaps they thought I was food. Then again, weren't horses vegetarian? But someone had once explained to me that horses were massively unpredictable things, being principally made up of half a ton of raw, unprocessed emotion, so I decided not to engage with any of them for the time being.

There were several horse rugs hanging on a hook on the wall, and I grabbed one of them and headed for the store room. The floor felt soft and surprisingly comfortable when I lay down on it with the rug wrapped round me to keep me warm, and within seconds I was fast asleep.

Chapter 9

I was dreaming that some nocturnal monster was slowly devouring me, starting for some arcane reason at the elbows, when I woke up to find that something was indeed nibbling at me in that exact spot. I sat up sharply and, in the dawn's early light, I saw a small, black-haired Shetland pony skittering away from me in alarm.

Jesus.

I stood up, holding the rug in front of me, toreador-style. I had a sudden, overwhelming, desire to get out of there as quickly as possible. The problem, however, was that the pony was now standing between me and the stable door. It was a curious-looking animal. As horses go, it was definitely on the short side and its legs were spindly and delicate, even if the hooves on the ends of them still looked as if they could cause substantial damage. However, from the top of its legs up it was built like a baby hippopotamus, and it was baring its teeth in a weird rictus that didn't look terribly friendly.

'OK, pony,' I said. 'Just let me out and we can still be friends.'

The pony made an odd kind of grunting noise, which didn't sound like anything a normal horse would make.

Trust me to end up in a confined space with some kind of evil demonic hybrid beast from hell.

'Hello,' said a small voice. I looked and saw a pair of eyes peering over the stable door at me. 'Are you the vet?' The voice was perkier than a human voice had any right to be at that time of the morning and belonged to a small girl with blond hair in ringlets.

'Er, yes, that's right,' I said, putting the rug down and brushing away some of the bedding off my scrubs. 'Come to see little…'

'Puff Blossom,' she said.

'What?'

'That's my horsey's name.'

'Oh,' I said. 'I'm guessing you had a hand in that?'

'Mummy says you're a useless twat,' said the girl, ignoring my question.

'Sorry?' I resented having my veterinary skills impugned by a random ten-year-old.

'And Daddy says the whole sodding lot are going to end up in a pie if those bastards don't give him a decent bonus this year.'

'Well, that would be a shame,' I said. He seems nice, I thought.

'But Daddy wouldn't really do that,' she said. 'At least I don't think he would.'

She opened up the door and came in to the loose box carrying a net full of hay. She hung it up on a hook on the wall and Puff Blossom began tearing eagerly at it. I saw my chance and followed the girl out, but not before I managed to tread in a gleaming heap of fresh horse droppings. I watched in amazement as she calmly walked into each of the other loose boxes in turn and put down a bucket of feed for each of the horses, every one of which was about fifteen times her size.

'Anyway, Puff Blossom seems to be doing just fine,' I said, but the girl was now busy with a bucket and shovel, picking up more of the stuff I'd just trodden in. This looked like slave labour, although she seemed to be perfectly happy about it. 'Shouldn't you be at school?' I said.

'It's half-term, silly,' she said, with a giggle.

'Right,' I said.

While she was occupied, I decided to sneak back towards the house. I needed to restore myself to civilisation. The side door was open and I could hear someone moving about upstairs, singing in a female voice. I took this as a sign that the coast was clear, so I nipped in and found the toilet. As I flushed it, a voice from upstairs called out 'Is that you, Annabelle?' I stood stock still, debating with myself whether or not I should try to imitate the girl's voice in reply. There was silence for several long seconds, and then I heard the sound of a shower.

Perfect.

I tiptoed upstairs, hoping that the sound of my footsteps would be muffled by the thick beige carpet. When I reached the top, I looked back and realised that the thick beige carpet was now dappled with occasional highlights of horse poo. I took my shoes off, even though I realised straightaway that it was a token gesture. The damage had already been done.

The shower was still going strong, so I searched around for the main bedroom. I located a wardrobe and rummaged around in it for a pair of men's trousers. I found a decent pair of jeans that looked around my size, plus a shirt and pullover. How much more time did I have? If I'd had any sense, I'd have simply run back down the stairs with the stolen clothes under my arm and got changed somewhere further down the road.

But in the heat of the moment, my desire to finally get free of my doctor's scrubs got the better of me and common sense flew straight out of the window and off towards Dover and the English Channel. I tore off my scrubs, throwing them onto the floor, and it was at that point, wearing my boxer shorts and absolutely nothing else, that I realised that the shower had stopped.

I froze.

The singing started again and I could hear it heading my way. Then a woman with long blonde hair bearing a distinct genetic resemblance to the girl from the stable passed the doorway wearing nothing but a pair of small towels – one spun around her head, turban style, and the other wrapped strategically around her middle.

'Morning,' I said.

'Morning,' she replied, continuing on her way.

Then I heard a scream.

Shit.

I opened a window and assessed the height of the jump. If I threw my new-found clothes out, plus the scrubs, there was a vague chance they might cushion my fall, but it was way too late for decision-making. I threw them out anyway, along with my shoes, but instead of landing in a useful homogeneous heap, the clothes scattered hopelessly in all directions.

Meanwhile, I could hear feet running downstairs, cutlery being rummaged for and then feet coming back upstairs. As the woman entered the room, holding an impressively evil carving knife, I grabbed the sides of the window, put one foot on the ledge and launched myself into the void.

I landed awkwardly and attempted to execute an authentic paratrooper-style roll in order to cushion the impact. This was partially successful, in that it limited my injuries to a twisted ankle and a severely gravel-grazed upper torso. I staggered to my feet and pulled on the trousers, stuck my feet back into my shoes without bothering to do up the laces, grabbed the rest of my clothing and limped off down the drive, pushing one arm into the shirt as I did so. By the time I reached the gate I was mostly decent, if a little untidy.

I still had no idea of where I was, but at least it was now getting light. I decided to head back the way I'd come, on the basis that it was probably going to get me closer to London. There was a chance that the lady of the house might decide to call the police, I suppose, but with any luck I would be halfway home by the time they got going. I somehow doubted that she'd come after me herself.

After a while I came to the picnic site where I'd found myself in the early hours of the morning, recognising it by the presence of the regurgitated contents of my stomach, now somewhat depleted owing to the attentions of some denizen of the night. At this point I became aware of a car approaching in the distance behind me, and some instinct made me throw myself under the bench just before a red Range Rover hurtled past. It seemed I was wrong about the lady of the house.

My phone rang. I fished it out of the pocket of my scrubs and answered it.

'Hello?'

'Where the fuck are you?' said Ali.

'That's a very good question,' I said, 'and not one amenable to an easy answer.'

'Try.'

'Somewhere in Kent. I went to try to talk to Benjamin Unsworth last night in hospital but I bumped into someone else who was kidnapping him or something and I ended up helping her and I think we may have shot someone along the way and then I got drugged and dumped by the roadside and so I spent the night in a stable with a Shetland pony and I borrowed some clothes and I had to jump out of a window and now the wife of the owner of the clothes is out looking for me and I've also got horseshit on my shoes.' There was silence on the other end of the phone. 'Ali?'

'Ah, fuck, I give up with you. As long as you haven't run off, then.'

'You really don't trust me, do you?'

'Why should I?'

'Because I'm your only hope, Ali.'

'Fuck me, I really am sunk, then,' she said. I ended the call and then ducked down again as I heard the sound of the Range Rover coming back. With any luck the woman from the oast house would try the other way now and then give up. I waited until she came past and then I was about to get up from my hiding place when a white van pulled into the lay-by. The driver got out, unzipped his fly and began to relieve himself.

I had a brainwave.

As quietly as I could, I slid out from under the picnic table and went round to the back of the van. I opened the back of it and saw that it was mostly filled with boxes but there was still space for a stowaway to hitch a ride. So I squeezed inside and gently pulled the door closed behind me. Not long after that, the van started again and we headed off towards London. Based on the journey the previous evening, I reckoned it would take us about an hour and a half to get to somewhere I could easily get home from. I only hoped he wasn't planning on making any deliveries before then.

For once, things went according to plan. It wasn't a pleasant experience, bouncing about in the dark in a cramped space, but we kept going. When the hour and a half was up, I risked a quick peek out of the back door of the van next time we came to a halt. We were sitting in a queue of traffic near London Bridge, and I was staring straight into the face of the driver of the taxi behind us. I decided to go for it. I opened the van door all the way and stepped out into the traffic just as it began to move off. I waved my hand at the taxi driver and gave a hopeful smile. The man just scowled and shook his head. No one else batted an eyelid.

'That's quite some smell you've got going on there,' said Ali, sniffing the air. She was sitting on the bed, scrolling through updates on her phone.

'It's horse, mainly,' I said. I'd scraped most of the mess off my shoes, but the aroma of the rug that I'd spent the night wrapped up in had soaked into the very pores of my skin and there would be no escape from the whiff until I'd spent a day or two under a shower.

'It's not going to catch on, pal.'

'No, you're right. I hope you appreciate the sacrifices I've been making for our cause.'

'Yeah, but what have you actually achieved? I take it you've come back with a whole load of new information.'

'Well, I know who Matheson is,' I said.

'Who's Matheson?'

'She's the one that Benjamin mentioned. At least I think it's her.'

'Is Matheson her real name?'

'Er... maybe?'

'So, what do you know about her?'

'She's a woman.'

'And? You've got contact details, perhaps?'

I sighed. 'No.'

'Who does she work for?'

'She didn't say.' Ali was staring at me. 'Look, it wasn't exactly easy to find out what was going on. Benjamin was out cold all the time I was with them and the Matheson woman wasn't particularly forthcoming. And she had a gun. I don't know about you but I'm not terribly comfortable about talking to people when they're waving guns around.' Ali was still staring at me. 'Well, what would you have done?'

Ali didn't say anything. She just shook her head slowly from side to side with a sympathetic smile. 'Never mind,' she said. 'At least it keeps you out of my hair.'

At this point, Patrice wandered in holding a plastic box. She walked over to the vivarium and slid the lid open. She took the lid off the box and removed something from it, before placing the box down next to the tank.

'Is that what I think it is?' I said.

'It's a mouse, yeah,' said Patrice.

'Right. Where do you get them from?'

'Oh, they come deep frozen.'

'Right,' I said. 'Right.' I had a spontaneous flashback to a time when I'd looked after a lizard belonging to a school chum whose diet consisted of live grasshoppers. The lizard, obviously, not the school chum – although looking back on it, he was the kind of kid who'd have been quite happy chomping on an insect or two if he ever got the chance. Anyway, the thing was, you had to deal with the whole food chain. You had to make sure the grasshoppers were fattened up ready for dumping into the lizard tank. Needless to say, given that my father got involved with the process, there were more grasshoppers bouncing around on the kitchen work surfaces at the end of it than there were providing nutrition to the lizard. Deep frozen mice seemed a much easier proposition, provided you didn't think too hard about exactly where they came from.

Patrice dangled the mouse by its tail over the tank and a slithery head popped up, opened up its jaws and accepted the proffered snack, before disappearing back into the depths. She put the lid back in place and picked up the box. Then she sat down on the bed next to Ali. The pair of them looked at me expectantly.

'Ah,' I said. 'I didn't realise I was interrupting something.'

'No worries,' said Ali.

'No worries,' said Patrice.

They both continued to stare at me. Patrice took Ali's hand.

'Look,' I said. 'I've had a bad night. I had to share a stable with—'

'A Shetland pony,' said Ali. 'I know. You told me.'

'Well, I'm knackered, if you want to know the truth.'

The two women exchanged the briefest of glances. Then they both got up and made to leave the flat.

'It's OK, we'll go to Patrice's,' said Ali, as if I'd just ruined her entire week.

'Cheers,' I said. Then I remembered something. 'What about Bertrand?' I said.

'He's cool,' said Patrice, with an innocent smile. 'He won't need feeding again for a couple of weeks. Just read him a bedtime story tonight and he'll be fine. He likes guys.'

Then they both left, leaving me and Bertrand to occupy the flat on our own. I crouched down and peered into the vivarium.

'So, what do you make of it all?' I said. Bertrand didn't make any attempt to reply, but continued to digest his mouse.

I spent the next few hours lying on the bed, half dozing and half trying to get my head round the events of the previous twenty-four hours. But it was all as opaque as ever. If only Dorothy was here to help, we'd have it cracked within a matter of minutes. But she wasn't, and for all I knew, she was part of it herself. What was she up to? Why hadn't she got in touch? Was she in danger? And what part did Benjamin Unsworth play in all this? What did he have to do with Helen Matheson? And who the hell *was* Helen Matheson, anyway?

About half past four I remembered I'd got a slot booked on a computer, so I left the flat and headed for the library. Checking through my emails would at least act as a kind of diversion.

Several members of the usual gang were there, along with a newbie I hadn't seen before who kept bothering each of us in turn, asking annoying questions about how to set up his email account. Despite the attentions of this bloke, who I decided to christen Newbie Neville, I spent a happy half hour deleting spam and catching up on the latest news about my mother's miniature alpaca herd in Tasmania. I'd missed out on several updates because whoever had stolen our computers had locked me out of my email account and I'd had to set up a completely new one, and – perhaps inevitably – most of the emails I sent out via my new address to inform my key correspondents of the change had gone straight to spam. Reading about her life out there, it all seemed rather idyllic, and for a moment I seriously wondered about abandoning all this madness and going out there to join her. I was sure I could work as an alpaca herdsman. How hard could it be?

But I couldn't just leave Dorothy behind. I was still clinging to a faint hope that she hadn't just run off with everything we had and that she still somehow needed me.

I was just about to finish up when I spotted one final email coming in, purporting to be from Rufus Fairbanks.

The next number, it said, *is 3.*

Oh, for crying out loud. 1, 2, 3 – anyone could work out what the next number is. Cut the portentous crap, mystery person. I opened up a reply.

Don't tell me. The next one's 4, isn't it? 1, 2, 3, 4. Well done me. Now what?

There, I thought. That'll show them, whoever they are. Don't mess with Winscombe. I began drumming my fingers on the table waiting for the reply to come through. Come on, come on. I've solved your little problem, I said to myself. Tell me what to do next. I looked up. Ramona the Romantic Novelist was glaring at me, so I stopped drumming.

Finally, the reply came through.

No, it said. *The next number is 5.*

What?

You've changed the rules, I wrote. *This isn't fair.*

I sat and waited for a full five minutes for the reply to come back. It didn't. If this was Dorothy, then since she'd been away she'd developed a seriously mean streak.

Was this some kind of test?

Well, obviously, it was some kind of test.

But what was I supposed to do?

I opened up another reply and sat for several minutes, trying to work out what to say. Eventually, I gave up and deleted the reply altogether. I thumped the table angrily, closed the session down and stood up. Everyone was looking at me.

'What?' I said.

'Are you all right?' said the boring, grey-haired family-tree man.

'What?' I said. 'Oh, yes, I'm fine. Fine.'

'You look terribly angry,' he said.

'No,' I said. 'Just very, very annoyed. Someone's messing with me and I've had enough.'

'Oh,' he said. 'Well, I'm sure everything will sort itself out eventually.'

'Oh yes, I'm sure it bloody will.'

I gathered my things together, stalked out of the library and began the walk home. Then I felt bad about snapping at the boring, grey-haired family-tree man. He wasn't to know I was being harassed by the ghost of someone my girlfriend and I had accidentally killed with a rogue blender. I picked up a takeaway pizza on the way back and, after some deliberation, I decided I could use a couple of cans of beer as well. And a four-pack of triple chocolate cookies. Sod the expense and sod my waistline.

After I'd consumed my supper, I lay down on the bed and the sleep that had been lurking around the corner ever since I'd made my escape from Kent pounced on me and I surrendered to oblivion. Even the despairing cry of 'I hate you, Keith' from the flat next door, signalling the start of another bout of shouting and shagging, failed to make any impact on my subconscious.

I awoke in the early hours to an odd shuffling noise. It was coming from the vivarium. Moonlight washed the flimsy curtains that covered our half of the French windows.

'Bertrand?' I called out. 'Are you all right?'

Well, it seemed a logical thing to do at the time. As did my next action, which was to get up and go over to the tank and push the lid to one side. My thinking was that, given that he had no way of replying to my question, I'd better take a look and see for myself. But as soon as I'd done so, Bertrand's head unexpectedly emerged, greeting my shocked expression with a quizzical grin. Before I could do anything else, the head had leaned out of the tank altogether and was now moving swiftly in the direction of the floor, followed by the rest of his body. My initial instinct was to grab at the passing animal, although this was very quickly countermanded by an overwhelming desire to give the passing animal as much distance as I could. I backed away.

'Bertrand,' I said, 'don't do this!'

Bertrand ignored me and continued to slither downwards. Once he reached the floor, he picked up speed and shot under the bed. Oh god. I was never going to be able to sleep in here again. Summoning up all my courage, I leaned under the bed and peered into the darkness. Something reptilian was lurking a couple of feet away. I reached in and grabbed at it, but my hand clutched at fistfuls of air. I found a shoe and threw it in the rough direction of where I'd seen the snake. There was a hiss and a rustling, and then Bertrand shot out the other side of the bed and headed for the opposite corner of the room, where he burrowed under the carpet and disappeared into a hole in the floor.

Shit.

Now what?

How long was it that Patrice said Bertrand went between meals? Two weeks? So it wasn't as if I was about to entice him out again with a tasty morsel. In fact, I frequently heard live tasty morsels running around under the floorboards, so it was entirely possible that Bertrand was now in a position where he could happily dine *al fresco* for the rest of his days.

Well, at least someone was happy.

I got back into bed and enjoyed a few fitful hours more sleep until the sun informed me that another day in the life of Tom Winscombe had dawned.

Chapter 10

'You did what?' said Ali.

'I was checking he was OK,' I said. 'I was looking after him.'

'You let him out.'

'I didn't mean to. He probably hasn't gone far.'

'Oh, like there isn't literally a whole fucking city he can run loose in now.'

'Slither,' I said. 'Snakes don't run.'

'Don't try to be fucking clever, pal,' said Ali.

'He'll come back when he starts missing Patrice.'

'Oh, will he?'

'Yeah. Animals develop a bond with their owners. Don't they?'

'Even snakes?'

'I bet they do.'

'How much? Fifty quid says they fucking don't, pal.'

'Yeah, well.'

Ali had come back mid-morning in a foul mood. Clearly she'd had some kind of row with Patrice, although she was unwilling to spill the beans and, in any case, she was understandably more exercised about the fate of Bertrand.

'I literally don't know what to say,' she said, shaking her head in fury. 'What the chuffing fuck am I going to say to Patrice?'

'I don't know. Maybe we could say that I've got something contagious, so it wouldn't be safe for her to come here any more.'

'The only disease you're suffering from is terminal idiocy. And, fortunately, that's not catching.'

This seemed unfair, and I was about to say so when she interrupted me.

'Oh, don't worry your thick head about it. I'll think of something. She doesn't need to come here for another couple of weeks and maybe Bertrand'll be back by then.'

'Well, that was what I was th—'

'No, don't try to pretend you were being clever. Chances are he won't be back, and you know it. Anyway,' she picked up her bag. 'I'm off to do some work. Some of us have things to do.'

'I'm doing things today,' I said.

'Like what?'

'I'm going to that crypto launch this evening.'

'And how does that get us closer to finding Dot?'

'It… doesn't. But I may work out what's going on with my father's money.'

'Yeah, well. Nothing to do with me, pal.'

Then I remembered about the messages from Rufus Fairbanks's LinkedIn account. 'Before you go,' I said, 'can you think of what this might mean?' I gave her a brief précis of what had happened.

Ali turned back and looked at me. 'You're sure you're not imagining this?' she said. 'Even by your standards.'

'Don't say that,' I said.

'Yeah, but come on, pal. It's a bit weird.'

'Look, I'm obviously not saying it's Fairbanks himself. That really would be weird. But it's definitely someone. And yes, I know this is wishful thinking, but it really does sound like Dorothy.'

Ali looked as if she was about to spit at the mention of Dorothy's name. She looked up at the ceiling as if searching for celestial inspiration. 'Oh, Dot,' she muttered to herself, 'if it is you, what the fuck are you up to?'

'I wish I knew,' I said.

Ali shrugged. 'Well, I haven't got time to deal with this now,' she said, turning back towards the door. 'Your best bet is to keep replying to them. Try to tease a bit more information out of them. See if they'll tell you what the next number in the sequence is, at least.'

'How's it going with you, by the way?' I called after her, but there was no reply. I had a strong impression that without Dorothy, Ali was floundering. But then again, so was I.

The first thing I did when I got to the library was check my emails. Inevitably, there was another one purporting to be from Rufus Fairbanks. *Hey,* it said, *I'm disappointed in you. I thought you were better than this.*

This was beginning to get annoying. Right, I said to myself, if you want to play at being mathematicians, Dorothy-or-whoever-you-are, I'm more than happy to join in. Ali was right. I needed to keep the conversation going.

I've almost got it, I wrote. *Just want to be sure, though. Give me another number.*

There was a long pause, and my hand started drumming again without me realising it. There was a deliberate little cough from Ramona the Romantic Novelist across the table from me, and when I looked up, she was glaring at me angrily again. Then without warning she stopped glaring at me and an evil grin took over her face instead. She looked back at her screen and there was a sudden burst of activity at her keyboard. I had a horrible feeling that I was going to end up in her next book, and not as the hero.

Another email arrived.

OK, one last try, it said. *The next number is 8.*

Oh, for heaven's sake. This didn't make any sense at all. I took out a scrap of paper and wrote them all down. 1, 2, 3, 5, 8. Actually, there was another 1, wasn't there? OK, so 1, 1, 2, 3, 5, 8.

Oh god, that was it! I punched the air with a quiet 'Yesss!' as the penny dropped, and Newbie Neville across the way from me tapped his hands together in mock applause. I stood up from my chair, bowed to him and sat down again.

The bloody Fibonacci sequence. I remembered now. In a misguided moment not long after we'd started going out together, Dorothy had decided that I really needed to know more about maths because it was really, really important and underpinned everything in the world. And the Fibonacci sequence was the thing she'd picked as an example.

As I understood it, the idea was that the next number in the sequence was calculated by adding the previous two together. So, 1 + 1 = 2, 1 + 2 = 3, 2 + 3 = 5, 3 + 5 = 8, and so on. I opened up Wikipedia to remind myself, and then I remembered the rabbits.

Rabbits.

Basically, it was all about the way in which an idealised rabbit population might expand over a period of time. You start off with one pair of bunnies. At the end of the first month they mate, and at the end of the second month, mummy bunny produces her first litter, making two pairs of rabbits. At the end of the third month, mummy number one produces her second litter, making three pairs. Meanwhile her offspring are at it too, so by the time the end of month four comes around, both mummies produce litters and we have five pairs.

And so on.

There was obviously some dangerous inbreeding going on here, but I did vaguely remember understanding it when Dorothy tried to explain it to me. Basically, you end up with this sequence where the next number is determined by the sum of the preceding two. So you get 1, 1, 2, 3, 5, 8, etcetera, etcetera.

And what got Dorothy so excited – although I began to lose her here, the same way as I always did whenever she got on her mathematics horse – was that Fibonacci numbers turned up all over the place. It was like it was all hard-wired into the universe. She did this thing where she found a piece of graph paper from somewhere and drew squares on it with sides the length of each of the numbers in the sequence, and the resulting pattern ended up like the kind of thing you see in sea shells. Then it turned out that the same thing turned up in leaves, animal markings and other stuff so, basically, you could quite easily convince yourself that everything in the universe was Fibonacci shaped.

So I opened up a reply to the email.

Shagging rabbits, I wrote. *The next number is 13.*

Because 5 + 8 = 13. Go me!

A reply came back a minute later. *Ah, we got there at last*, it said. *Poetry in motion.*

Sorry, how was I supposed to respond to this?

What do you mean? I wrote.

I think you know what I'm talking about, came the reply.

What? I wrote. *21's the next number, if that's what you're looking for, but I don't see any poetry in there.*

You know what I'm talking about, came the reply.

I thought long and hard about this. And then I remembered. Dorothy had composed what she called a Fibonacci poem – one that had, oh god, one syllable in the first and second lines, two in the third, three in the fourth, five in the fifth and so on. She'd sent me a copy to read and I'd saved it somewhere on my laptop, wherever that was now. It was something about nanotechnology and she'd thought it was terribly clever. I seem to remember just thinking it was terrible.

Well, there wasn't anything more to say. I couldn't remember any of the stupid poem and, in any case, there were too many other unknowns to deal with right now. I decided that I could really do with leaving Zombie Fairbanks at the side of the road for the time being.

I was still no closer to working out what Dorothy was up to and why she'd suddenly scarpered with all our stuff. Who was helping her? What was Benjamin Unsworth up to at the Vavvies? What did Helen Matheson – if that was indeed her real name – have to do with it all, and what did she mean when she told me I had no idea what I was mixed up in? On reflection, however, that was an easy one to answer: I did indeed have absolutely no idea whatsoever what on earth I was mixed up in.

I resolved to put all this onto one side and concentrate on the most pressing matter, which was tonight's Tulpencoin Super Plus launch. I decided to prepare for this by googling Kevin Wilberts. His YouTube channel turned out to be every bit as terrible as I'd been expecting, although I was quite taken with the video where he described how he'd decided to abandon the unnecessary and unmanly frippery of cooking in favour of an exclusively raw meat diet. I especially enjoyed the link, provided by a helpful commenter below the line, to a piece written by one of his ex-girlfriends that went into great and somewhat unnecessary detail about his resulting issues with tapeworms and the prodigious amounts of industrial-strength antibiotics and other pills he'd ended up taking to try to maintain some semblance of good health.

The rest of it was a mishmash of inspirational homilies and dubious science purporting to back up his wild theories about white male superiority and I eventually gave up watching. I really wasn't looking forward to sitting through an entire evening of him, especially if I was going to be sitting slap bang in the middle of an adoring audience. But I was going to have to face up to it if my father was going to have any chance of ever seeing his life savings again.

The foyer at the Old Rococo Theatre was buzzing with hordes of twenty- and thirty-something, mostly white men scurrying around eagerly exchanging business cards with each other. Long posters depicting a performatively serious and combative Kevin Wilberts hung from the ceiling, adorned with gnomic quotes from the great man himself: 'Do not be ashamed of the power of your masculinity.' 'How can it be wrong for men to demand rights?' and 'The Heart of Humanity is MAN'.

Tulips were in abundance, both in the many floral displays that adorned the walls and in the design of the mini-dresses worn by the small army of almost entirely blonde women wearing Tulpencoin sashes and carrying prospectuses, who swanned in and out of the assembled crowd.

One of them came up to me.

'Hi,' she said, flashing me a smile that could have burnt a hole in a telephone directory at thirty paces. 'Can I interest you in a prospectus, sir?'

'Sure,' I said, taking one from her.

The smile doubled in intensity. 'I bet you're a Tulpencoin investor already,' she said, 'I can tell.'

'Well, sort of—'

'I knew it!' she said, almost ecstatic with joy. 'Can I interest you in our convertible options? We're really excited about them.'

'Well, maybe, but—'

'Or what about—' I was spared the remainder of her patter by an announcement over the tannoy to the effect that Kevin Wilberts would be taking the stage in five minutes.

'Sorry,' I said. 'I have to go.'

'Well,' she said with a hint of desperation now, 'maybe you'd still like to think about them and talk later?' She held out a card, but I was already on my way.

'Sure, definitely,' I said over my shoulder as I located the entrance to the stalls.

I ended up sandwiched between a chap on my right who looked as if he hadn't quite started shaving yet and a weird ungainly monster of a man on my left who looked as if he was mostly composed of beard.

'Your first time at a Wilberts talk?' I said to the beardy monster.

'Uff gfuff deflurf uff guff,' came the softly-spoken reply, modulated by several layers of facial fluff.

'Right,' I said.

'Uff guff,' said the man, nodding.

'This is my first time,' said the other guy.

'Mine too,' I said.

'Exciting, isn't it?' came the reply.

'I guess so,' I said.

Silence enveloped the auditorium as the lights dimmed. The curtains drew back to reveal a bare stage. Then the music started: the opening drum motif from Queen's 'We Will Rock You' on a continuous loop, crescendoing towards a wild climax, until the whole room was joining in, stamp-stamp-clap, stamp-stamp-clap. Suddenly, the music cut out altogether as the announcer's voice boomed out: 'The Kevin Wilberts Foundation, in association with Tulpencoin International and the Institute for Progress and Development, presents – live on stage – KEVIN WILBERTS!'

The crowd went ballistic as Wilberts hit the stage. He milked it as long as he could, dashing from one side of the stage to the other, alternately waving at the audience and punching the air. Then finally he signalled with his arms that enough was enough and the hall went quiet once again.

'Hello London!' he shouted to another burst of applause. 'It's good to be back! ARE YOU FEELING GOOD?'

There was a general roar of agreement. But Wilberts was having none of it.

'Why are you feeling good?' he said, suddenly sounding concerned. His voice was deep and sincere, with the slightest shading of Afrikaans. 'I look out at this magnificent room, full of magnificent, heroic people and I see a vision of the oppressed. Do you feel oppressed?'

The audience clearly weren't quite sure how to respond to this, and the reaction was somewhat equivocal.

'Let me break this down a little for you,' said Wilberts, dropping his voice a little. 'There was a time – not that long ago – when the world was ruled by red-blooded men. And yes, many of those men were white, let's not shy away from that. And let's not shy away either from the fact that many of the things those red-blooded white men did were not good things.'

Here he made a dramatic pause.

'But sometimes good men need to do bad things. This is our burden.'

Somewhere behind me there were sounds of a scuffle and raised female voices. I turned round to see three women being hustled out of the theatre by burly security guards. Wilberts had clearly noticed the altercation.

'Ah! I see I have upset the women already!'

A ripple of laughter spread round the audience.

'Do not worry, ladies!' he said, with a chuckle. 'I am proud to call myself a feminist. I support you in your struggle! My most fervent wish is to put women back on their pedestal. For too long, our sisters have been forced to debase themselves by taking jobs and engaging in an unedifying tussle for power. For too long, the stultifying smog of—' he spat out the words '—Political Correctness has enveloped the world, forcing ordinary people into roles they neither comprehend nor desire.'

There were several boos when he enunciated the words 'Political Correctness', including one from the chap on my right. I turned to him and raised an eyebrow.

'This is better than sex!' he exclaimed, wide-eyed. I was surprised he was in a position to make the comparison.

The bearded bloke on my left was equally enthusiastic. 'Huff gfuff flurf!' he muttered.

'Ah yes, Political Correctness,' continued Wilberts, reflectively. 'A tool developed by the elites who would shape our destinies and whose sole desire is to crush us with our guilt. They want us to feel guilty for being men. Guilty for being white. Guilty for wanting to have sex with women. Can you imagine that?'

The audience, who only a few minutes previously had been happily clapping and stamping along to the music of a gay man from Zanzibar, roared their appreciation at this. As Wilberts continued his rant, he began to lay out the mathematical basis behind his argument for white, male supremacy, and I had to admit it all seemed terribly convincing, apart from the fact that I failed to understand a word of it. At some point during his discourse, however, the topic shifted subtly towards the necessity for the decentralisation of wealth and how the blockchain was going to remove the need to trust anyone else ever again. This was, of course, the cue for Wilberts to wrap up his speech with an introduction to Tiger de Montfort to explain all about the revolutionary features of the Tulpencoin Super Plus.

Kevin Wilberts left the stage to a standing ovation. A queasy wave of guilt swept over me. I'd sat there listening to all this dreadful stuff and I'd done nothing. I hadn't said a peep, not even to the guys sitting next to me. I hadn't been much of an ally, had I? What would Dorothy have thought of me? Then again, did it matter any more what Dorothy thought of anyone? Was she even still alive? What did—?

'Scuzz ma flurf,' muttered the beardy, breaking my train of thought as he made to push past me towards the way out.

'Oh, right,' I said, standing up and leaning back to let him out. In fact, a good percentage of the audience were now heading for the exits, presumably because either they'd only come to hear Wilberts or they were already convinced of the brilliance of the Tulpencoin Super Plus concept. De Montfort did his best to retain the crowd's interest with a long and detailed presentation delivered in a dry Australian drawl, but it was clear that the exciting part of the evening's proceedings was well and truly over. The applause as he left the stage was perfunctory, and delivered by a crowd that was already on its feet and shuffling out.

Chapter 11

The queue to register for Super Plus Tulpencoins circled all the way round the foyer now, and I overheard at least one potential buyer panicking that he'd left it too late. I ignored all this and headed for the door to the backstage area. A bouncer with the build of a plus-size sumo wrestler who looked as if he was just about to explode out of the dinner suit he was wearing, Incredible Hulk-style, inspected the backstage pass that Matt Blank had given me and gave me a surly nod and a rearward jerk of the thumb.

As I walked down the corridor, I heard a familiar voice from one of the side rooms. I was about to call out to him, but then I realised that Matt Blank was talking to someone on his mobile. I paused by the doorway to listen. He was using a loud stage whisper, and sounded jumpy.

'No,' he was saying, 'you've really got to pull me out now. It's only a matter of time before... yes, I know that... sure, I know what I signed up to... but you promised you'd... no, that's not fair, we had an agreement... we had a fucking agreement!' There was a long pause, and then he started again, in a more conciliatory tone. 'OK, I understand... sure, sure... just do whatever you can, and I'll do whatever I can at this end… gotta go, it's time for the debrief… yeah, sure… I will.'

Something about his conversation unnerved me, so I decided not to engage with him right now. Instead, I hung back as he emerged from the room, allowing a safe distance to open up between us before I followed him down the corridor. He turned into another dressing room at the end and pulled the door to behind him. I nudged it open a fraction and peered into the room.

There were five men in there apart from Matt Blank. The two who were standing were of similar build to the fellow who'd checked my backstage pass and were presumably part of the security detail. The rest of the party were seated. I recognised Kevin Wilberts and Tiger de Montfort from the show earlier, but the remaining guy was new to me. He was in his forties and built like a whippet. He wore glasses with pebble lenses and spoke with a patrician accent.

'Well,' he was saying, 'I think we can all congratulate ourselves on an exceptionally fine piece of work this evening, and I was particularly pleased that I could be there to experience it myself for once. Oratory of the quality demonstrated by Mr Wilberts here is a rare and precious thing. Sir, you are indeed a *rarissima avis*.'

Kevin Wilberts looked mildly nonplussed at first, but accepted the compliment with a smile and a deprecatory wave. 'It's nothing, boss,' he said. 'I'm only happy to do whatever I can to further the cause of the Institute. The project is very close to my heart.'

'Indeed,' said the man with pebble glasses. 'And Tiger, my friend, you have surpassed yourself with the Super

Plus. You are a gifted man with a gifted development team.' Then he turned to Matt Blank. 'And you, sir, I don't think we have met, have we?'

'No, sir,' said Matt. 'All of my dealings have been with Tiger to date, so I'm very pleased to meet the guy who's been paying my bills.' No one laughed. 'I'm Matt Blank, by the way,' he added, his voice faltering a little. He held out his hand, but the man with the pebble glasses ignored him.

'Yes, we have been paying your bills, haven't we?' he said. There was an odd undertone to his voice – almost a threat. 'And you have indeed repaid us with some excellent work. Correct me if I'm wrong, but there wasn't a seat to be had tonight for love or money – *ni amor ni pecuniam*.'

'That is very true.'

'Hmm.' The patrician man stood up and surveyed the men in front of him. 'And yet,' he said, 'despite this semblance of success, we seem to have a problem. To be precise, we appear to have sprung a leak. Which is most unfortunate at this stage when full knowledge of our operation needs to remain entirely *intra muros*.'

Kevin Wilberts, Tiger de Montfort and Matt Blank all began loudly to assert their innocence until the boss raised his hand for silence. Then he gave the slightest of nods and the two heavies took up positions either side of Matt Blank.

'I'm not talking about you, my dear Tiger and Kevin,' he said. 'Treachery would be entirely *infra dignitatem* as far as you're concerned. However, I would appreciate it if you would empty your pockets, please, Mr Blank.'

'I don't know what you're talking about,' said Matt. There was more than a hint of desperation in his voice.

'I rather think you do. Please comply with my request.'

Matt Blanc tried to stand up and make for the door. But the security thug on his left grabbed his arms and quickly secured them behind his back with a cable tie around the wrists. Then he held him firm while the other one began to frisk him.

'This what you were looking for, boss?' he said, extracting an iPhone from Matt's trouser pocket. He passed it over to the man with the pebble glasses, who took it from him and examined it, turning it over in his hands as if he'd never encountered anything like it before.

'Interesting,' he said. 'Correct me if I'm wrong, but it appears to be recording our little meeting. Is this perhaps in lieu of making notes? I know some of you less well-educated chaps often struggle with this kind of thing.'

'It must have switched itself on by accident,' said Matt.

'Oh! Well, that is an unexpected ploy. *It must have switched itself on by accident.* Do you know, my dear fellow, I don't think I've heard a defence that poor used before. But to be honest, it seems more like a case of *insita hominibus libidine alendi de industria rumores.*'

'You what, mate?' said de Montfort.

'Man's innate desire to propagate rumours,' came the reply. 'Livy, my dear chap. Do keep up. Well, it won't wash. It won't wash at all.' He seemed to deliberate for a moment. 'I'm terribly sorry about this,' he said eventually, 'but I seem to have no alternative. The law, or at least the law where I come from, is quite clear on the penalty for spying.' He turned to the security guy. 'Gunther, my dear fellow,' he said, 'would you please take care of the necessary? And Dirk, be a good chap and give him a hand?'

Before Matt could say anything more, the thug called Gunther quickly tied a gag over his mouth, so that all I could hear from him were desperate groans. Then the one called Dirk produced a sack from out of his pocket and placed it over the still struggling Matt's head. I took a step back from my viewing position. I definitely didn't want to watch this. I heard Tiger de Montfort utter a half-hearted 'Strewth, mate' and then there was a muffled shot followed by a dull thud like the sound of a body hitting the floor.

A long silence followed, broken by Kevin Wilberts. 'I never liked him much,' he said.

A cold sweat enveloped me. I hardly knew the guy, but I'd spent a pleasant enough evening with Matt Blank. He didn't deserve this. No one did. A sequence of thoughts began to spin through my head. First of all, any question of me confronting the guys in that room about my father's difficulties had just gone straight out of the window. Secondly, what the hell was going on here? Who was the guy with the pebble glasses? Who was Matt really? Should I have done something to help him? Oh god, I should have done something to help him. Yes, but what? Oh, I don't know, something. But I hadn't. I'd just skulked outside the door while he got whacked. Thirdly…

Thirdly, I had to get out of there. Quickly. If anyone came out of that room and found me lurking outside, I would be bumped right up the list of people to be taken care of. Trembling, I stepped back another couple of paces, straight into a trolley I hadn't previously noticed, piled high with enough crockery to handle the tea and cake requirements of the feeding of the five thousand. Following my intervention, the contents of the trolley wobbled for a tantalising couple of seconds before spilling onto the concrete floor, behaving in exactly the way that a large collection of crockery would be expected to behave on impact with a solid, inelastic, horizontal surface. The long, high-ceilinged corridor picked up the resulting cacophony and threw in a liberal sprinkling of echo and reverb for good measure so that the entire backstage area of the Old Rococo Theatre was treated to a performance that wouldn't have sounded out of place at the *Internationale Ferienkurse für Neue Musik* in early 60s Darmstadt.

Shit.

I had roughly two-thirds of a picosecond in which to decide which way to run. The choice was between heading back the way I'd come, with the mild advantage that I did at least know which way to go and the strong disadvantage that I would have to somehow deal with the plus-size sumo wrestler who would now be barring my way out, or to blunder onwards in the hope that I'd find a way out somewhere else. I decided to blunder onwards.

I hurtled down the corridor, hoping that I'd somehow get to the corner before Gunther and Dirk emerged. With any luck, they'd split up so that I'd only have to deal with one of them. Then again, chances are that they were both armed, so it didn't really make a lot of difference whether it was one or two of them on my tail. I heard footsteps a second after I'd turned left at the end, so I hunted around for somewhere to hide. The first door I tried was locked, but the second one opened and I found myself in a room full of theatrical props. There had to be something here I could make use of.

There was. Leaning against the wall was a scary-looking Roman-style spear. I hefted it in my hand. It felt good. There was something primeval about it. Sure, it would be hopeless against a man with a gun, but at least I'd go down with honour. I also noticed a balaclava on a shelf and, on a whim, I took it down and pulled it over my face, in the hope that this might make me look a bit scarier. I switched off the light and took up a position behind the door.

It wasn't long before the doorknob rattled and then slowly turned. A shaft of light from outside spilled into the room, throwing the intruder's hand and the gun it was carrying into sharp relief. Without a moment's hesitation, I brought the spear down onto the man's wrist. There was a yelp of pain and the gun skittered out of his grasp onto the floor. Then the door burst open and Gunther launched himself into the room in its wake. My spear was quite heavy and its momentum was still carrying me downwards at this point, but I just about managed to swing it around so that I caught him at ankle height.

Now Gunther was on the floor, flapping his arms around trying to find his gun. The point of the spear was at roughly the right height now for impaling him. I hesitated for a moment and then raw adrenaline kicked in and I rushed him. At this point, however, the papier mâché tip of the spear gave way, acting as a helpful crumple zone to cushion the blow. Gunther scuttled backwards, uninjured and laughing at me as I followed through behind the spear, out of control. Then I watched in horror as he got to his feet and raised his right hand, with a gun once again held firmly in it.

Chapter 12

I know they say your life flashes before you when you're facing death, but all I could think of as Gunther fired the gun was Dorothy. How I'd never find out where she'd gone to, what was behind her sudden disappearance, why she hadn't said anything to me by way of an explanation, whether she even cared for me any more, whether I even cared for her any more – given the existence of the preceding four questions – and why—

Hold on.

I was still alive.

Gunther noticed that I was still alive, too, and we both realised why at the exact same moment. He'd picked up the wrong gun. The one in his hand was a prop. Almost immediately, I spotted the real one out of the corner of my eye. I consciously made a herculean effort not to actually look at it, so as not to draw Gunther's attention to it, but I managed to ascertain that it was lying on the floor just out of reach to my left, underneath a pile of hats.

I propelled myself towards them, fumbled briefly with an outsize sombrero and then rolled over, clutching the gun to my chest. Then I stood up and pointed it at

Gunther, who obliged in the traditional manner by putting his hands up, dropping the fake on the floor.

'Right,' I said, and then paused. I had absolutely no idea what came next. For one thing, I'd never actually fired a gun in my life, apart from an inept attempt at clay pigeon shooting on a corporate bonding weekend a couple of years previously. In any case, there was no way I was going to shoot a man in cold blood, regardless of what he'd done to Matt Blank, and for a few seconds, there was an uneasy stalemate between us. Then I noticed that there was a key in the back of the lock. Keeping Gunther firmly in sight, I edged towards the door and delicately removed it.

'Stay where you are,' I warned Gunther, as if he was going to take any notice of me. I slid my body around the outside of the door, and then slammed it shut behind me as I exited the room back into the corridor. I tucked the gun under my arm and held the door firm against the jamb while I struggled to insert the key in the lock from the outside. There was a brief tussle as Gunther began tugging at the doorknob on his side of the door, but I managed to hold it firm until the door was properly locked. With any luck, it would hold for long enough for me to make good my escape.

As I ran off down the corridor, I heard more footsteps rounding the corner behind me. Shit. I wasn't in the clear quite yet, because Dirk was about to come into the reckoning. Wherever this corridor led, I was unlikely to get to the end of it before I had company, and the chances were that he was also armed. So I dived through the next doorway on my right and found myself in a cramped area surrounding a spiral staircase that led up into the darkness above.

Putting my fear of heights to one side for a moment, I began the ascent. I was nearing the top when Dirk burst through the doorway below. He looked up at me and I could see the anger in his eyes as he brought his gun up to point at me. I briefly considered waving Gunther's gun back at him, but I wasn't sure if I could bluff it out without actually firing it and there was always the danger that I might actually hit something with it if I did. I hauled myself onto the landing at the top of the staircase and looked around for somewhere to run.

As I was trying to make up my mind where to go, a shot ricocheted off a steel beam above me, reminding me that I didn't have the luxury of time to make decisions. Picking a direction at random, I ran along a lighting gantry that led over the stage. If I could somehow abseil down, there was a decent chance that I'd be able to make my escape through the back of the theatre to the foyer. This plan came apart almost immediately when it became clear that there was no rope available. To be honest, I'd never actually abseiled before in my life, so it wasn't a great plan to start with.

As I carried on running towards the far end of the gantry, I turned round and saw that my assailant had also made his way up the stairs and was now once again bringing his gun up to take a shot at me. I glanced back towards where I was heading and realised to my horror that my pathway didn't end in another spiral staircase as I'd hoped, but a dead end.

Shit.

It was time to take a more grown-up approach to this. This man had fired a gun at me. There was every chance he was about to do so again. So I was entirely within my rights to fire at him. Come on, Winscombe. Man up.

I turned to face the man, pointed the gun roughly in his direction and squeezed the trigger.

In the heat of the moment, I'd temporarily forgotten what guns did when you fired them. There was, after all, a reason why cops in films used both hands when aiming at a villain. It wasn't just because it looked cool. This realisation came to me as the recoil from my hopelessly wild shot propelled me backwards into the void beyond the edge of the gantry and I found myself heading rapidly towards the stage below. I dropped the gun and reached out with both hands, desperately grabbing at anything I could find to slow my fall. Somehow, I found the curtain. I gripped it tight and for a moment I hung there in space, staring up at the thug, who had now taken up a position above me. As he aimed, I felt a slight 'ping' and the curtain dropped to one side and the gunman's shot missed me by inches. Then another 'ping', and another, as eventually the whole thing came 'ping-ping-ping-ping-ping' off its runners and lowered me gently towards the ground.

When I was a few feet above the side of the stage, I let go and dropped down, landing awkwardly, but miraculously with no bones broken. This was a good thing as I was still being shot at and I needed to keep moving. I cowered behind some flats at the side of the stage for a moment, assessing my optimum escape route. Then another bullet whistled past my ear and reminded me to stop making assessments and get the fuck out of there. There was an exit at the side of the stalls below where I was standing, so I jumped down and started to head for it, just in time to see the door open to permit the plus-size sumo wrestler to squeeze his massive frame through.

I scanned the auditorium. Every other exit required me to cross the floor of the theatre to get to it. Not for the first time that day, my options were looking decidedly limited. I turned and looked upwards at Dirk. He looked back down at me and essayed a grin. However, he clearly hadn't picked up a wide variety of facial expressions at thug school, because the resulting rictus didn't suit him at all. He grasped his gun firmly in both hands and took aim at me once more.

Before he could take the shot, however, his attention was taken by a commotion at the far end of the auditorium. One of the doors had crashed open and someone was standing in front of it. It was the beardy bloke who'd been sitting next to me during the presentation earlier.

'Gflurf!' he announced. 'Floff ma fladge.'

The plus-size sumo wrestler exchanged baffled glances with Dirk.

'Ma fladge,' repeated the beardy man, with exaggerated emphasis.

I suddenly had an idea. It was absurdly risky, and it depended on the desire of the psycho on the gantry to avoid unnecessary collateral damage, but it was my only chance.

'Can I help you?' I called out.

'Gflurf!' He'd started to rummage under the seat. I suddenly realised what was going on.

'Ah!' I said. 'Have you lost something?'

'Flurf gflurf!' he said, standing up again and nodding eagerly at me.

I glanced up at Dirk, who was frowning now. It suited him better than the grin. He was still pointing the gun at me, but he was still hesitating about taking his shot. He was clearly still processing this unanticipated exception to the rules of engagement. I was pretty certain that it was against standard protocol to shoot the punters, but I fervently hoped it was also against standard protocol to shoot other people in front of the punters.

I began to walk forwards towards the beardy man, fully aware that two of the remaining pairs of eyes in the room were tracking my every move. The other pair of eyes belonged to the beardy man, who was still looking for whatever it was that he'd left behind, completely oblivious to the drama that was unfolding around him. I just hoped he wouldn't find what he was looking for any time soon.

When I reached the row where we'd been sitting, he was still groping around on the floor. I knelt down next to him and pretended to search myself. It was unpleasant work, as the carpet in the theatre looked like it hadn't been changed since the place had been built and the accumulated debris of several generations of theatre-goers had been well and truly ground into it. Unexpectedly, however, I quickly spotted a couple of things my companion had missed: a discarded scarf and a badge with an 'I' followed by a heart and the Tulpencoin tulip symbol.

'Is this what you're looking for?' I whispered, showing him the badge.

'Gflay!' he cried. 'Ma fladge! Ma fladge!'

'Sssssh!' I said, putting my hand on his arm for emphasis. 'What about the scarf?'

He shook his head.

'Good,' I said. 'Look, we're in a bit of a situation here. The guy standing on the gantry above the stage – NO, DON'T LOOK AT HIM NOW – is trying to kill me.'

'Gflurf!'

'Yes, exactly. Now, what I want you to do is make your way carefully to the door you came in by. I'll walk next to you, close enough to spoil his shot. He won't want to risk shooting you instead.'

'Flurf?'

'I think so. You're going to have to trust me here.'

'Gfloof.'

'Yeah. When we get near the door, don't hesitate for a moment. Just dive through and I'll follow you. OK?'

He nodded. I got the impression that he was finding it all quite exciting.

'OK,' I whispered. 'Three... two... one... go!'

We both got up and moved briskly towards the exit. As we approached it, I pushed the beardy man forwards with all my might and then dived down to enable myself to roll through the doorway. As we left the auditorium, a single bullet smashed into the exit sign.

'Cheers, mate!' I said, shaking the beardy man's hand. 'Great work.' He gave me a confused thumbs-up. Then I tore off my balaclava and hurtled down the stairs two at a time into the foyer and straight out into the street. A bus drew up alongside me, and I jogged next to it as far as the next stop, a few yards down the road. I hopped on, nervously scanning the front of the theatre for signs of any emerging gunmen. But the bus pulled away before anyone appeared, and, for the moment anyway, I was safe. As it happened, the bus was going roughly in the direction of our flat, so it didn't take me long to get back home. I walked in, slumped on the bed and began to tremble uncontrollably. That had all been a bit too close.

I had recovered sufficiently the next morning to think about what I should do next. I really needed to tell someone about poor Matt Blank, but I had no idea of anyone who might know him, apart from Narendra. I gave him a call and gave him a brief summary of what I'd seen, leaving out the description of my subsequent flight from the theatre.

'Shit, mate,' he said. 'That's terrible. I mean, I hardly knew the guy, but still.'

'I know.'

'Someone's got to do something.'

'Do you have any contact details for him? A home address or something?'

'No, nothing. All I've got is a scrunched up business card. It was the only one he had left when I met him. Hold on, let's have a look.' There was a long pause at the other end. 'Nope, nothing. Just his phone number and email address. Oh, hang on. There's another number scribbled on the back.'

'What?'

'Another mobile number.'

'Read it out.'

He gave it to me.

'Cheers,' I said.

'Look,' said Narendra, 'we need to tell the police about this.'

'They probably won't believe me. It all sounds way too weird.'

'But there'll be evidence in that room at the theatre, won't there?'

'That's true. Blood and stuff. Look, I'm still a bit shaken up. Can you report it for me?'

'Of course. Which theatre was it?'

'The Old Rococo.'

'Ah.' There was a long silence. 'That would be the Old Rococo that burned to the ground last night?'

'You're kidding.'

'Nope. All over the news this morning.'

'Shit.' After a moment or two of silence during which I couldn't think of anything else to say, I said goodbye and hung up. I sat for a moment, holding my phone in my hand. Then I decided to call the number on the back of Matt Blank's business card. It rang twice and then a crisp female voice answered.

'Matheson,' it said.

Chapter 13

For a moment I was completely lost for words.

'Sorry?' I said. 'Did you say Matheson?'

'Well, it's my name. Who is this, please?'

'It's… never mind. Look, do you know a guy called Matt Blank?'

'Do I know you? Your voice sounds awfully familiar.'

'No, listen to me please. Matt Blank is dead.'

'Is this some kind of threat?'

'No, it's a fact. He was killed yesterday afternoon. At the Old Rococo Theatre.'

'Oh dear.' There was a long pause. 'Are you sure I don't know you?'

'Well, we have met,' I said. 'Just the once, though. You sprayed something in my face and dumped me by the side of the road. I've had better first dates.'

'Ah! The man who calls himself Jim Beam! I knew it was you! I was picking up all sorts of chemicals when I heard your voice. Synaesthesia's an absolutely bloody curse sometimes, but occasionally it comes up trumps.' She paused. 'God, poor Matt. He was a useful asset, and he was getting so close.'

'He wanted you to pull him out. I overheard him talking to you.'

'Well, as that rather sadly shows, he was also bloody careless. And now he's wasted a whole operation.'

'He's dead, Matheson.'

'That as well.'

'Who are you really?' I said. 'What's going on?'

'I'm afraid I can't tell you that.'

'I think I have a right to know what's going on. I nearly got killed myself yesterday.'

There was a long silence.

'Tell me more about what happened,' she said. 'Please.'

'You don't really want to know, do you?' I said. 'Sorry, but I've got things I need to be getting on with.' Actually, I had no idea what I was going to do right now, but she didn't need to know that.

'I do. Really, I do. What happened to Matt?'

'He was in a meeting,' I said, 'you know, with Tiger de Whatsit, Kevin Wilberts and the other bloke.'

'Which other bloke?'

'You know. The weedy one with glasses who speaks Latin all the time.'

'I have no idea who you're talking about.'

'But he's their Mr Big. You must know.'

'That's the thing. We don't know who Mr Big is. Look, I've probably told you too much already.'

'Well, it was Mr Big who ordered the heavies to shoot him. Said that where he came from, that was the penalty for spying.'

'Where he came from?' repeated Matheson. 'Did he have some kind of accent, then?'

'Only when he was speaking Latin,' I said.

'Well, that's even more baffling.'

'OK, then. I've given you some choice information there. The least you could do is throw me a hint as to what's going on.'

'Sorry, darling. It doesn't work like that. What were you doing there anyway?'

'I don't need to tell you that either,' I said. 'As I said, I nearly got myself killed, though,' I added. 'I'll tell you that much.'

'But you clearly didn't.'

'No.'

'Well, remind me about that next time I'm in the market for an asset who isn't in the habit of getting topped.'

'That's a bit tasteless.'

'Well, I'm sorry, sweetheart. I'm not in the taste business, I'm afraid.'

'What kind of business are you in, though?'

Matheson ignored me. 'This chap with the glasses. He was definitely in charge?'

'Definitely.'

'Interesting.' She paused for a moment. 'Well, I think this conversation is at an end. Thank you for your information. We won't be talking again, so please dispose of my number.'

'Hold on,' I said. 'Just tell me who you are and who you work for.' But the line was already dead. I hadn't even had a chance to ask her how Benjamin Unsworth was getting on.

As I took the phone away from my ear, something clicked in my brain. That was it! That's what Matt Blank's operation was all about. Matheson's organisation, whoever they were, had sent him in undercover to find out who Mr Big was and now he'd gone and got killed and wrecked the whole show.

I sat on the side of the bed and stared out at the cats marauding around outside. There were too many unanswered questions for one man to cope with. Confusingly, the ones about Dorothy had, temporarily at least, been pushed to the background by recent additions to the set. Even more confusingly, the enigmatic Matheson had now re-emerged from the shadows as a common factor. Then I glanced at the empty vivarium and remembered that there was still one more outstanding conundrum: where had Bertrand slithered off to?

I bent down and peered under the bed on the off chance that he'd returned. He hadn't. However, I fully understood where he was coming from. Right now, I was developing an intense desire myself to slither off somewhere and start afresh. Sure, there were certain aspects of the herpetological lifestyle that I'd probably struggle to habituate myself to, but I was sure that I'd get there eventually. There were worse things to be than a feral urban snake.

Unfortunately, right now if I was a feral urban snake, I was a feral urban snake that was trapped in the body of a poor confused human.

My phone rang. It was Ali.

'Good morning, PR boy!' She sounded unreasonably perky.

'Hi.'

'Everything OK?'

'As a matter of fact, no. I spent last night being shot at and—'

'Good, good. How's little Bertrand doing?'

'Bertrand? He's gone missing, you know that.'

'Jolly good. Patrice says to give him a kiss from her.'

'Ali, he's fucking missing. M-I-S-S-I-N-G. Vanished. Disappeared. Vamoosed.'

'Good. And you can even give him a kiss from me if you like.'

'Ali, are you listening to a word I'm— ah, right.' I realised what was going on. This conversation was not being held for my benefit at all. 'Look, Ali,' I said, lowering my voice, 'next time you can spare me one of your brain cells, I could do with a chat. Might need a whiteboard or something. It's all getting a bit complicated.'

'Oh, how sweet,' said Ali, gushing. I'd never heard her gush before, and it was more than a little unsettling. 'I'll tell Patrice how well he's settling in.'

'Yeah, you do that. Seriously, we need to talk.'

'I'll come round on Monday to see for myself,' she said.

'Monday?! Look, I—'

'Yes, I'm busy busy busy!'

'Great.'

It galled me to have to ask Ali for help, but as things currently stood, she was the only person available. I didn't even have ready access to the internet, as I hadn't bothered booking a slot at the library, and the computers there always filled up towards the end of the week. If only I still had that ancient laptop of mine. Sure, Dorothy and Ali used to laugh at it, but it did everything I wanted it to do. More importantly right now, it had Dorothy's bloody stupid Fibonacci poem on it. Why did those bastards take that as well as all the high-end machines the other two used for development? It couldn't have been of any value to them, surely?

I said as much to Ali when she turned up the following Monday, but she wasn't remotely interested in the fate of my shitty laptop.

'Let's face it, pal,' she said. 'I'd struggle to play fucking minesweeper on that thing, so it's no great loss to the world of game development.'

'I still think they could have at least left it behind.'

'I think you're the one that needs to leave it behind, pal. Anyway, can we get on with the main event? I haven't got all day.'

I took Ali through the events of the previous Thursday, which she absorbed with little interest until the arrival of Matheson in the final frame.

'Wasn't she the one you bumped into in the hospital?' she said.

'Yeah.'

'OK, I think I need a diagram now.'

I turned towards the whiteboard that she had unexpectedly brought with her and then wished I hadn't. It was filled with a frightening rat's nest of equations that was sending my brain into a fierce tailspin.

'What's all that?' I said.

'Oh, something of Patti's. She doesn't mind if we wipe it off. She's abandoned that line of attack, apparently.'

'Right. So, Patrice—'

'Is another mathematician, yes.'

'Right.'

'Mathematical biology.'

'Is that a thing?'

'Apparently so. She's actually some kind of professor.'

'Right.' Not for the first time, I had an image of myself paddling around in the shallow end of the gene pool while everyone else was performing elaborate swan dives from the high boards into the deep end. 'Do you want to just—?'

'Wipe it all off? Yeah, it's freaking me out, too, to be honest, pal.'

Ali grabbed a paper towel and wiped the board clean.

'OK, fire away,' she said, handing me a marker pen.

I wrote the word DOROTHY in the middle and drew a circle round it. Just above it I wrote OUR STUFF and drew a circle around that too. I connected it to DOROTHY. Then I wrote VAVVIES and connected it to DOROTHY. I also connected VAVVIES to BENJAMIN. Continuing to expand the diagram, I connected BENJAMIN to MATHESON, MATHESON to MATT and MATT to TULPENCOIN.

'Very nice,' said Ali. 'The only problem is that if you tug at the TULPENCOIN end of it, it just unravels into a straight line with OUR STUFF dangling off the end.'

'I know. Oh, hang on, there's one more thing I need to add.' I added FAIRBANKS at the bottom of the board. As an afterthought, I put inverted commas around the name.

'That doesn't help.'

'Yeah,' I sighed. 'I know that too.'

'OK, let's think for a minute. Whoever this Zombie Fairbanks person is, whether it's Dorothy or someone else altogether, they've only contacted you since the break in, right?'

'What are you saying?'

'What I'm saying is that this person, whoever they are, is almost certainly somehow connected to it.'

'It's possible, I suppose.'

Ali took the marker pen from me and drew a dotted line from "FAIRBANKS" to OUR STUFF.

'So now if we pull on TULPENCOIN,' I said, 'we get a straight line leading to "FAIRBANKS", right?'

'It's your fucking diagram, pal.'

'OK, chill,' I said. There was a long silence between us as we contemplated the contents of the whiteboard. Eventually, I shook my head.

'Nope,' I said. 'This is telling us nothing new, is it?'

'You're not wrong. How's it going with Zombie Fairbanks, anyway?'

'Well, that's it, you see. I'm a bit stuffed right now, because whoever it is behind that account is asking me about a stupid poem that Dorothy wrote.'

'I'm sorry, what?'

'Yeah I know. Dorothy wrote this poem – this Fibonacci poem – and I think they want me to recite it to them or something. I think it must be like there's something hidden in the words.'

'Oh, good grief. But you know the poem, right?'

'Do I look like the sort of person that memorises poetry?

'Fuck knows, pal. Up to thirty seconds ago, I wouldn't have said that Dot was the kind of person who fucking *wrote* poetry, so what do I know?'

'Anyway, the answer is no. Can't even begin to remember the damn thing.'

'Couldn't you just make one up?'

'Ali, do *I* look like the sort of person who writes poetry?'

She didn't say anything.

'You see, it was on my laptop. It's one of the reasons I'm so bloody annoyed and upset about those bastards taking it.'

'Didn't you make a backup?'

I paused. 'No,' I said. 'Dorothy was always going on at me about that.'

'Yeah, well, I can't help you.'

'I just don't understand why they didn't leave it behind. It can't have been of any value to them, can it? Half the keys were missing, the screen was cracked, the fan kept cutting out, in fact the only thing that worked properly was the disk drive and that was because I'd had to replace it. Oh, hang on.'

Ali looked at me. 'What?' she said.

'If I could get hold of the old disk drive, would I be able to get access to that document?'

Ali whistled softly. 'You're kidding me,' she said.

'No, I'm not.'

Ali went quiet for a moment. 'Possibly,' she said eventually. 'If we could find it and if we could somehow persuade it to give up its contents to us. But those are two fucking big ifs there, pal.'

'Surely it's worth a shot?'

'Well, let's take a look at the first if. What actually happened to the old drive?'

By the time we got to Mad Mickey's Hardware Exchange in Watford, it was almost five o'clock and he'd gone home for the day.

'Fuck,' said Ali.

'Bugger,' I said.

'Another wasted journey. I still don't see why you brought it here, anyway.'

'Dorothy suggested him. Seemed a nice enough bloke. Bit intense, but no more than the rest of you techie types.'

'Oh, he's a decent enough bloke. Bought a fair bit of kit from him myself back in the day. But last time I heard of him, he seemed to be devoting most of his energy to restoring meltdowns.'

'Meltdowns?'

'Crypto mining rigs that ran a bit too hot. Did your man explain all that to you?'

'He went on about crypto mining causing global warming, or something like that.'

'Yeah, well, your hardcore backroom miners build their own rigs, using the fastest overclocked graphics cards they can get their hands on and run them to the max without proper cooling. Fucking disaster. Also plays fucking havoc with the price of graphics cards, which is not good for my blood pressure. Not that it matters any more.'

'Thought you were close to getting everything back up and running?'

Ali went uncharacteristically quiet. 'Yeah, well,' she said eventually. 'No point in hanging around here now,' she added. 'We'll come back tomorrow morning.'

'What are the chances, though?' I said. 'He's probably reconditioned it and sold it on by now.'

'Not if I know Mad Mickey. Odds are it's still in there somewhere. Classic computer guy. Hopelessly over-optimistic. Buys far more drives in part-ex than he can turn round. That's why he's called Mad Mickey. 'Cos he's an idiot. Lovely guy, but basically an idiot.'

'Fair dos. Still can't imagine what there is in that poem that's so bloody important.'

'Nope, me neither. But we won't have long to wait, will we?'

But when I met Ali the next morning outside Mad Mickey's, however, it was clear that we were going to have to work a little harder to find out what was on the drive.

'This sort of thing happen to you a lot, does it?' she said. She was trying to remain cool, but there was no disguising the tremor in her voice.

'Lately, yes,' I said.

'I might think about maintaining a safe distance from you then, pal.'

Mad Mickey's body lay on the floor behind the service counter. There was a neat hole in the middle of his forehead.

Chapter 14

'Careful where you tread,' said Ali, leading me through. 'It's a bit sticky down there. Best not to leave any footprints.'

'Is this because of us?' I said.

'Probably. God knows how, though.'

'Well, it scarcely matters right now. So, what are we going to do?' I was scanning the shelves on the wall behind the counter. Last night, they'd been piled high with equipment. Now they were completely empty. The place had been ransacked.

'What did Mickey do when you brought the drive in?' said Ali.

'Sorry?'

'What exactly did he do?'

'He opened up the laptop, undid a whole load of screws and took the drive out. Then he looked at it, turned it upside down and then made a note of the serial number. Then he came up with a pathetically small price and knocked it off the cost of a reconditioned replacement. Then he fitted the new one.'

'Where did he write the serial number? In a spreadsheet, right?'

'No, a big red book. I remember thinking that was odd.'

'Ah, I remember now. He didn't trust computers.'

'I can see his point.'

'Well, that means all we've got to do is find a big red book. Can't be hard. Got any gloves?'

'Gloves?'

'Fingerprints, pal. Don't want your dainty little pinkies getting recognised, do we? And I'd rather not have mine on the register, either.'

'Basically, no. But there's a hardware shop across the road.'

'Like that's not going to arouse suspicion,' said Ali. 'Look, we haven't got very long. I'll just have to do it myself, I suppose. Keep an eye out for any other customers. Don't fancy being disturbed.'

Ali fished a pair of leather gloves out of her bag and put them on with a certain amount of ceremony. I had a distinct impression that she was enjoying herself. She leant over the counter and began to rummage about the shelves underneath it, before emerging in triumph with a big red book that matched my recollection of the one Mad Mickey had used when I brought my drive in.

'OK, OK, we're doing well,' she said. 'So roughly when did you bring the thing in?'

'Month or so ago,' I said.

Ali riffled through the ledger as fast as her gloved hands would allow her. Then she stopped and went backwards. And then forwards again. And then backwards once more. Then she looked hard at the inside of the book.

'Fuck me, they've torn the page out,' she said.

'Bastards. Well, that's it, then, isn't it? They'll have found it by now.'

Ali was rummaging in a drawer under the desk.

'Not necessarily,' she said, holding up a set of keys. 'Take a look at the inside front cover of the ledger.'

I looked. The cover had the single word 'Overflow' written on it in black ballpoint pen. Then Ali dangled the keys in my face and I could see that the fob attached to them also had the word 'Overflow' written on it.

'Nice work,' I said. 'So all we need to do is find out where Mad Mickey's overflow store is, and then try every single one of the disk drives we find in there. Not wishing to rain on your parade, but I'm not a hundred per cent sure we've actually moved on very far here.'

'Ach, there's always one ready to put a dampener on things. OK, what about this?' Ali waved a flyer for a pizza delivery company in my face.

'Huh?' I said. 'Bit early for lunch.'

'Look at the address.'

'I am looking at it. It's a very nice address. Not a place I'd choose to live if I had the option, but—'

Ali snatched it back from me. 'Jesus, is it "slow twat day" or something? OK, I'll spell it out. The address on this flyer is several miles west of here. Why would Mad Mickey keep a flyer for a place several miles west of here?'

'Unless that was where he lived—'

'Or where he stored all the stuff he couldn't fit in his shop. Or, most likely, both.'

'Well, what are we waiting for?' I said.

Three-quarters of an hour later, we were standing outside The Gobfather's Mega Pizza Palace, an establishment that looked as if it prioritised portion size over taste, and although it was now mid to late morning, I wasn't tempted.

'Somewhere around here, I bet there's a row of lock-up garages,' said Ali.

'Why do you think that?'

'Take a look at the key. That's a garage door key if ever I saw one.'

'How do you know?'

'Trust me, pal. I know shitloads of things.'

'So where is it?'

'Can't be far away. Let's try over the road.'

A side street led off from the main road almost opposite from where we were standing. We crossed over and began to walk down. There was a row of terraced houses on each side and no sign of any garages. But then we came across a small alleyway on the right-hand side and lo and behold, there were half a dozen lock-up garages in a neat row, just as Ali had predicted.

'Come on, admit it,' she said. 'I'm good at this.'

I didn't say anything.

Ali glanced around, looking for CCTV cameras, and then, satisfied that we weren't about to audition for our slot on *Crimewatch*, she began to try each of the locks in turn. The first few didn't yield to her efforts, but door number five did, allowing Ali to press the handle in to unlatch the door.

'Open sesame!' she said with an air of triumph, gently raising the door to reveal Mad Mickey's overflow store.

'Bloody hell,' I said, gaping at the stuff in there.

'OK, goldfish boy,' said Ali, 'find the light switch.'

I felt around on the wall, gathering the webs of several long-departed spiders on my hands, until I found it.

I pressed the switch and the place was illuminated. Ali pulled the door back down again behind her.

'Right,' she said, pulling on her gloves. 'Let's get cracking.'

The garage was filled from floor to ceiling with plastic crates perched on top of industrial shelving units. The shelving was organised in five rows, two along each of the long walls and three at equal intervals in the middle. It soon became clear that Mad Mickey was quite the entrepreneur, and it wasn't just hardware that he was dealing in. One entire row of shelves was devoted to DVDs, and Ali picked one out and showed it to me.

'That's… quite specialised,' I said.

'You're not kidding,' she said, turning the cover round several times. 'How the fuck did they even get into that position?'

I shrugged and Ali continued searching the shelves.

'Bloody hell,' she suddenly announced. 'Look at these!' She was holding up a stack of enormous floppy disks. 'Five and a quarter inch floppies! This is AWESOME. This place is a fucking museum!'

I failed to share her enthusiasm. 'Ali,' I said. 'Can we just find my drive and get out of here? I'm worried that our man with the gun will get the same idea as you and head this way.'

'No chance,' said Ali. 'No one's as smart as I am.' But she put the floppy disks down with a theatrical display of reluctance and continued working her way along the shelves. "OK,' she said eventually. 'Here we are.' She grasped a large cardboard box off the shelf that ran along the opposite wall to where I was standing, hauled it over and placed it at my feet.

I stared down into the box. It contained thirty or forty disk drives of various sizes and makes.

'Recognise yours?' she said.

'Well… not exactly.'

'Well, let's try to pin it down. What was the make?'

'No idea.'

'Size?'

'Well, it was a similar size to that one there.' I pointed to one that had a Western Digital label on it.

'I meant capacity, you numpty.'

'Ah. In that case, nope. No idea at all. I seem to remember it was quite big at the time when I bought it. They made a big deal of that when I bought it. Didn't entirely understand what they were saying.'

'I bet you didn't.'

'Why don't you look at the dates on the labels?'

'What?'

'They've all got sticky labels on them with dates. I know when I brought it in.' I told Ali the date. She rolled her eyes and began to rummage through the box. Eventually she came up with three options.

'OK this one,' she said, holding up the largest of them, 'is definitely not your disk. Won't fit in a laptop for starters. So that leaves these two. My money's on this one, but sod it, we'll take both. Stick them in your bag and let's get moving.'

I didn't need any encouragement to do this. Ali put the box back on the shelf and went towards the door. I switched off the lights and we emerged blinking into the daylight.

'Job done,' I said.

'It's only just started, pal,' said Ali.

We grabbed a couple of slices of pizza from the Gobfather's Mega Pizza Palace for lunch, which turned out to be every bit as unpleasant as I'd anticipated. Then we headed back to the flat. I dumped my bag on the floor and sat down on the bed. Ali busied herself with texting.

'So, what do we do now?' I said.

Ali held up her hand to stop me talking, then continued texting. When she had finished, she looked up at me.

'You were saying?' she said, looking at me expectantly.

'What happens next?' I said. 'Now we've got the drive, I mean. We can't just attach it to the mains and run it up, can we? Or can we?'

'Almost. If I can persuade Patti to let me open up her desktop machine, I can probably rig something up.'

'And what then?'

'Possibility one is that the drive is still unreadable. Possibility two is that Mad Mickey actually managed to recondition it, in which case he'll have reformatted it so that the data isn't on there any more.'

'But that means we've wasted our time, doesn't it?'

'Ah.' Ali raised a significant index finger. 'Possibility three is that we can somehow persuade the drive to cooperate with us long enough to locate and extract the data we need to keep Zombie Fairbanks talking, whoever he or she may ultimately turn out to be.'

'So, what are the chances of you persuading the drive to talk to you?' I said eventually. For a moment I had a curious flashback to the time when Dorothy and I attempted to interrogate μ the cat to find out who had murdered her owner, Mrs Standage. It hadn't been entirely successful.

'You're forgetting, PR boy,' said Ali, 'that you are in the presence of a total fucking wizard.'

I looked at her and shook my head.

'I hope you're right.'

'Oh, I'm right about that, don't you worry. Anyway, I'm off round to Patti's now to square everything off. I'll pick up all the cables and shit I need on the way. When I'm ready, I'll give you a call and you can bring the drive round.'

'Why don't you just take it with you?' I said.

Ali shook her head. 'Don't want to appear too presumptuous,' she said.

'You really are taking this relationship seriously, aren't you?'

'Too fucking right I am.'

I swear that Ali winked at me as she left the flat.

I lay back on the bed and began to go through the events of the day, beginning with finding Mad Mickey's body. I'd hardly known the guy, but it was still a hell of a shock. Had we inadvertently brought him and his killer together?

The sound of my phone jerked me awake. I looked at the time on it – I'd been asleep for an hour.

'Hello?' I said.

'Hey, Rip van Winkle,' came Ali's cheery voice, 'this is your wake-up call!'

I sat up, rubbing my head.

'I wasn't asleep,' I said.

'Don't lie to me, PR boy. You were spark out. I can tell these things.'

'Pah. What do you want, anyway?'

'I'm ready and waiting for you to bring that hard drive over.'

'Oh. Right.'

'You'll be needing an address.'

'Yes. Yes, I will.' I'd been in a deeper sleep than I'd initially thought. I shook my head to try and clear the cobwebs. This didn't help. Instead, it had the effect of making my incipient headache slightly worse. Ali gave me Patrice's address and ended the call.

I picked up the bag with the disk in and went out. It was now twilight on a chilly, drizzly night and the streets were full of commuters finding their way home. About a hundred yards from the flat I began to be aware of footsteps right behind me. Not long after that, someone barged into my left-hand side and I felt something cold pressing on my ribs.

'Stay cool,' said a rasping, male voice in my ear, 'and everything's going to be just fine.'

Something told me that the second half of this sentence was quite likely to be one hundred per cent inaccurate.

Chapter 15

'Next turning on the left,' said the man.

My instinct was to lash out at this stranger, but a more rational part of me had concluded that this might end very badly indeed and had taken precautionary steps to override the default reaction. I decided to play along.

'This turning here?' I said.

'What do you think, mate? Don't try to act clever.'

I turned off the high road and found myself in a badly-lit alleyway. There was no one else around.

'Keep walking,' said the voice, giving me another nudge in the ribs. Our footsteps echoed off the walls on either side.

After we'd gone a short way, the voice ordered me to stop. Whatever had been poking me in the ribs was now relocated to the back of my neck.

'Right then,' said the man. 'Put the bag down now. Nice and gently.'

'What do you want?' I said.

'Just put the fucking bag down, sunshine, and no one's going to get hurt.'

'I don't believe you.'

I felt a sudden sharp pain on the back of my head and my vision went temporarily blurry.

'Jesus!' I said, instinctively putting my hand to my head. The hand was brushed away with something cold and metallic.

'Just get on with it,' said the voice.

I took the bag off my shoulder, bent down and placed it on the pavement. 'Now walk away,' said the man.

I took a few steps forward, fully aware that whatever had been pointing at the back of my neck was almost certainly still pointing at it and still capable of doing a lot of damage to me.

'OK, that's far enough,' he said. I stopped walking and began to turn around, getting my first glimpse of my attacker. In the poor light of the alley, his features were hard to make out, although there was something about the way he was standing that seemed vaguely familiar for some reason. He was a short, spindly guy wearing a hoodie and the gun in his right hand was pointing in my direction. He had a slight nervous twitch and he was jigging from side to side. Was this the guy who had killed Mad Mickey?

He crouched down on the pavement, transferring the gun to his left hand while rummaging in my bag with his right. Suddenly he yelped and withdrew his hand, which now had blood running from it.

'Bastard!' he shrieked, standing up and jamming his hand in his mouth. Then he took it out again, roaring with rage, and grabbed the gun from his other hand. Then he took aim at the bag but, in his panic, he missed completely and succeeded only in shooting himself in the foot.

'Fucking hell!' he yelled, before collapsing onto the ground, firing randomly into the air a couple of times as he did so. Then he threw the gun away, clutching at his shattered, bloody leg. I hesitated for a moment, wondering what in god's name was going on, before running back towards him. I grabbed hold of the bag and continued onwards, hoping against hope that the gunman's attention was now entirely focused on his own problems rather than myself. This did indeed turn out to be the case.

When I reached the end of the alleyway and emerged onto the High Road, I paused for a moment to catch my breath. Then I took my phone out and called 999, asking for the police, before explaining to the bemused person at the other end that I had just escaped from a dangerous gunman who had shot himself in the foot in the course of the proceedings and who they could still probably nab if they got a move on. Then I peered into my bag to check that nothing was missing and immediately closed it again. I opened it up a crack to confirm what I'd just seen and then shut it once more.

The good news was that Bertrand the ball python had come back. The bad news… well, for once there wasn't any.

Patrice lived in a purpose-built flat in a smart new block half a dozen underground stops away from our nearest station. As I turned into her street, I already felt that I had moved significantly up in the world from chez Tom'n'Ali. Even the air smelt fresher. I checked the list of names on the doorbells and found the one for P. Ambrose. I pressed it and announced my presence. The front door buzzed open and I went upstairs.

As Patrice opened the door to the flat, she gave me a warm smile.

'Thomas,' she said, waving me in. 'Welcome.'

'Er, hi,' I said, offering her the bag as I walked in through the door. 'I brought the disk drive. And Bertrand.'

She gave me a puzzled look.

'Bertrand the whatsit, you know, the ball python, snake thing.'

'I was assuming that was who you were talking about. But what's he doing in your bag?'

'Protecting my disk drive from attack,' I said. OK, this was playing a little fast and loose with the truth but, in my defence, this was precisely what Bertrand had, in fact, done. However, my explanation was immediately undermined by Ali bounding up behind Patrice and saying very loudly, 'He came BACK?'

Patrice looked at me with the vaguest hint of amusement in her eyes.

'Yeah, well,' I said, 'Ali's right. I sort of lost Bertrand a couple of nights ago. But he's back now, so it's all fine. And he really did save the drive from attack.' I gave them a brief summary of what had happened on the way here.

'Clever Bertrand,' said Patrice. 'May I?' she said, turning to me.

'I – sorry?' I said.

Patrice gestured towards the bag.

'Oh, sorry,' I said, handing it to her. She passed it to Ali, who realised too late what was about to happen.

'Alison,' said Patrice, 'could you possibly tuck Bertrand up in bed and read him a story? There's a free tank next to Gottfried.'

A look of pure terror scurried across Ali's face and then her usual bravado reasserted itself. 'Sure, Patti,' she said. 'No problemo. No problemo at allo.' Ali disappeared into a room at the back that emitted an eerie fluorescent green glow as she opened the door.

Patrice showed me into the front room and we sat down in adjacent leather armchairs. The room was like any other living room, I supposed, apart from the vast whiteboard that spanned the entire wall over the fireplace. This was covered in mathematical equations that threatened to make my head spin if I looked too closely.

'So, then,' said Patrice. Before she could say anything else, however, she was interrupted by a torrent of high-energy Anglo-Saxon emanating from the direction of Ali in the other room.

'Do ball pythons usually bite?' I said.

'Only when stressed. Poor love's had a bad day.'

'They're not poisonous, then?'

'No, Thomas,' said Patrice with gleaming eyes. 'They constrict.'

'Right,' I said. 'Right.'

There was an awkward silence between us.

'So—'

'Alison is completely safe with him.'

In the background, I distinctly caught the words 'you', 'little', 'fucking' and 'slimeball'.

'Quite some bedtime story,' I said.

'She'll get used to it.'

'I'm sure she will.'

A few moments later, Ali appeared in the doorway, holding a tissue to her fingers.

'Thank you, Alison,' said Patrice.

'No problem,' said Ali, failing to suppress a wince. 'He was quite docile really.'

'How did that bloke know you were going to be there?' said Ali. Her hand was now covered in sticking plasters.

'I don't know,' I said. 'That's what I've been trying to figure out. That, and how they managed to work out that the drive had gone to Mad Mickey's. Call me paranoid, but I can't help feeling that someone is watching us.'

'Have you checked the bag for bugs?' said Patrice. I was quite impressed with the way she was getting up to speed with the way of life that we'd been enjoying lately.

'Well,' said Ali, 'unless young Bertrand found one and swallowed it, nope, it's clean.'

'It's so weird that it all happened at exactly the same time that I was trying to get hold of the drive for Zombie Fairbanks,' I said.

'Ain't it just,' said Ali, with heavy sarcasm.

'What do you mean?'

'What I mean, pal, is that I'm not a great believer in coincidences.'

'You're surely not suggesting that Zombie Fairbanks, whoever he or she may be, is behind this nutter with the gun?'

'Right now, pal, I'm not excluding any possibilities.'

'But, hold on… I mean… how?'

Ali shrugged. We both turned and looked at Patrice, who was regarding us with some curiosity.

'Who's Zombie Fairbanks?' she said.

'Didn't Ali explain to you that's what this is all about?' I said.

'Not exactly,' said Ali.

'Not at all,' said Patrice. 'Would one of you care to explain?'

I told her about all my interactions with my mysterious counterpart on LinkedIn.

'And where were you when you were doing all this?' said Patrice.

'On a computer at the library,' I said.

'I see.' Patrice gave a slow nod of the head as if that explained everything.

'What?' I said.

'But all your communications were via LinkedIn messaging, right?' said Ali. She seemed anxious that she might have missed something. I was certainly missing something.

'Well, not exactly, but—'

'But what?' said Ali. 'Come on, PR boy. Tell me you didn't switch to direct emails.'

'Well, that was the odd thing,' I said. 'After our initial contact, Zombie Fairbanks was quite insistent that we switched away from LinkedIn. Said there was a chance that someone could be listening in. Seemed plausible to me.'

At this point, Ali and Patrice executed a simultaneous facepalm, accompanied by a cry of 'Aargh!' It was a performance that wouldn't have looked out of place in a synchronised swimming contest.

'What?' I said. 'What have I done now?'

'Winscombe, you tit,' said Ali, 'by replying via open email, you exposed the IP address of where you were working. All they had to do was look at the raw headers and – bingo – they could tell exactly which library you were sitting in when you sent it. Possibly even which chair your stupid arse was occupying.'

'Yes, but still—'

'And then they hired some local hoodlum and gave him a contract to hang around the library until they found out how you were going to get hold of that disk drive.'

'Oh shit,' I said. I'd just realised why the gunman's face seemed familiar. It was Newbie Neville. He wasn't an innocent computer user after all. 'But that means—'

'What it means, pal, is that whatever Zombie Fairbanks is after has almost certainly nothing to do with that daft poem you thought they were after. That was just a ruse to send you off on your hunt for this.' Ali held up my disk drive. 'There's something really valuable on this little piece of kit. Something you probably don't even know about. But something worth killing for. And I'm going to go out on a limb here and suggest that it's very likely it was Zombie Fairbanks and his or her chums who broke into our office and stole all our kit. And chances are, the only thing they really wanted was your scuzzy little laptop. More specifically, your scuzzy little laptop in the state it was before you replaced this manky old disk drive.'

'You're kidding me.'

'Nope.' Ali turned to Patrice as if for confirmation. Patrice shrugged.

Ali rubbed her hands together. 'So then,' she said. 'Shall we take a look and see if we can find out what it is that's on there?'

Chapter 16

Ali took the drive out of the bag and placed it on the desk. She plugged in a couple of cables that were also attached to Patrice's desktop machine and the drive responded with an unhappy scraping noise, as if a coffee grinder was attempting to deal with a consignment of industrial grit. Ali winced.

'Ooh, that's not good,' she said. She picked up the drive, shook it from side to side, as if to try and settle the grit into a more grinder-friendly formation. Then she put it back down again, whereupon it resumed the exact same noise as before.

'Shit,' said Ali. She stood watching the drive for a moment, deep in thought with her head resting on her chin.

'Why don't you—' I began.

'Leave this to me?' said Ali. 'Yes, I think that would be a VERY good idea, PR boy. Now fuck off and let the expert do the thinking.' She waved me away with a flick of the wrist. Patrice frowned at her.

'Alison,' she said, very quietly.

Ali stared back at her and looked as if she was about to say something. Then she gave a deep sigh and turned to me.

'Look,' she said, 'I can handle this myself, is all I'm saying. OK?'

'Sure,' I said, holding up both hands. 'Sure.'

Ali picked the drive up again and put it on its side. The sound modulated itself slightly, as if the grit had been leavened with a five per cent solution of WD40.

'Better,' said Ali, before finally turning the drive on its back. The noise lowered still further to a dull, irregular rumble. Ali moved her hands away, holding them over the device as if she were some kind of faith healer. All three of us held our collective breath. There was a brief squeal as if a cat was being attacked with sandpaper, and then the disk drive relaxed to a contented hum.

'OK,' said Ali. 'I think we're ready to dive in.'

Patrice and I exhaled.

'This could be really disappointing, you know,' I said.

'Oh, I don't know,' said Ali. 'If nothing else, we'll all get to read a fucking poem.'

'Well, there is that.'

'Anyway,' said Ali, 'this is the really boring bit. Now that I've got this drive of yours talking, I'm going to backup as much as I can from the thing to Patti's computer so that if and when we have to read it the last rites we've at least got something we can work on.' She peered at the monitor. 'Looks like it's going to take an hour or so. OK?'

'OK by me, Alison,' said Patrice.

I shrugged. 'OK by me too.'

'I wasn't asking you,' said Ali. 'So, then, any food in the house, Patti?'

It wasn't until I'd tasted Patrice's unbelievably delicious goat curry that I realised how long it had been since I'd eaten a decent meal. I immediately decided that I would quite like to live here for a while. Unexpectedly, this was exactly what Patrice was about to suggest.

'I think you should both stay here for a while,' she announced. Ali clearly hadn't been expecting this, because she choked on her wine.

'What?' she said, once she had recovered at least something of her composure. She wore the expression of someone who had just been informed that she would be required by law to wear a five-millimetre-thick layer of raspberry jam on her face for the next month. 'This is the man who almost lost Bertrand!'

'Bertrand came back, Alison. At Thomas's hour of need. There is a bond between them now.'

'Oh, for fuck's sake.'

'Alison.'

'Yes, but—'

'But the point is, Alison,' said Patrice, 'we have to assume that your delightfully bijou pièd-a-terre is unsafe for the foreseeable future. Whoever it was who tried to get hold of Thomas's disk drive must have followed him home from the library.'

'Oh god,' I said. 'Really?'

'How do you think he got to you so soon after you left the flat?' said Patrice.

'Maybe he was just lurking around on the High Road?'

'I don't think so, Thomas. He probably followed you all the way from where you live, waiting for the right moment.'

'Scumbag,' I said.

'But he's out of commission now, right?' said Ali, who was clearly still coming to terms with the idea of me invading her love nest.

'Assuming the police got to him before he managed to crawl away,' I said.

'But he could have passed the information on to whoever contracted him,' said Patrice. 'By the way, I'm assuming you weren't followed here, Thomas?'

'I... don't think so,' I said. Then again, I couldn't really be sure. My sixth sense wasn't reliable at the best of times.

'Well, that's something.'

Ali looked at her watch and cleared her throat. 'Probably finished copying now,' she said. 'I'll go take a look and see what you've got lurking on your drive.'

'I still can't believe there's anything important on there.'

'Tell that to Mad Mickey,' said Ali.

Ali left the kitchen and Patrice leaned over and topped my wine glass up.

'So how long have you been in the Vavvies?' I said, trying to make conversation.

'That was my first meeting,' she said. 'It was more eventful than I'd anticipated.'

'I don't think they get many professional mathematicians along.'

'No, Thomas. I don't think they do.'

There was something remote and self-contained about Patrice, as if she was constantly working on something in her head, but was only willing to discuss it when she'd finished thinking it through to its logical conclusion.

'Why the reptiles?' I said.

'Why not?'

'Because they're reptiles?'

'I think you're forgetting the service that Bertrand provided for you.'

'But that was an accident.'

'Are you sure?'

'Fairly sure. I certainly don't remember getting down on my hands and knees and calling through the floorboards "Bertrand! I need you to come back so you can sit in a bag and guard a disk drive against a nutter with a gun who is waiting to pounce on me as soon as I leave this flat. Pretty please, Bertrand!"' I accompanied this speech with a humorous gesture or two in order to emphasise the absurdity of the whole idea.

'Thomas,' said Patrice. She had a way of looking at you that suggested that she wasn't angry, just very, very disappointed. I immediately shrank back in my chair. I hadn't felt this small since I was wearing short trousers and Start-Rite sandals.

'Oh, all right,' I said eventually. 'I am very grateful that Bertrand chose that moment to show up. If it hadn't been for him, we wouldn't have the disk drive with us now. Or me either, most likely. And if he ever wants a special treat next time he gets fed – I dunno, maybe some kind of rare, festive rodent – I'm very happy to provide one for him.'

Patrice was looking at me again, but this time there was a hint of a twinkle in her eyes. 'I might take you up on that,' she said.

As she finished talking, Ali burst in through the door, looking agitated.

'Well, PR Boy,' she said, 'have *you* gone and fucked things up this time.'

'What?' I said.

'You know,' she continued, 'I did wonder what all the sudden interest in cryptocurrencies was about. All that crap about your stupid father getting involved in them.'

'I don't know what you're—'

'Yes, you do, pal. The only one who was putting everything he had – and I'm willing to bet, everything the fucking COMPANY had too – into bitcoins and any other dodgy crypto shit that came along... the only one who was doing that—' here she stabbed a finger in my direction '—was you, pal. YOU.'

A terrible silence fell over the kitchen table.

'I—' I began. Two faces were staring hard at me. 'I literally have no idea what you are talking about. Are you saying there were bitcoins on my laptop?'

'Not just bitcoins, pal, but loads of other crypto shit. Even those Tulpencoins you've been going on about lately. It's quite a portfolio you've built up there, and it wouldn't surprise me in the least if we find out that *that*'s where the contents of our bank account have gone.'

'Well, at least that means we haven't lost everything,' I said, 'now we've got the drive back.' It turned out that this wasn't a helpful remark.

'Thomas,' said Patrice, 'are you really saying this has nothing to do with you?'

'Nothing,' I said, spreading my arms wide. 'Honest to god, nothing at all.'

'He's lying,' shouted Ali, thumping the table. 'I knew he was trouble as soon as Dot brought him home. I've never liked him.'

'Alison,' said Patrice. 'Please.'

'Look,' I said, standing up, 'if I can get a word in edgeways—'

'Don't let him,' said Ali. 'The little creep'll weasel his way out of it. He always does.'

'Alison,' said Patrice, holding up a hand.

'Oh, but—'

'Alison. Let him speak.'

'Thank you, Patrice,' I said.

'Please sit down,' she said, motioning to both of us to take our seats again. 'This isn't helping.' She paused. 'Thomas,' she said, 'please go ahead.'

I took a deep breath. Then I took another one.

'OK,' I said, 'first of all, until I found out last week that my father had started dabbling in Tulpencoins, the word cryptocurrency wasn't even in discussions about joining my vocabulary. So there's absolutely no possibility whatsoever that I had anything to do with bitcoins, Tulpencoins or anything like that ending up on my laptop. Honestly. Look at me, Ali. Do you really think I'm the sort of guy who'd get involved with that sort of thing? It involves technology, for god's sake!

'Also, why would I go to the trouble of making up some implausible story about being mugged and then somehow being saved by a snake? Surely if I had something to hide I would have let them have the bloody thing? And please don't try to tell me I was the one who arranged to have Mad Mickey bumped off. Do I look to you like someone who could set up a contract killing?'

There was a long silence.

'Alison?' said Patrice.

'Well, it wasn't me, if that's what you're thinking,' said Ali.

'No one's saying that, Alison.'

'I might be,' I said.

'Oh, FUCK OFF,' said Ali. There was a brief pause while we all looked at each other. Then Patrice shook her head. 'Look,' continued Ali, 'it's on a disk drive that's only ever been attached to your laptop. What am I supposed to think?'

'What about Dorothy?' said Patrice. 'Could she have done it?'

'Dot?' said Ali. 'Possibly. But I can't somehow see her stopping to use a shitty little laptop like PR boy's here. Not her style at all.'

'Wait a minute,' I said. 'Maybe that's it.'

'What?' said Ali.

'She did borrow my laptop once. When I was accidentally confronting Rufus Fairbanks in his home. She used it to hack into his home internet. And just before we left, she was digging into his other systems to try to work out what he was up to. Before I told her it was time to get out of there, that is. What if Fairbanks was a crypto head?'

'Are you saying Dot might have copied Fairbanks's digital wallet?'

'Why not? It's the sort of thing she might have done for a laugh. Just to prove she could. I doubt if she had any intention of stealing anything. It would just have appealed to her as a hacker.'

Ali looked at me. It was as if her features were trying to arrange themselves into something approaching a look of conciliation, but something powerful was still putting up resistance. 'That's the first plausible explanation for anything I've heard from you for some time,' she said. 'Possibly ever.'

'Thank you,' I said.

'Yeah well, I'm not anticipating a repeat performance any time soon.'

Patrice was deep in thought. 'I still don't understand how these people came to know that it was on Thomas's laptop. And why they've gone to all this trouble when they've got the laptop anyway.'

'Ah, I can answer that one,' I said. 'I was very selective about what I backed up and restored onto the new disk. I didn't bother about anything I didn't understand. But you're right about the first question. How did they know I had it in the first place?'

Ali stood up. 'Got an idea,' she said, leaving the room. We followed her into the study. She sat down at Patrice's desk and we took up positions behind her as she clicked her way around the system.

'Aha!' said Ali eventually. 'There we go.' She was pointing at a window on the machine full of lines of dense-ly-packed text in black on a white background.

'What are we looking at?' I said.

'That file is executed as part of your boot sequence. When your scuzzy little laptop wakes up to face another shitty day in the office. And look at that line there.'

I peered closer. I couldn't make out anything particularly odd.

'Shouldn't be there at all,' said Ali. 'That line there is kicking off something well iffy that's going to lurk in the background and do stuff that you don't want it to do.'

'Do you mean a virus?' I said.

'Yup. A virus almost certainly caught from your man Fairbanks. And Dot – oh god, Dot, why oh why oh why? – brought it back to the office right inside our firewall.'

'It was quite an emotional day,' I said. I didn't mention that Dorothy had advised me to give my laptop a good clean in order to remove the illegal hacking tools she'd installed in order to break into Fairbanks's intranet. I'd always meant to do it, but I'd somehow never found the time.

'Yeah well, fuck emotion. Never did me any good.' I snuck a glance at Patrice. She remained poker-faced.

I had a feeling Ali hadn't yet told the whole story. 'Go on, then,' I said. 'What kind of virus are we talking about?'

A look of triumph spread over Ali's face. 'One manufactured by Tulpencoin,' she said.

Chapter 17

'Tulpencoin?' I said.

'Yep,' said Ali. 'Definitely them. Now, normally in the case of a crypto-based virus, I'd suspect it was some kind of mining bot.'

'What do you mean?'

'Something that sits on your computer, stealing your CPU to mine bitcoins. Great example of distributed processing, although not such a good example of distributed consent.'

'Good grief, does that happen?'

'You'd be surprised.'

'Actually, before I had the drive replaced, my laptop was beginning to run a bit slow.'

'Yeah, but I don't think it was a mining bot, pal.'

'What then?'

'Well, take a look at these logs here.' She tapped at the screen.

'What of them?' I was still struggling to work out what was going on.

'It's running through an attack sequence. It's trying to crack open Fairbanks's crypto wallet.'

'So kind of like a mining bot, but a bit more local?'

'Precisely. I reckon the whole Tulpencoin thing is a hacking scam. Sure, they'll raise a wad of cash via their ICOs, but I'll bet you anything most of the funds on their balance sheet are represented by pilfered crypto.'

I considered the implications of this. Also, what a weird coincidence it was that my own father had got involved. I said as much to Ali.

'No coincidence, pal,' she said. 'Chances are this little bot has had a scan of your address book too. Most of your chums will have chucked it straight in the trash, but the more gullible ones would have been in there like a shot.'

Shit. So that was all my fault too. He'd told me it was one-eyed Kev who'd got him into it, but the ground had already been well and truly prepared. I had to do something. My father was a fool, but I was the one who'd introduced the scammers to him. My head was spinning.

'Run through it all again, Ali. I'm struggling here.'

Ali looked at me and took a deep breath.

'Patti,' she said, waving at the whiteboard on the wall. 'Is all this shit important to you?'

Patrice shrugged. 'I can reproduce it in a few minutes,' she said. 'So no. Go ahead, Alison.'

'Ta,' said Ali, moving over to the board and wiping it clear. 'Right,' she said, picking up a marker pen. 'Here we go. First of all, your man Rufus Fairbanks is a big deal investor, right? So he's bound to have an interest in anything new and wacky going, such as bitcoin and all that shit.'

'Seems fair,' I said.

'And then the Tulpencoin boys come knocking. They spin him a good yarn and he agrees to invest in their first ICO. The Tulpencoin management software – or whatever they call their little virus – gets installed on his system and off it goes on its merry way, maybe even reporting back to base when it finds something interesting. Fairbanks's machine starts to run a bit hot, but he puts it down to outdated equipment or the weather or something.'

All the time, she was scribbling on the whiteboard, drawing boxes and pictures of computers and annotating them as she went along.

'Then you and Dot walk in and everything ends badly for him. Your laptop, which Dot has been using to hack into the Fairbanks intranet, gets infected with the Tulpenbot. Dot gets excited by the chance to get into Fairbanks's system and sets a bulk copy program going. But then you sensibly tell her to stop arsing around and get out of there, so she abandons the download, but not before she's accidentally grabbed hold of his crypto wallet,'

'So, at that point,' I said, 'my laptop has Fairbanks's crypto whatsit sitting on it, but it has also been infected with the Tulpenbot virus.'

'Correct.'

'So, what happens then?'

'My guess is that Fairbanks's system goes dark. A light flashes up on some kind of dashboard at Tulpencoin HQ to that effect, and they decide to hold a little conference. The last report from the bot says that it still hasn't done its job and the wallet remains uncompromised. But they know who they're dealing with here, because all sorts of ID stuff has been scraped – including, of course, the password to Fairbanks's LinkedIn account, in case you were wondering. And they know that Fairbanks is a big player. So they decide to implement Plan B.'

'And Plan B is?' I said.

'Plan B involves nothing short of burglary: the theft of every single computer they can find at Chateau Fairbanks.'

'But that didn't happen, though, did it?'

'No, because right on cue, PR boy's scrofulous little laptop pops up the very next day and says "Hey guys, yoo hoo! Look at me, I've got the wallet you're looking for right here!"'

'Bloody hell. I think I know what happens next.'

'Yup,' said Ali. 'First of all, it logs your keystrokes when Dot lends you our bank account details to order more coffee because she's too busy – don't deny it, because I bet it fucking happened, pal – so it's primed and ready to clean us out when they give the order. Next, your manky machine's disk drive collapses under the strain of having to run the Tulpencoin software and you take it away to Mad Mickey's to trade it in for a reconditioned one. When it comes back, you restore all the stuff you really needed, accidentally cleaning your machine of any reference to bitcoins, Tulpencoins and Uncle Tom Cobbleycoins. In short, Fairbanks's wallet has gone dark for the second time.'

'And this time they actually implement Plan B.'

'They sure do. Now they could just break the door down and shoot the lot of us, but that's a bit messy in an area like Hoxton and the whole thing could go tits up. But from reading your emails and stuff, they know the kind of thing that'll clear each one of us out of the office while they do it. Me to a concert – which was really shit, by the way – you to try and impress Dot by presenting her with the fucking Vavasor papers, and Dot to some conference when they were about to announce the solution to the Riemann Hypothesis.'

'Well, that didn't happen, either,' said Patrice.

We both looked at her.

'It's an area I'm interested in,' she said. 'Did you really see the Vavasor papers, Thomas?' she added.

'Not on this occasion, no,' I said. 'They were complete fakes. But I did see them once. I also saw them get blown up. Possibly.'

'Perhaps that would be the best thing for them,' said Patrice.

'Surely you don't mean that?'

'They seem to have caused a lot of trouble, one way or another.'

'Anyway,' said Ali. 'Back to the story. We're nearly there. The Tulpencoin Bros start off by cleaning out our bank account just for the hell of it. Then they take a long, hard look at all this kit they've stolen and realise there's absolutely fuck all of use to them on it. They take a few things apart and notice that your laptop has a nice shiny new disk drive. So they put two and two together and work out that Fairbanks's crypto wallet is sitting on the old drive. Which is most likely now in some landfill somewhere. On the off chance that it isn't, however, the only one who can lead them to it is PR boy here. So they hatch a plan to lure you in via Fairbanks's LinkedIn account and we end up leading them right up to Mad Mickey's door.'

Ali finished by scribbling a crude drawing of a body lying on the ground.

'Did you have to remind me of that?' I said.

'You weren't to know,' said Patrice, touching me on the shoulder.

'The point is, though,' said Ali, 'for once we're ahead of them now. We've got Fairbanks's bitcoin stash. Christ knows what we do with it, though.'

'Sell it?' I said. 'Couldn't we use the money to get the company back up and running again? Replace your equipment?'

'Who can we sell it to, though? It's not easy to launder crypto, pal. Sure, I could probably repurpose the Tulpencoin virus to hack into Fairbanks's wallet without sending the details back to Tulpencoin Central, but it wouldn't do us a lot of good if all we end up with is a load of easily traceable hot bitcoin.'

'And, in any case, we're missing something important here,' I said. 'Don't get me wrong, I appreciate your analysis and everything. But we're not after Fairbanks's cash, are we? We're trying to find out what's happened to Dorothy.'

Ali sighed. 'Yeah, I guess we are.'

'You sound reluctant,' said Patrice.

'Yeah,' said Ali. 'I'm still not sure whose side she's on.'

'You can't really be serious,' I said.

'Yeah, well, maybe I am. I'm still not convinced she's not somehow involved in this.'

'Surely not?'

'Yeah, well, whatever.'

'Oh, come on, Ali,' I said, standing up. I'd had enough of this. But I'd forgotten how much wine I'd had with my supper and I misjudged the transition from slouch to vertical so that there was a brief moment when I teetered on one foot threatening to collapse into the fireplace. A brief windmill impression with my opposite arm restored my balance, but the impact of my manoeuvre wasn't quite as impressive as I'd hoped.

'Don't "Come on, Ali" me, PR boy,' said Ali, looking at me with some contempt. 'I've known her a lot longer than you have. Just 'cos you've seen her with her kit off doesn't mean you know everything about her, pal.'

Now it was Patrice's turn to stand up. She was significantly shorter than either of us but she nonetheless succeeded in taking control of the space between Ali and myself with very little apparent effort.

'Guys,' she said. 'Cool it. Look, we're all tired. You've both had a difficult day. Let's call it a night and work out what to do next tomorrow. OK?'

'OK,' I said, relaxing a little.

Ali shook her head, then gave a deep sigh. 'Ah, fuck it, Patti,' she said. 'Just for you, then.'

Next morning, I awoke to sunshine streaming in through the lace curtains. The sofa had been reasonably comfortable and I felt suitably rested. All was not entirely well, however, as there was an alien presence on my chest, staring at me with unblinking, judgmental eyes. The face had hints of many colours about it, although mostly it seemed to be matched with the blanket I'd thrown over myself. A fly buzzed around my head for a moment or two before coming in to land on my nose. Without a moment's hesitation, the alien flicked out a disgustingly long tongue and removed it.

'Cheers,' I said.

'Ah,' said Patrice, wandering in to the room, 'I see you've met Maryam.' She came over and picked the creature up, cuddling it as if it were some kind of fluffy thing. 'Now who's a naughty girl, then?' she said.

'So that's Maryam, then,' I said, wiping the end of my nose. 'The one who has issues with Bertrand.'

'Yes. That's probably why she decided to go for a walk last night. She probably wasn't expecting Bertrand to come back.'

Well, that was at least something she and I had in common.

'She's a chameleon,' said Patrice.

'I'd sort of guessed that.' I looked at Maryam again, trying to think of some kind of intelligent remark I could make. 'That tail of hers,' I said. 'It's a bit like a Fibonacci spiral, isn't it?'

Patrice gave me a sympathetic smile, the kind that teachers tend to reserve for the slow kids in the class. 'No,' she said. 'Once you find out about Fibonacci spirals, it's very tempting to see them everywhere, as if their existence is an indication of some kind of underlying order to the world. But sometimes all you see is something that just looks like a Fibonacci spiral. And Maryam's tail just looks like one, I'm afraid.'

'Oh,' I said. I found this quite disappointing.

Ali was conspicuously quiet over breakfast. I got a distinct impression that Patrice had had some kind of word with her. Like 'chill', for example.

'Who are these people behind Tulpencoins?' said Patrice. 'I mean, what was their initial coin offering intended to raise money for?'

'I don't know,' I said. I hadn't even considered that. I thought ICOs were just a thing that happened in the crypto world for no ostensible purpose. 'There was something at the launch about "The Institute for Progress and Development" if that's any help,' I added.

'Ah,' she said. 'Them.'

'You sound like you've heard of them.'

'Yes,' she said quietly. For the first time since I'd known Patrice, I heard real anger in her voice. 'I sometimes get little billetsdoux from them,' she said, 'explaining in great detail how my very existence offends them. I tick a lot of boxes for people like that.' She paused. 'Alison,' she said, 'I was going to ask if I could have my computer back, but if there's anything you need it for right now, it's yours. As long as you need it for. I want you to bring these people down.'

Ali sat deep in thought for a while. 'Give me a minute,' she said. Then she got up from the table and went into the study. I got up to follow her, but Patrice touched my arm.

'No,' she said. 'Let her get on with what she has to do. If I'm going to be involved, you need to bring me up to speed on all of this.'

I sat down again and spent the next hour distilling the essence of the last few months of my life. By the end of it, the expression on Patrice's face suggested that she now deeply regretted any involvement with (a) the Vavvies, (b) Ali and (c) most of all, me. She was staring at me, slowly shaking her head. Eventually, she spoke.

'What do you really think's happened to Dorothy?' she said.

I sighed. 'God knows,' I said. 'Despite everything Ali says – and I know she has her reasons, because Dorothy was behaving very oddly before it all happened – I don't think she's a part of this. I think she's a victim as much as any of us. But it's just so weird that she hasn't been in touch with us since then.' I paused. 'I suppose the absolute worst case scenario is that she left her lecture early and interrupted the gang as they were emptying our office and something happened to her as a result.'

'Well, I don't remember seeing anyone leave early. But then, I didn't know what she looked like, so I don't even know if she was there. Tell me again what this Matheson woman said to you, Thomas.'

'She said I had no idea what I was getting involved in.'

'Well, she was right there,' said Patrice. 'Although there are some aspects of it which, unlikely as it may seem, we know more about than she probably does. I think you should give her a call. Hand over everything you know and leave it to the professionals.'

I found this advice unexpectedly disappointing. Now that we seemed to be getting close, it seemed a dereliction of duty to simply abandon the project. There was something else as well.

'I'm not sure I trust Matheson,' I said. 'Also, she doesn't seem to look after her staff very well. I really hope Dorothy hasn't got mixed up with her.'

'I still think you should call her, Thomas. Maybe just to keep the communication lines open.'

'But seriously, Patrice, I don't think—'

'Call her, Thomas.'

'I guess so.' I took out my phone and called the number I'd got from Narendra. This time, however, I got the 'number unobtainable' tone. I put the phone down on the table. 'Looks like we're on our own, Patrice,' I said, but she was busy tapping away at her own phone.

'Ah,' she said. 'Here we are. The Institute for Progress and Development seems a little shy about revealing where it's based. There's some contact details here, but they look more like just a forwarding address.'

'Well, that explains why Matheson was struggling to get at them.'

'I wonder if the key to it is your Mr Big chap. It would be helpful to know who he is.'

'Matheson certainly didn't know. And neither did her man Matt Blank – at least not until it was too late.'

At that point Ali came back into the room, trembling with excitement.

'I've found it,' she said.

'You've found what?' I said.

'The server for the virus.'

'Really?'

'Yeah. But it's really, really weird.'

'Why?'

'Because it's in the middle of the fucking sea.'

Chapter 18

We clustered around Patrice's computer, watching as Ali explained what she'd done.

'Y'see,' she said, 'I suddenly had this totally awesome idea. Why can't I turn their virus back against them? First thing I had to do was crack their IP address, right? So I moved their little virus thing onto a spare CPU in the cloud, just so as they don't come to hunt us down if a little red light starts flashing on their dashboard. Then I ran up a Wireshark session – sorry, Patti, I've downloaded all sorts of shit onto your machine, but it's all good stuff, don't worry—' Patrice grimaced '—and finally I set the little fella running. And guess what the first thing it does is? It reports back to base. "Hey, guys! Look at me! I'm up and running again!" So, Wireshark captures the transaction and Ali gets the IP address.'

She concluded by leaning back in her chair and glancing up at each of us in turn, smiling encouragingly.

'You're allowed to congratulate me,' she said.

'Well done, Ali,' I said. 'But how does that get us any nearer to locating the server? Is there some kind of IP phone book we can look it up in?'

'Well, I tried an rDNS but that was blocked, so no, basically. However, I thought to myself, why not try and telnet into the thing? Chances are they've spent all their waking hours twatting about writing viruses and not bothering to cover their own arses. There's always some kind of back door. So I tried a few of the usual suspects for usernames with default passwords and whaddya know? I'm in.'

'Are you following this?' I said to Patrice.

'Mostly,' she said.

'Oh,' I said.

'Yeah well, anyway,' continued Ali. 'So I FTP a few choice tools I've got lying around, get myself root privilege and have a scout around. Guess what, the server's GPS-enabled? So I grab the location and that's when it all gets a bit weird, because when I stick it into Google Maps, it turns out it's about five miles off the coast of Burnham-on-Sea.'

Ali sat back in her chair again and this time we didn't wait for her to ask us to congratulate her.

'That's amazing,' I said.

'I'll take amazing, yeah,' said Ali.

'You're a star,' said Patrice. 'But what does it mean?'

Something was lurking in the back of my mind.

'It's not a boat,' I said.

'What?' said Ali. 'It's got to be. 'Cos if it's someone's house, they're going to have a fucking awful damp problem.'

'It's a rig.'

'Are you mad?' said Ali. 'There's no fucking oil in the Bristol Channel.'

'Not an oil rig. A rig to transport construction materials. One that walks. I remember now, there was a story a couple of years back about some bunch who'd acquired this thing from the wrecker's yard and walked it out into the middle of the Bristol Channel and declared independence from the UK. Didn't pay a lot of attention to it at the time, but I'll bet you anything that's it.'

'Channellia?' said Patrice, who had been tapping away at her phone.

'That's it!' I said. Ali immediately put the word into Google and brought up the website of the Autonomous Bailiwick of Channellia.

'Whoa,' said Ali. 'That's some seriously deranged shit.' There was a kind of manifesto on the main page of the site which gave a summary of the Autonomous Bailiwick's laws, which essentially amounted to an extreme statement of libertarianism, starting with the freedom from political correctness and then proceeding via, amongst other things, the freedom to smoke, to the freedom to discriminate against anyone on any grounds that took your fancy. Most importantly, the manifesto included the freedom for the Seigneur of the Autonomous Bailiwick to do whatever the hell he goddamned liked.

'So, who's this Seigneur dude?' said Patrice.

'Hold on, there's bound to be a picture of him,' said Ali, hunting around the screen. 'Ah, here we go.'

'Shit,' I said.

'What?' said Ali.

'I know him.'

'You *know* him?' said Patrice.

'Well, no,' I said. 'I don't actually know him to speak to. But I've seen him. Quite recently, too. He was the third guy in the room at the Tulpencoin launch. The one who ordered the killing of Matt Blank.'

'Ah,' said Ali. 'Well, I guess that completes the triangulation process.'

'Sure does,' I said. Ali opened up a new tab in the browser and found his page on Wikipedia. 'What a guy,' she said. It turned out that the Honourable Sholto Chelford-Bickerton, after completing his education at Eton and Balliol College, Oxford, used his, not inconsiderable, trust fund to build up an advertising agency responsible for a series of 'edgy' campaigns resulting in a record level of complaints from the Advertising Standards Authority. Having sold his stake a couple of decades later for what was, by now, a small fortune, he'd decided that what he really fancied having was his own personal fiefdom.

So he'd acquired this rig, built a settlement on top of it and walked it out to sea. Even though it was still within territorial waters, no one in the UK government seemed entirely sure what to do about it. Of special concern was the fact that Channellia had managed to build up an impressive arsenal of high-tech weaponry without anyone noticing until it was too late to do anything about it without causing a bloodbath. Also, it was rumoured that the Seigneur had friends in high places.

'Go back to the Channellia page,' I said. Ali flicked to the other tab. 'There,' I said, pointing to the screen.

'What?' said Ali.

'The stuff about weekend breaks.'

Ali sighed. 'Look, pal,' she said. 'I know we're all of us in need of a holiday, but—'

'No,' I said. 'Seriously. They have a hotel on there. It's got to be their cover story, right? Look. There's a casino on board. Laser tag. Clay pigeon shooting. They do corporate events. Training weekends. Team building. And look at that, Ali. Stag parties. They host stag parties.'

'And?' Ali was looking at me with genuine bewilderment.

'I've got an idea,' I said.

'No,' said Patrice when I'd explained what I intended to do. 'That's a terrible idea. You'll get yourself killed.'

'Well,' said Ali. 'Every cloud, and all that. But Patti's right. You'll never do it.'

'Please, guys,' I said, 'humour me? Ali, have you got Twitter there?'

'Twitter?' she said. 'What kind of numpty do you think I am?'

'Just go to the website, please, Ali.'

'Fucking Twitter,' muttered Ali. 'Playground for fucking Nazi twats who can't get laid. I hate fucking social media, you know.'

'I'd never have guessed,' I said. 'But just this once—?'

Ali sighed, opened up another tab and after another burst of low-level muttering, pulled up Twitter.

'Now search for mentions of Channellia,' I said. 'Yes, there it is. That'll do. That's perfect.' The tweet simply said 'Whoa! Two sleeps till #Channellia #lads #stag #bantz'.

'Jesus,' said Ali. 'You really aren't going to go through with this. Are you?'

'Click on his profile,' I said.

'Oh, Christ, do I have to? He said "bantz". With a "z".'
'Please, Ali.'

The profile that came up was absolutely perfect. It was just what I'd been looking for.

The shuttle boat to Channellia was scheduled to depart from Bristol docks at five p.m. on Friday evening, so at around three o'clock I scoured the pubs in the vicinity for groups of twenty-to-thirty-something men who were obviously drinking much more than they were used to and had no intention of returning to their place of work. The atmosphere on the waterfront was febrile, as if something exciting was about to happen, even if it was just the start of another weekend.

Eventually, I came across a likely bunch, outside a bar on the waterfront opposite the Arnolfini gallery. There were three of them, late twenties or early thirties, all wearing matching striped rugby shirts emblazoned with the words 'Todger Squad' and sporting a badge depicting a smiling cartoon penis. They were arrayed like the front row of the least convincing scrum ever to take part in a fifteen-a-side match, with the two on either side swaying unsteadily from side to side while the one in the middle vomited copiously all over the pavement.

'Come on, Piers!' shouted the tight-head prop on the right. 'Better out than in!' Meanwhile, the loose-head on the left started up a chant of 'Chunder! Chunder! Chunder!' His colleague quickly joined in with this, although the hooker in the middle declined to do so, having other things on his mind. It was impressive to see how much sick one man could produce on his own. Eventually, he decided to sit down on one of the outside chairs and the other two disappeared back into the bar. I snuck in past them and observed from a discreet distance.

The bar was mostly populated by lone drinkers who had clearly decided to give the day up as a bad job, along with three larger clusters. The first of these was clearly some kind of leaving do although, given the toxic atmosphere it was giving off, I detected more of a mass redundancy vibe. Then there was an exceptionally loud hen party, all wearing tulle skirts, sparkly make-up and angels' wings, apart from the one in the middle sporting an outsize L plate and ruined mascara, telling everyone that Dane was a fucking bastard and that she was only going through with this for the sake of the unborn kid.

Finally, there was my target group. The two props had joined a group of five others, in varying states of intoxication, from pretty much off their face right through to not having any serviceable knowledge of what a face actually was. They were all wearing identical rugby shirts, although I could now see that they had nicknames on the back, which enabled me to establish that they would like to be known as Badger Pubes, Ham & Tongue, Furball, Gobshite, The Jizz Bandit, Pisspot and Tampon. They were all conventionally dressed below the waist, apart from the one called Furball, who was wearing a mini-skirt, stockings and suspenders, not all of which were attached. I assumed he was the bridegroom. Badger Pubes and The Jizz Bandit, who I'd already encountered outside, seemed to be giving some kind of report on Piers's health, following which the entire group broke into a spontaneous chant of 'Chunder! Chunder!

Chunder!' followed by a convincing impression of the sound of seven men throwing up. Then they ordered another round of drinks.

I was pretty certain this was the right lot because I'd recognised Piers from his Twitter profile picture. And here he was again, wobbling from side to side as he attempted to traverse the challenging terrain between the front door and the bar. As it happened, he missed the bar altogether and hurtled straight on past towards the gents, at which point I noted that he was going under the name of Titface. It was becoming increasingly clear that Piers was not going to be capable of playing much of a role in the weekend's activities, which created exactly the opening I had been anticipating.

I decided to make my move. I bought myself a pint and sidled over to the stag party. By now, they had abandoned interest in Piers's well-being and were now competing to see who could successfully flick a pork scratching into their mouth. No one had so far succeeded at this, despite the considerable encouragement that the others were giving, in the shape of a chant of 'Porky! Porky! Porky! Oink! Oink! Oink!' As a result, it was getting quite crunchy underfoot.

After a couple of rounds of this, I grabbed the bag and chucked one towards my face. In my state of relative sobriety, swallowing it wasn't anything like as hard as it had appeared, and I was unexpectedly successful. The group erupted as one, changing the chant to 'Oink! Oink! Oink! Oink! Oink! Oink!' and several of them patted me on the back with quite some ferocity.

'Who the fuck are you?' shouted Ham & Tongue in my ear. He was six foot six and muscular with it.

'Mate of Piers,' I shouted back. It was very unlikely that this assertion would be challenged. Not today, anyway.

The bloke looked at me for a moment and then started chanting 'Piers is a wanker! Piers is a wanker!' very loudly. Everyone joined in with this, too, finishing with a universally-recognised hand gesture and a series of grunts.

'The thing is,' said Ham & Tongue, 'Piers is a bloody good chap. Bloody good chap. But he's a wanker. Right?'

'Right,' I said. 'Right.'

At this point, Tampon managed to knock his pint glass over, spilling its contents all over the floor, mixing with the spilled pork scratchings to form a sticky render. Ham & Tongue pointed at him and shouted, 'Forfeit! Forfeit!' The group reconfigured with Tampon in the centre, all roaring at him and shouting 'Forfeit!' Badger Pubes was delegated to go to the bar, returning with two pints of beer, both of which he handed to the hapless Tampon. Now the chant of 'Chug! Chug! Chug!' started up while Tampon attempted to down the first pint in one. He just about succeeded, but the second pint proved a beer too far and he dumped it down on the table next to him and lurched out into the street.

Ham & Tongue shouted 'Lightweight!' after him. Then he looked at each of his remaining five fellow team members in turn and seemed to be considering what to say next. 'Shots!' he announced.

'Mate,' said Badger Pubes quietly, 'we've got a boat ride ahead of us. Don't you think—'

'FUCKING LIGHTWEIGHT!' bellowed Ham & Tongue by way of response, and Badger Pubes shrank away and headed back to the bar. This time he came back with seven small shot glasses, each filled with a colourless liquid, presumably vodka. He handed one out to each of them, plus one for me. We each held our glass in our hands, awaiting a signal. When everyone was ready, Ham & Tongue called out 'Three... two... one!' and we downed them in one. Yep, it was vodka, and cheap vodka too. I'd had some really bad experiences with vodka in the past, but I was some way behind the rest of the group with the amount I'd drunk, so I reckoned I'd be reasonably safe.

Suddenly, Ham & Tongue looked at me, as if seeing me for the first time. As I looked into his unfocussed eyes, I realised he was in fact very, very drunk indeed.

'Where's your shirt?' he said.

'What?' I said, feigning innocence. 'This one?' I took hold of my collar by way of demonstrating which shirt I was talking about.

'No, you twat,' said Ham & Tongue. 'Your rugger shirt.'

'Ah, you see, Piers didn't tell me about that. I've only just found out about the weekend, you see.' I was hoping that the combination of my confidence and his extreme inebriation would go some way towards convincing him that I really was supposed to be there.

'Oh,' said Ham & Tongue. 'Well, I said Piers was a wanker. Tell you what, why don't you have his shirt?'

'Won't he be wearing it?'

'Not if we take it off the fucker.'

'Right.'

Ham & Tongue stormed off towards the Gents, with me tagging along behind. We found Piers, aka Titface, still crouched over the bowl in the second cubicle along.

'Oi, Piers, you wanker,' said Ham & Tongue. 'Give us your fucking shirt.'

'Donwanna. Leamelone. Whoaaaaaaagh.' Another bout of retching interrupted his pleas, although there seemed to be precious little left to come out.

'Come on, give us a hand,' said Ham & Tongue. I looked at him and then between us we manhandled Piers off the floor and on to the seat.

'Wassgoinon,' said Piers. 'Leamelone. Buggroff.'

Ham & Tongue grabbed the right sleeve and I grabbed the left one and between us we managed to remove Piers's shirt. Then we left him still sitting there, slumped and wondering what to do next.

'There you go,' said Ham & Tongue. 'There's a splash of chuck on the front there, but it'll come off with a bit of water.' He gestured towards the sinks.

'Cheers,' I said, as Ham & Tongue disappeared back into the bar, where a roar from his mates greeted his return. I took Piers's shirt over and ran it under the tap and then attempted to dry it using the air blower. I took my own shirt off and put Piers's on. It fitted me reasonably well. Great. I was now officially Titface. I returned to the bar and bought myself a beer, taking extra care not to spill any of it as I walked back to where the others were still congregated.

I was halfway through my pint, listening to a distinctly off-colour story about the experiences of one of their mates in the police, when a generously-bearded chap in a sou'wester walked in, carrying a scrunched-up slip of paper.

'Er… "Todger Squad"?' he said, consulting his note. He had a broad Bristolian accent, and appeared not to be in the mood for any nonsense.

This was the cue for everyone present to start up a 'Rar! Rar! Rar!' chant, and the man responded by signalling with both arms that they should stop.

'All right, me lads, calm down. Now, I've got a Mr Kerrigan down here as the primary contact.' He looked from one member of the group to the next as if waiting for one of us to own up to being Mr Kerrigan. Finally, Ham & Tongue raised his hand.

'That would be me, old chap' he said.

'All right, Mr Kerrigan, then,' said the man in the sou'wester, spitting out the name with contempt. 'Get your lovely lads to follow me. And tell them that if there's the slightest bit of arsing about on the way over, the perpetrator will end up over the side. I'm not joking, either. No bugger's going to miss you, I can tell you. Not even your lovely girlfriends, 'cos they've already got something much better than you lined up, am I right? You know I'm bloody right.'

The seven of us staggered outside, collecting Tampon on the way, who seemed in a marginally better state for having had a breath of fresh air. We followed Captain Birdseye as far as a jetty, which had a small motor launch tied up to it. We wobbled down the steps and into the boat.

'Oh god,' said Badger Pubes as he saw the size of the tiny boat. 'Don't think I can handle th—' he broke off to start retching over the side.

'That's right,' said the captain. 'Let it all go, me lovely. Just get rid of it before you get on board and I might just let you stay. But any accidents and you'll be finding your own way there. And it be a long swim, I can tell you.'

Chapter 19

The journey through the Avon Gorge and out to the Bristol Channel passed without major incident, apart from The Jizz Bandit losing his mobile phone while trying to take a selfie.

'Don't worry about that,' said the captain, 'you'll not be needing him whilst you're on the ABC. No signal, see. Not unless it's two o'clock in the morning and there's a strong south-westerly blowing, anyway.'

I hadn't thought of this. Just because the rig was the hub of a massive bot net, it didn't necessarily mean I'd be able to communicate with anyone myself. If I needed to raise the alarm if something untoward happened, I was going to struggle. Maybe I should have brought some flares with me or something.

Eventually, the Autonomous Bailiwick of Channellia loomed ahead of us. Now that we were up close, it seemed even bigger than I'd imagined from the photos on their website. It was actually possible to imagine that someone could really think of this as their own tiny little kingdom. As we approached, the captain sounded a horn. This was more for our benefit than anything else, as he seemed to be in radio communication with the ABC already.

We tied up to one of the legs of the rig and bobbed up and down in silence for a moment. Then the captain pointed up to something which looked like a harness of some sort coming down towards us on the end of a rope.

'You're not getting me in that thing,' said Badger Pubes, a flicker of green crossing his complexion.

'Ooh, I think we will,' said the captain, grabbing the harness as it arrived in the boat. Before Badger Pubes could complain any more, the captain, assisted by most of the others in the group, had strapped him in. Then he gave a wave and Badger Pubes began to rise, but not before Ham & Tongue had given him a gratuitous shove at the last minute so that he swayed wildly from side to side as he went up. In the boat, an impromptu sing-along of 'Come Fly with Me' accompanied his ascent, although the effect was somewhat ruined by Badger Pubes throwing up on the assembled party from approximately halfway up.

'Little bastard,' muttered the captain, wiping his cheek. 'You know, I've half a mind to dunk the lot of you.'

'Whoa. Sense of humour failure or what?' said Ham & Tongue, smirking at the others.

'Sod it,' said the captain, knowing he was outnumbered. 'I'm getting too old for this lark.'

Once we were all on deck, I took stock of our surroundings. I'd noticed on the way up that what looked like the livable area of the rig began several floors below deck, although there were hardly any windows in this part and it had a decidedly functional look to it. The part of the rig that sat on top of the deck was divided into a number of areas. Directly in front of us was an empty space with a large letter

H identifying it as a helicopter landing site. Behind it, to our left, was a three-storey building that had the ambience of an out-of-town industrial unit that someone had made a half-hearted attempt to repurpose as a motel.

To our right was a more stylish two-storey circular building with a steel and glass observation deck perched on top of it. A hyper-realist bas relief sculpture adorned its base, featuring an absurdly muscular Poseidon waving a trident around like a drum majorette, in an attempt to scare away a shoal of marauding water-nymphs. A long wooden pole protruded out of the middle of the building, flying what I recognised as the Channellia flag, which consisted of the business end of Poseidon's trident against a symbolic wave motif.

I scanned the infrastructure for cameras, although it wasn't as if I could do anything about them – I was just feeling paranoid. Gunther and Dirk had only ever seen me wearing a balaclava, so it was unlikely that they'd recognise me. The plus-size sumo guy had got a glimpse of me when he scanned my backstage pass, but he didn't strike me as the kind of guy who'd be employed for his photographic memory, if they let him on the rig at all. As for the others, Matheson had taken down the guy who'd poisoned Benjamin Unsworth and the guy who'd tried to steal the disk drive had taken down himself. The only other way in which I might have been spotted was if Zombie Fairbanks was hanging out here, although my LinkedIn profile picture was several years old and dated back to a time when I'd experimented with an ill-advised goatee beard.

A blonde woman wearing a pin-stripe suit and high heels click-clacked her way across the metal deck towards us. Ham & Tongue stepped out and she shook his hand.

'The Best Man?' she said, flashing a synthetic smile.

'The very best,' said Ham & Tongue, essaying a lascivious wink that didn't quite come off owing to a belch that surfaced at just the wrong moment.

'And you must be the groom,' she said to Furball, who offered her the sheepish grin of a man who had just sobered up sufficiently during a half-hour boat trip to transition from thinking that wearing women's clothes for a day was a hilariously edgy jape to feeling a bit of a prat.

'Well,' she said, maintaining an inscrutable expression, 'Welcome to the Autonomous Bailiwick of Channellia. I'm Katya and I'll be your hostess for the weekend. If there's anything you require during your time with us, you will find my number in the information pack in your room.'

One or two of the lads nudged each other and sniggered when she said this. Her features made an infinitesimal adjustment for a moment to register her disgust before reverting to normal.

'So, if you'd all like to follow me,' she continued, 'I'll show you to your accommodation.' She paused, as if considering the state of the sample of manhood that she had been presented with, before adding, 'The steps to the upper levels can be a little slippery, so I'd advise you to hold on tight to the handrails.'

We all nodded and shuffled after her. As we reached the bottom of the first set of stairs, I found myself behind Badger Pubes, who stumbled several times and muttered 'Oh god, oh god' to himself all the way up. I left a couple of clear steps between us just in case.

When we reached the upper deck, Katya directed each of us to our rooms and left us, informing us that dinner would be served in the main restaurant on the top deck in half an hour. I dumped my bag on the floor and lay on the bed, wondering what I'd got myself into. Then I got up and surveyed my surroundings. The room was a small capsule with a dainty porthole for a window. I peered out of it and saw the lights of what was presumably Burnham-on-Sea in the distance. It was a lot further than I was capable of swimming, even without the treacherous sandbanks to negotiate along the way. There was a definite chance that this would be a one-way mission.

The evening meal drew its inspiration from the great British tradition of overcooked comfort food, albeit with descriptions that had been put through a gastronomic vocabulary blender. Our group of eight – or rather seven, because Badger Pubes had failed to re-emerge from his room – sat round a circular table in one corner, scoffing away at our trios of sausages with distressed potatoes and onion jus, washed down with several jugfuls of rough Rioja.

The restaurant had a vaguely nautical theme to it, with antique charts and other shipping memorabilia hung on the walls. There were large windows on all sides, giving a magnificent view of the sunset. In any other circumstances, I would have been thoroughly enjoying myself. As it was, I was struggling to concentrate on my food.

There were maybe a dozen other guests in the restaurant, including one I recognised, sitting on his own at the table next to us but one. He was trying hard to look inconspicuous, but there was no mistaking Kevin Wilberts, and I now realised that the Tulpencoin Super Plus launch wasn't the first time I'd actually seen him. He'd been lurking at the back of the Vavasorologists' convention in the Dog and Fishbone. Was it him who'd set the poisoner off on Benjamin Unsworth's trail?

As I was studying him, he suddenly looked back at me and I wondered for a moment if he had recognised me after all. There was a reasonable chance, after all, that he was the man behind Zombie Fairbanks – he had the mathematical background, for one thing. But after a moment he went back to picking at his food. I noticed with interest that he seemed to be eating a salad. If Wilberts was here, there was no doubt whatsoever that I was in the right place. I was slap bang in the belly of the beast.

'Oi, you,' said Gobshite, nudging me in the ribs and interrupting my train of thought. 'Was asking you a question.'

'Sorry, what?'

'Which one,' he slurred, 'would win between a lion and an octopus? Fair fight. Unarmed combat. One on one.'

'I don't know—' I began.

''Cos I reckon it'd be the octopus,' he continued, waving his knife about and ignoring me.

'What?'

'Octopus,' he repeated, stabbing his knife wildly for emphasis. 'It'd drag the lion all the way down, all the way right down, to the murky depths and drown the fucker.'

'Yes, I mean, you're probably—'

'I mean, fucking lions. Fucking rubbish. Octopuseseses are the best.'

'Octopi,' I said, instantly regretting it.

'What?' said Gobshite, turning to stare straight at me. 'Fuck off.' He paused. 'You sure?'

'I'm pretty sure.'

'Well, fucking right, then,' he said. 'You're a good man,' he added, slapping me on the back. 'Piers is a wanker, you know.' He picked up his wine glass and attempted to take a swig from it. He missed his lips by several inches and most of the liquid went over his shoulder. Then he put the glass down heavily and the remaining wine spilled over the tablecloth. Without missing a beat, he grabbed the nearest bottle and topped himself up again.

'To Piers!' he said to everyone, raising his glass.

'Wanker!' shouted everyone in response.

Dessert arrived in the form of spotted dick and custard ('pouding éponge, smattered with desiccated grapes and drizzled with sauce anglaise') and the assembled company dived in with great relish.

'Soggy oggy!' shouted The Jizz Bandit, flicking custard at Tampon.

'Come on, chaps,' said Ham & Tongue. 'We're not at school any more.' Then he paused. '*This* is how you do it,' he added, scooping up an entire heaped dessert spoonful of the stuff and chucking it in the direction of Tampon, who ducked, just in time to collect a custard shampoo. 'Soggy oggy!' shouted Ham & Tongue.

'Oggy oggy oggy!' replied the others, joining in until the bemused Tampon's face was covered.

'You bastards,' he said, wiping his face with his serviette.

'Ooh!' said Gobshite, adopting a camp tone. 'Get him.'

'Banter! Banter! Banter!' cried the others.

Tampon shook his head, muttering to himself, and went back to eating his spotted dick.

When we'd finished eating, the port arrived and then our waiter asked us if we'd care for a spin in the casino. My heart sank. Knowing the way my luck usually went, there was no way I was going to do anything other than lose heavily. Given the state of my finances, I was barely capable of putting up any kind of stake, and I came very close to making my excuses and turning in for the night. But, in the end, I forced myself to follow the others swaying down the stairs to the casino, which was located on the main deck.

'Casino' was a somewhat inflated term for a small low-ceilinged room with subdued lighting containing a couple of gambling tables staffed by young female croupiers wearing lowcut black dresses. A couple of thickset guys in dinner jackets stood either side of the door. I recognised them as my old sparring partners Gunther and Dirk, and I hoped neither of them had sufficient brain cells to recognise me without my balaclava on.

One of the tables was set up for blackjack and the other for roulette. As I exchanged my last fifty quid for ten five pound chips, I closed my eyes and prayed that my group didn't head for blackjack, because I didn't have the first clue as to how to play that one. Fortunately, there were already half a dozen men clustered round the blackjack table so we all headed towards roulette, where I would almost certainly get just as fleeced, but at least I would know how and why I was being fleeced.

As we took our places round the table, our croupier looked up for the first time, smiled at us and asked us to place our bets. When she caught my eye, there was the slightest flicker of surprise before her face resumed its previous impassive demeanour. As for me, my mouth had suddenly gone as dry as the Sahara Desert after a massed army had spent a day treating every single grain of sand with a hot air gun. I looked at her again, but there was no mistaking it. The woman standing on the other side of the roulette wheel was exactly who I thought it was.

She had a blonde wig on and her name badge said 'Tabitha Li', but I knew her as Dorothy Chan.

Chapter 20

I took a few deep breaths to steady myself. My immediate reaction had been to either shout out or run out of the room altogether but, somehow, I had to remain cool for the next hour or so until I could get a chance to talk to her. I took a single five pound chip from my pile and held it in my hand until I stopped trembling. Focus, Winscombe. Focus.

'Place your bets, gentlemen,' said Dorothy, with a barely detectable quaver in her voice, as if a small moth was bouncing backwards and forwards between her vocal cords.

I decided to start with a low risk stake, so I placed the chip on black. Dorothy gave the wheel a nonchalant spin and dropped the ball in, sending it in the opposite direction. The ball bounced around for an agonisingly long time before finally settling on... five. Red. Great start, Tom. I wasn't alone among our group, as the drunker members of the party – meaning, basically, all of them apart from myself – had adopted more ambitious strategies, none of which had actually come off, although The Jizz Bandit took a significant amount of persuading that five was not in fact an even number.

Maybe colours were unlucky for me, so I decided that my next gambit would be to try the odd numbers. I placed a couple of five pound chips on the baize cloth and pushed them with my thumb towards the square marked 'Even', as if this was the kind of thing I did every Saturday night. Dorothy spun the wheel again, sent the ball rolling and this time it settled on… thirteen. There was a cheer from Gobshite, who had staked everything on thirteen to twenty four. Tampon groaned. He'd tried the same strategy as me.

The safe plays clearly weren't working, so it was now time to try something a bit riskier. I took four more chips from my rapidly-diminishing pile and pushed them towards the box that said twenty four to thirty six. The wheel spun, the ball flew and this time it ended up in eight. Come on, Dorothy, I said to myself, give us a break?

'Come on, darling,' said The Jizz Bandit with a leer, 'give us a break, will you?'

Dorothy looked at him and smiled. He responded by reaching out at her, flailing and missing by several feet. I was about to break cover until I noticed that Gunther had taken a couple of steps forward. The Jizz Bandit backed off very quickly indeed and Dorothy gave a quick shake of the head in Gunther's direction. He resumed his position by the door.

'Sorry,' muttered The Jizz Bandit. 'Got a bit carried away.'

'Twat,' muttered Ham & Tongue.

I took another chip from my pile and held it in my hand while I looked up at Dorothy. She caught my eye and nodded very slightly.

What was that all about? Had she just given me a clue?

Then I realised something. What did five, eight and thirteen all have in common? They were all Fibonacci numbers, weren't they? As Ali would have pointed out to me, that was very unlikely to be a coincidence. The only explanation was that the game was rigged. The corollary to this was that Dorothy was playing with me. It wouldn't have surprised me.

It was time to be bolder still. I took the four chips that I had left and put the whole lot on twenty one.

'Are you sure, sir?' she said.

'Quite sure,' I said, just avoiding adding 'Dorothy' on the end.

'Risky,' said Ham & Tongue, with a hint of admiration in his voice, putting a couple of chips on 'Even.'

'Wuss,' I said, feeling that I should engage in some banter.

'Hark at Mr Macho Man,' said Gobshite, glaring at me and placing a pile of ten chips on twenty two. 'Your turn,' he said, turning to Tampon.

'Nah,' said Tampon, collecting his chips together. 'Had enough.'

'Put a bet on,' said Gobshite.

'I said no.'

'Put a bet on,' said Gobshite again.

'No.'

'Put a fucking bet on.'

'No.'

'Leave it,' said Ham & Tongue. 'He doesn't want to play. If Mr Wussy Pants wants to run away, let him.'

'Lads,' said Furball. Everyone ignored him.

'I'm not a wuss,' said Tampon. 'It's just not running right for me tonight.'

'It's fine,' said Ham & Tongue. 'If you want to spoil his big weekend,' he added, pointing to Furball, 'go ahead. I'm sure he won't mind.'

'Lads,' said Furball. Everyone ignored him.

Tampon took out a single chip and put it on 'Odd'. 'OK?' he said.

Everyone else shrugged.

'Are we all ready?' said Dorothy. Everyone nodded, so she spun the wheel and set the ball rolling once more. It bounced around for about twenty-five times as long as it had on previous occasions before finally settling on... twenty one.

'Fuck,' said Gobshite.

'Bloody hell,' said Ham & Tongue.

'Well,' said Tampon.

'Good grief,' I said.

Everyone apart from Gobshite clustered around me to congratulate me on my good fortune. Gobshite just muttered something about having had enough for one night and then disappeared. Dorothy swept away all the failed bets and then tipped a whole pile of chips onto mine. As I collected them, our fingers briefly touched and I felt a bolt of electricity shoot through me.

I had an idea.

'I think I'd like a bottle of champagne sent to my room to celebrate,' I said. They were almost certainly the cheesiest fourteen words I'd spoken in my entire life, but Dorothy got the message.

'Which room, sir?' she said, raising her eyebrow by roughly the width of an eyelash.

I gave her my room number and left the table to cash in my winnings. I bought a round for the remaining five members of the Todger Squad, then left them still gambling hard and looking for that elusive win. Knowing Dorothy, the odds on any of them winning big that night were somewhat on the low side. Especially The Jizz Bandit.

An hour and a half later, there was a knock on my door.

'Room service?' came the voice.

I opened the door to see Dorothy standing there holding a tray. On the tray was an ice bucket containing a bottle of champagne and two glasses. I waved her in and shut the door.

'So, what in god's name's going on?' I said. Dorothy's eyes widened to the size of dinner plates and she put a finger to her lips. She hunted around in the room for a while and then eventually found a pen and a pad of writing paper in a drawer. She tore a sheet off the top.

probly bugged, she wrote, handing the pen to me.

I looked at her and pulled a face. She responded by grabbing the pen back, circling the word 'bugged' an unnecessary number of times. She waved the piece of paper in my face before thrusting the pen back at me.

ok, fine, I wrote below this, *but wtf r u doing here?*

cd say same of u, she replied, snatching the paper back from me. *bit rich of u 2 show up now*

what u mean?

u know exactly what I mean

no I dont

wheres the money tom?

I was going to ask u that

WHAT, wrote Dorothy, the pen almost going through the paper.

I dont know where it is do I?

well either u or ali does + shes not here

ali doesn't know either

Dorothy looked temporarily lost for words, spoken or written. *don't believe u*, she wrote eventually.

well its true, I replied.

wtf r u you doing here anyway? she wrote again eventually, turning the page over.

I came to find u

WHY

had to

well u did – well done – now piss off + let me finish

U CANT DO THIS, I wrote. I waved the paper in her face for emphasis.

CAN. She waved it back at me.

why r u here? I wrote. *why just run off? u upset me*

had to

WHY

its my problem

mine too

She thought about this. Then she scribbled, *cdnt trust anyone – odd traffic on network – everything stolen – bank account emptied – only you, me + ali know password.* This last sentence started off at the very bottom of the page and then went up the side.

I tore off another piece of paper. *its not me or ali*, I wrote. *really it isnt*

WELL NOT ME, wrote Dorothy.

why didnt u trust me? why did u think it was me? how did u get here?

Dorothy gave a deep sigh before writing, *tired – long story – explain tomoz – find somewhere 2 talk*

ok – u ok tho?

been hard – better now

god, D – missed u – actually can we have sex pls?

Dorothy put up her hand to forestall any attempt on my part at intimacy.

how did u find me? she wrote.

v long story, I wrote. Then I added, *want a drink?* I went to pick the champagne bottle out of the ice bucket.

Dorothy just shook her head.

ok, I said.

got 2 go now, she wrote. Underneath she added, *level b2, cold store, 11:45 tomoz.*

I nodded, mouthing 'See you then,' to her as she left the room.

Next morning, there were even fewer members of the Todger Squad down for breakfast. In fact, the squad basically consisted of Ham & Tongue and myself. Dorothy was presumably breakfasting in the staff canteen, if such a thing existed.

'Quite fancy that Katya,' he was saying. 'What do you reckon? Think she'd be up for it?'

'I… have no idea,' I said, cautiously.

227

'Then again, have to say I was rather taken with that little roulette girl.' I tried not to choke on my granola. 'I'm sure she was giving me the eye. Pretty certain I might be in with a shot if we go back there tonight.'

'Right,' I said.

'Yah. Bet she's red hot. Those – you know – ones usually are. Although I'm usually more for the normal girls, me.'

'Normal?'

'Yah. Straight up, white, Caucasian, whatever you call it. I mean, I'm no racist, but—'

'I know what you mean,' I said. Yeah, I knew exactly what he meant.

'Take my current significant other, for instance,' he continued. 'Lovely, gorgeous girl. Natural blonde. Not much in the brains department, but good solid homegrown stock.'

'Right,' I said. He paused to go and fetch a full English from the hot counter. When he came back, he continued with his musings.

'Thing is,' he said. 'Sometimes a man feels the need for something a bit more – how shall we say? – exotic. And what happens in the Autonomous Bailiwick of Channellia stays in the Autonomous Bailiwick of Channellia, does it not?' He took a mouthful of sausage and bacon. 'Seems churlish not to try, really.'

I went to get my own cooked breakfast in the hope of breaking up his flow. If he carried on like this, there was a decent chance that I might feel forced to challenge him to a duel or something to defend Dorothy's honour. Even though he'd probably beat the crap out of me and Dorothy was quite capable of defending her own honour. Fortunately, the tactic worked.

'How did you know that wanker Piers, anyway?' he said.

I'd been dreading this question. I was fairly sure I couldn't claim that we'd been at school together, because the 'Soggy oggy' incident the previous evening had made it pretty clear that most of the others in the group had a shared education. I decided the best way was to make a joke of it.

'I bumped into him in the toilets, didn't I?'

Ham & Tongue gave me a puzzled look for a moment and then burst out laughing.

'You know what? You're fucking hilarious.'

'I know,' I said, joining in with his laughter.

'In the toilets,' he repeated. 'Bloody Piers. In the toilets. I like you, you know. You're a bloody good chap.'

'I know,' I said. 'I know.'

Chapter 21

After last night's inconclusive attempt at conversation with Dorothy, I was anxious to meet up again, preferably in an environment more conducive to speech. But first I had to get through the morning's activities, which involved a game of laser tag. This took place in a space consisting of several dimly lit interconnected rooms on the lower deck that had been painted black and filled with smoke. All eight of the squad reassembled for this, although most of them were still in pretty poor shape. In theory we were divided up into two teams of four, one with red lasers and one with green. However, in practice, the game basically involved everyone ganging up on Tampon, who, while clearly annoyed, still seemed to accept this as the natural order of things. It wasn't made any easier when one of the party threw up about twenty minutes in, making the floor unpleasantly slippery. No one owned up to this.

I snuck out a quarter of an hour early and went off in search of our rendezvous point, two levels down from the main deck. Dorothy was waiting for me when I got there. She ushered me inside and pulled the heavy insulated door closed behind us.

'Jesus,' I said. 'You didn't tell me it was going to be this cold. It's bloody freezing in here.' I noticed that she was wearing a heavy pullover.

'I wrote "cold store", Tom,' she said. 'Didn't you see that?'

'Well, yes, but—'

'It's basically a walk-in fridge.'

'Nice choice of venue.' She was wearing gloves too. And a woolly hat. And a wig. How could she do this to me?

'It's the only place I could think of that is outside the surveillance network, Tom. Think about it.'

'I am. But it's still bloody cold and I'm not dressed for it.'

'Well, that's your problem,' she said. 'Look. Tell me everything you know.'

'Only if you tell me first,' I said.

'Tom. Please. We haven't got much time.'

'Oh, all right,' I said. I wanted to get this over quickly too. 'OK, where to begin? Ali and I have been sharing a shitty bedsit together and no, it wasn't really working out, but anyway Ali's now moved out and is currently living with her new girlfriend Patrice who's some kind of mathematical biologist and keeps reptiles.'

'Cool. I like reptiles.'

'So, someone got in touch with me through Rufus Fairbanks's LinkedIn account—'

'You're on LinkedIn?'

'Yes, what of it?'

'How quaint. Go on.'

'Jeez, it really is sodding arctic in here, Dorothy. Can we turn the heating up or something?'

'Tom, it's supposed to be like this. If we turn the heating up, all the food will go off.'

'Wouldn't be a great loss, though, would it?'

'Tom.'

I clapped my hands together a few times and stamped up and down. This didn't have much effect, but at least I felt I was doing something. 'OK, where were we?' I said.

'LinkedIn.'

'Yeah. OK, to be honest, I thought you were Zombie Fairbanks, because all that happened was they sent me a whole load of emails counting up in a Fibonacci series. It's the sort of thing you'd do, and don't deny it because you did it last night too.'

'That was different,' said Dorothy. 'I was just using a bit of maths I'd taught you, right? And it worked.'

'Yeah, well, mainly it worked because I'd been reminded of it by the stuff that Zombie Fairbanks sent me. Anyway, that reminded me of that stupid Fibonacci poem you wrote, and that made me think there was something significant in it that might lead to you and so I thought I'd better find it and of course I didn't have it 'cos my laptop had been nicked and then I remembered the broken disk drive so we managed to track that down – really long story there, by the way, but never mind – and Ali ran it up and it turned out Rufus Fairbanks's bitcoin wallet was sitting on it – did you realise that, by the way?'

Dorothy was staring at me, amazed. 'You're kidding me,' she said. 'I didn't have time to look at any of that stuff.' Then her hand shot to her mouth. 'Oh god, Tom,' she added. 'I know what you're going to say next.'

'Yeah. There was a virus. The Tulpencoin virus that we acquired when you connected my laptop to Fairbanks's network. Fair play, it did lead us here, once Ali had worked out how to track it back to its base.'

Dorothy was silent for a moment.

'I'm sorry, Tom,' she said, quietly. 'It was all the crypto traffic I was seeing on our network that made me suspicious of you and Ali. So when everything got stolen I thought you were involved. Seems mad now.'

'We thought the same, Dorothy.' My hands were numb. I stuck them into my pockets to warm up.

'And the bank account?'

'Well, if it's none of the three of us, Ali reckons the virus did a bit of sly key logging too.'

'Plausible. How is Ali, by the way? I mean is she—'

'She's furious. If you ever see her again, wear Kevlar.'

'I'll bear that in mind.'

'But how did you end up here, D?'

'I got back early from that lecture – which was rubbish, by the way – to find them putting the last of our machines into a white van. I took a note of the number as it drove off. Then I called someone I knew at the PNC—'

'PNC?'

'Police National Computer. Basically, I called in a favour. Don't ask. Found out who the van belonged to. Turned out it was a small office fitting company based in Bristol. So I bought the wig, got on a train down here, found a room in a cheap hostel and looked for a way in.'

'Not sure the wig suits you,' I said. 'Just thought I'd put it out there.'

'Me neither. It's itchy as well. Anyway, after a few days of staking out their warehouse, I noticed there was a temporary vacancy for a clerk. As you can imagine, I can find my way around a spreadsheet with my eyes shut, so it was a pretty straightforward interview.'

'So how long did you spend there?'

'Too long. I'd forgotten what a nightmare it was working for other people. What was worse was that I couldn't find any of our equipment. It had all been moved on before I got into the warehouse. Given what we now know, I'm guessing most of it got wiped and sold on, apart from that crappy laptop of yours, which is probably still on this rig somewhere. Unless they chucked it in the sea when they found out that their little ruse to get hold of the drive had failed. That's what I would have done.'

'I liked that laptop.'

'Even the ugliest babies are loved by their mothers, Tom. Doesn't mean they're not ugly. By now, I'd seen enough of the books to work out that there was something seriously odd about that warehouse. Constant references to transferring equipment "offshore", for example, although these transfers only ever happened at the evenings and weekends when none of the regular staff were there. Everyone told me not to ask too many questions, which naturally made me even more suspicious. Anyway, I had to work one weekend in order to get that quarter's VAT filing ready, and I spotted a consignment of equipment being loaded up. I nipped out and put on my best officious tone, asking the guys if this was authorised by senior management and so on, and one of them let slip that the load was destined for this place.'

'Bingo. So, what did you do next?'

'Before I did anything else, I deactivated every online account I still had access to. I'd lost access to my emails the day after the burglary, but I'd managed to hang on to a few things by changing my passwords before they noticed. But if I was going to be out of contact for a while, I thought it best to shut as much as possible down altogether.'

'We noticed you'd deactivated your *vavasorology.com* account,' I said.

'Yep. Anyway, I spent the next week trying to work out how I'd get myself on board here. I thought about signing up as a guest, but there didn't seem to be any way of doing that without ringing a lot of alarm bells. But then I noticed an advert in the *Bristol Evening Post* for a croupier and it seemed just too good to be true.'

'You never told me about Third Uncle,' I said. My hands still weren't warming up. In fact, my upper thighs were also freezing now. I took my hands out of my pockets and stuck them under my armpits.

'Yeah, well. You don't know everything about me yet, Tom.'

'I'm beginning to realise that. Also, what's with the "Tabitha Li" stuff? Is that your porn name or something?'

'Tom.'

'Oh, all right. I have skills you don't know about too, you know.'

'Such as?'

'I can flick a pork scratching straight into my mouth.'

Dorothy shook her head in what I hoped was amazement. 'You never cease to astonish me, Tom. And the point of this skill is?'

'I used it to establish my bloke credentials in order to smuggle myself here. You wouldn't understand. It's a guy thing.'

'I'm not sure I'd want to understand. Who are all those guys anyway?'

'My new best friends. One of them fancies you, you know. In a slightly racist sort of way.'

'I'm flattered,' said Dorothy. 'Still, we need to get back to business. We've basically sussed out how the scam works, right?'

'Mostly. But the missing piece is how they launder the crypto once they've harvested it. Look, could I just borrow your hat?'

'No.'

'Or your wig? I'd be happy with just that.'

'No.'

'There's probably room for two of us inside that pull-over, you know.'

'No.'

'I've gone off you, D.'

'No, you haven't. Anyway, you were asking about laundering. Two doors along from here, there's another storeroom that very few people have the key to, but I managed to sneak a look in there one day when they'd accidentally left the door open. Basically, this place is actually a clearing house for drugs. Most of the cocaine in the South West flows through this place.'

'Oh, bloody hell. Because the easiest place to dispose of bitcoin without anyone asking too many questions—'

'—is on the dark web, yes. So, they buy the stuff with bitcoin and then sell it for cash. The perfect three-way transaction.'

'But why bring the drugs here? Couldn't they just move it on straight away?'

'I wondered that. I think it's because they don't like holding onto bitcoin. Too volatile. Once they've siphoned a batch off, they're keen to offload it straight away, without having to wait for a buyer for the drugs.'

'But why not just keep their stash on shore, then, in somewhere like that office fitter's warehouse?'

'Here they can see anyone coming for them several miles off. They've got line of sight and radar.'

'Right.' I thought for a moment, 'So you're basically telling me that they don't actually hold crypto at all?'

'Nope. Like any sensible dealer, they don't touch their own stuff.'

'Bastards.'

'Yep.'

'I take it you've got pictures of all this.'

Dorothy took out her phone and waggled it. 'Oh, yes.'

'So, basically, we get out of here sharpish, send it to the police or whoever and that's job done, right?'

Dorothy shook her head. 'We're unlikely to get our money back if we do that, Tom,' she said. 'You know we can't talk to the police right now. Maybe one day we'll have to face up to it but right now we're on our own. We can't trust anyone else.'

I narrowed my eyes and looked hard at her. 'So, what are you suggesting?' I said.

Dorothy took a deep breath, looked me straight in the eye and told me what she'd decided we were going to do. When she had finished I was shivering, and not just from the cold. I was quite convinced that she had gone completely out of her mind. It was crazy, wild and dangerous.

But there was also the tiniest, outside chance – a chance so far outside that it might as well be sitting in the bottom of a deep crater on the dark side of the moon – that it might just work.

Towards the end of lunch, the Todger Squad's hangovers had largely dissipated and they were in a boisterous mood. There was a lot of playful punching and banter, and then someone accidentally remembered that you could have a lot of fun thumping the business end of a fork so that it launched into the air. An impromptu competition very quickly developed, with each member of the team trying to outdo the others, regardless of the irritation it was clearly causing to the other diners in the restaurant, including Kevin Wilberts, who was once again sitting on a table near us, nibbling at an avocado and parsnip sandwich.

'Reckon I can get one in the ceiling,' said Gobshite, looking up at the polystyrene tiles above him.

'Bollocks you can,' said The Jizz Bandit.

'Nope. Reckon I can.'

A ragged chant of 'Fork! Fork! Fork!' started up and Gobshite, with great ceremony, rolled up his sleeve, pulled his fist back and, with what he clearly hoped was a terrifying roar of 'Aieeeeee!', brought it back down on the fork

– or at least where he expected the fork to be, because the waiter had intervened at the last minute and removed it. The waiter then proceeded to remove all the other cutlery on the table, in a manner that suggested he had seen all this, and much worse, many times before.

'Ow,' said Gobshite, nursing his hand. 'Spoilsport.'

'Coffee, gentlemen?' said the waiter, in a weary voice.

As we drank our coffee, there was a brief flurry of activity outside as a helicopter touched down on the main deck. The door opened and two men bowed their heads and stepped out. I'd seen both of them before: Tiger de Montfort and the Honourable Sholto Chelford-Bickerton, otherwise known as the Seigneur of the Autonomous Bailiwick of Channellia. Gunther and Dirk trotted up and fell into step either side of them, while Katya strode forward to greet them. Then they all disappeared into the circular building at the other end of the rig. Back in the restaurant, Kevin Wilberts mopped his mouth delicately with a serviette to remove any crumbs and then got up from his table, presumably to join them.

Well, I thought to myself, the gang's all here. Just as Dorothy had predicted.

A few minutes later, Katya appeared in the dining room to lead us to our afternoon activity, which involved a bungee jump over the side of the rig, down towards the forbidding waters of the Bristol Channel. To be more precise, it involved the spectacle of eight fully-grown men being strapped in turn into a harness and putting on a demonstration of preposterous machismo and bravado that wouldn't have disgraced the stage of the National

Theatre. As we were each goaded towards the edge, however, our body language told quite a different story – the story of a body that dearly wanted to be somewhere else altogether, possibly with a slightly reduced volume of bodily fluids.

At around five o'clock, the group assembled in the bar and I began to get the sense that, a day and a half into the weekend, they were all beginning to get heartily sick of the sight of each other. There's only so much aggressive camaraderie that a man can take, after all, and the cracks were beginning to show. By the time the boat came to take them home tomorrow, they would be close to boiling point.

However, none of them was consciously aware of this yet, and they were all happily downing pints with whisky chasers as if the law on prohibition was just lining up for its second reading. There was, however, the occasional dispute as to whose turn it was to pay for it.

'Oi, you,' said Gobshite, prodding Tampon in the chest, 'isn't it about time you bought a round?' He waved his glass threateningly in Tampon's face.

'Yeah,' said The Jizz Bandit, 'he's always been a skanky bastard.'

'That's not true,' protested Tampon.

'Fucking is,' said The Jizz Bandit.

'Lads,' said Furball. Everyone ignored him.

'All right,' said Ham & Tongue, 'if he's too tight-arsed to pay for a round, I suppose I'll have to do it.' He began making his way to the bar with unnecessary ceremony, elbowing the others out of the way as he did so.

'No,' said Gobshite, grabbing hold of Ham & Tongue's shoulder, 'make him pay. It's his fucking turn.' As he said this, he managed to spill Badger Pubes's beer down his front.

'Oi,' said Badger Pubes, backing away and narrowly avoiding sending Pisspot's pint into oblivion.

'Oh, shut it,' said Gobshite. 'Should be drinking a bit quicker, you twat.'

'I was enjoying that,' said Badger Pubes.

'Wanker,' said Gobshite.

'Lads,' said Furball. Everyone ignored him.

'Calm down, chaps,' said Ham & Tongue, now that he'd reached the bar. 'What are you all having, then?'

There was a brief pause, and then everyone thrust their glasses towards him. He paid for the beers and passed them out.

'Hey,' said Tampon. 'Where's mine?'

'Get it your fucking self,' said Ham & Tongue.

'Bastards,' said Tampon.

I noticed that Kevin Wilberts wasn't at his usual place at dinner – presumably he was dining with Tiger de Montfort in the Seigneur's private quarters. The other guests, a posse of ball-bearing salesmen on a training break, had all left that morning, leaving us with the run of the place. This was fortunate, given what was going to happen tomorrow if everything went to plan.

The team was a little subdued by the time we got to the casino, although Ham & Tongue brightened visibly when he saw Dorothy behind the roulette wheel, and he began flirting with her outrageously. At least, I think that was what he was trying to do, although it mostly consisted of him adding the word 'inches' every time he placed a bet on any number higher than nine.

As Dorothy had planned, however, Ham & Tongue had a wretched night and failed to win anything beyond a feeble couple of chips on 'Odd' and another couple on 'Black'. I also contrived to throw away a modest amount of last night's profits, but I managed to spin it out so that it didn't look as if I was shying away from taking part, unlike Tampon, who once again gave up early in the proceedings. The big winner of the night turned out to be Gobshite, who – exactly as predicted – also turned out to have his eye on Dorothy.

'Hey, my gorgeous exotic beauty,' he said, after an absurd punt of ten chips on twenty one yielded an unexpectedly generous win, thanks to Dorothy's manipulation of the wheel. 'You feeling lucky? No? Well, give us a kiss an' you can have some of mine.'

I almost threw up, but fortunately Gunther noticed the potential trouble and took a step towards the table. Gobshite put his hands up and backed away.

'Jus' a joke!' he said. 'Jus' little joke. Gonna pick my chips up now, OK?' He scooped the chips from the table, dropping several on the floor and failing to notice as The Jizz Bandit stole half a dozen of them. Struggling to carry them all at once, he wobbled over to Dorothy and whispered his room number in her ear. She smiled innocently and raised an eyebrow, making sure that everyone noticed. I caught a brief glimpse of Ham & Tongue's face. If looks could kill, the way he looked just then was ready to contemplate genocide.

After Gobshite had cashed in his chips and bought us all a celebratory round, everyone else decided that they'd had enough excitement for one evening. I gave a slight nod to Dorothy as I left the room and she gave the tiniest of nods back. The real work of the day was just about to begin.

Chapter 22

An hour or so later, there was a knock on my door and Dorothy came in. I'd already prepared a few written conversation cards while I'd been waiting for her.

got an hour or so 2 kill, I'd written, *so just wondering if we cld have sex first?*

Dorothy rolled her eyes and produced her own piece of paper. She'd clearly been working on this too.

NO, it said, *stuff to do – need to prepare*

Bugger. Was I really that predictable?

It seems I was.

An hour later I was standing in the corridor outside Ham & Tongue's room. I was wearing the darkest clothes I'd brought with me and Dorothy's woolly hat, which she'd finally relinquished, now that it was no longer necessary to keep her warm. I looked to left and right, as if I was about to enact the Green Cross Code, then slid the duplicate card key that Dorothy had stolen from the main desk into Ham & Tongue's lock. The door clicked softly open and I tiptoed in, nudging the door shut behind me.

Now that I was in, I began to wonder why I was worrying about keeping quiet, because the noise coming from the other side of the room wouldn't have disgraced a crash of in-season rhinos relaxing after a day out on the savanna. Then I walked into a chest of drawers and the noise spontaneously mutated into a rapid series of staccato snorts. I held my breath until everything settled down again.

I decided at this point to crouch down on the floor and wait for my eyes to adjust to the light. After a couple of minutes, the configuration of the room became clearer and I could make out the silhouette of Ham & Tongue's figure in bed. I went over to him, and established that his phone was on the bedside table as I'd hoped. However, both his hands were underneath the covers, which was most definitely not as I'd hoped.

Dorothy's plan to deal with this eventuality was one of the flakier elements of the whole concept, but as I hadn't managed to think of anything better, I'd gone along with it, trusting that this was one contingency that wouldn't arise. I sighed inwardly and quietly removed the feather from my inside pocket. Kneeling down again, I moved the feather to underneath Ham & Tongue's nose and gently wafted it back and forth. Once again, the snoring shifted gear, but crucially Ham & Tongue's right hand also appeared, trying to nudge away the source of the irritation.

I quickly withdrew the feather and put it back in my pocket. Dorothy had been most insistent about this, as it belonged on one of her favourite hats. Ham & Tongue's snoring had now settled back into its usual rhythm and his hand was now lolling freely by the side of the bed. Before he could move it back again, I grabbed his phone and pressed the home button against his thumb. After a couple of attempts, the home screen appeared and I scurried back to the door. I pulled the handle towards me and eased it downwards to open. Two seconds later I was back out in the corridor. I disabled the lock screen as Dorothy had reminded me to do, twice, and then took it back to my room.

I handed the phone and Ham & Tongue's key card silently to Dorothy. She took them from me and gave me a thumbs up.

One down. One to go.

Gobshite's room was down the corridor in the opposite direction. I let myself in and paused by the door this time, waiting to orient myself. Gobshite was significantly less full-throated than Ham & Tongue in his choice of night-time vocalisation. In fact, it was closer to singing than anything else, or perhaps a kind of reedy hum. I hoped this didn't mean that he was a lighter sleeper than Ham & Tongue, because that would put our brilliantly conceived plan in jeopardy.

The first problem was that his phone was on the table on the far side of the bed, so I was going to have to get down and wriggle my way across the floor at the end, a task which wasn't made any easier by the randomly scattered clothing and ear-splittingly loud carrier bags that he'd dumped there too. Halfway through my traverse, the humming stopped. I slowly lifted my head above the end of the bed, in a move that, if Gobshite really was awake, I sort of hoped would remind him of Killer Bob from *Twin Peaks* and, with any luck, scare him back to sleep again.

'Martha!' he called out. Or was it 'Mother'? I stopped, stock still, staring straight at him, trying to look scary.

After a moment, however, he relaxed back into slumber and resumed humming. It was safe to proceed. I dropped down again and continued crawling to the other side of the bed. I shuffled along to the bedside table and retrieved Gobshite's phone. At this point, the second problem presented itself. Gobshite's right thumb was firmly stuck in his mouth. Now what? Even if I did somehow persuade him to remove it, it was going to be so covered in dribble that there was very little chance it would succeed in unlocking his phone.

While I was considering this, my own thumb unconsciously strayed to the home button and when I pressed it, quite unexpectedly the home screen appeared. The idiot hadn't bothered adding a password or a thumbprint. I vaguely remembered him saying something over dinner about not being able to remember that sort of thing and who'd want to hack into his phone anyway?

Well, I knew one person who was *very* keen to.

Back in my room, I handed the phone and Gobshite's key card to Dorothy. Now the real fun was going to start.

Or, as Dorothy wrote: *this, tom, is going to be MUCH better than sex*

As she worked on it, I could sort of see her point. Sort of. She began by scrolling through Ham & Tongue's photo stream until she found a picture that might work. She looked up at me and raised an eyebrow. I nodded, and she transferred it to her own phone. Then she did the same with Gobshite's photo stream, but came to an abrupt halt over one particular group photo.

'Holy shit!' I said out loud, before Dorothy put her hand over my mouth. Because there, in that picture of the entire Todger Squad, including the original Titface – before I temporarily took over the role – was my former girlfriend Lucy.

I grabbed a piece of paper and wrote down, *piers.*

what? wrote Dorothy.

thats the name of lucys new bloke + thats her there

well

I took his place

well

well

shall we carry on?

OK

I wasn't sure what to make of this latest snippet of information. It was quite pleasing that the last time I'd seen him, he was face down in the toilets puking his guts up. Childish of me, I know, but it was still pleasing. But it was more than a little awkward that I'd somehow adopted his persona for the weekend. I really, really hoped Lucy wouldn't find out, because I'd never hear the last of it.

Dorothy continued searching through Gobshite's photos and then suddenly a large grin slowly spread over her face. She'd found the one she was looking for. She handed the phone over to me, pointing to the image on the screen.

She was right. This was going to be awesome.

Having transferred the photo onto her phone, Dorothy got down to business. The relish with which she approached the task gave me a strong impression that there was a definite element of revenge by proxy in what she was doing. It took another half hour before she was finished, but when she showed the results to me, I was gobsmacked. This really was going to work.

that's amazing, I wrote.

of course it is, she replied.

Then she uploaded the results and handed the phones and key cards back to me.

over 2 u, she wrote.

Gobshite was still humming to himself in his sleep when I got back into his room. I was about to put the phone back on the nearside table when I remembered all the hassle I'd had getting it from the other side. Even he might be a bit suspicious if he found it had magically traversed from one side of the bed to the other during the night. So once again I got down on the floor and began to crawl round to the opposite side of the bed. Unfortunately, by the time I got there, I realised that I'd managed to get my foot caught in the covers, and I was slowly dragging them off the bed. I felt a fierce tug from above, and felt myself being flipped over onto my back.

Bloody hell. Gobshite was awake.

I tried to slide underneath the bed, but in doing so, I managed to pull the covers away from him again. There was another tug, and I felt my leg being dragged away from me again into the open. I heard Gobshite grumbling sleepily above me and then with another yank, he turned over heavily, his buttocks bouncing on my face through the mattress as he did so. As he settled on his side again, my ankle was caught awkwardly on the corner of the bed and as I tried in vain to extricate myself, I realised that our frenzied tussle had only served to tighten the knot.

The only good thing about my present position was that Gobshite's face was, at least, turned away from me, so I was able to lessen the agony by sliding out from under the bed again. I eased myself into a more comfortable posture by rotating myself until I was now at a right-angle to the bed. Having done that, I settled down to wait for a few minutes until the gentle hum of Gobshite's snoring told me that he was once again in the land of nod.

The forced inactivity had calmed me a little, and I now realised that all I had to do was untie my laces and slip my shoes off. That done, I succeeded in extricating my feet, and having done that, it was a simple matter to disentangle my trainers. I abandoned all pretence of crawling and scurried to the door as fast as I could. I eased it open again and very soon I was back in the corridor outside.

At this point I realised I was still holding Gobshite's phone.

I had to stick my fist in my mouth to avoid howling out in rage, but after counting from one to, well, around seven hundred and thirty-two, I felt in a calm enough frame of mind to try to return his phone again. This time I removed my shoes first and left them outside the door, and the operation went off without a hitch.

Ham & Tongue was next. Still holding my shoes in my hand, I walked back down the corridor to his room and unlocked his door. Ham & Tongue's snoring was still similar in effect to having your head cut open with a chainsaw, but this didn't bother me, because at least it meant he was still spark out. As I waited by the door for my eyes to adjust, though, his phone suddenly vibrated and I nearly dropped the thing out of shock.

Jesus.

I stared at the screen, hoping the light from it wouldn't invade Ham & Tongue's consciousness in any unhelpful way. A text had just come through from 'Piers', who was apparently still awake and very angry at two o'clock in the morning - the time when the boatman had said there might be a mobile phone signal if there was a strong south-westerly blowing. I listened hard. There was definitely a bit of a gale brewing outside. Fortunately, I'd forgotten to reset the lock screen timeout, so I could read the entirety of the message, the gist of which was that he'd worked out who that twat who stole his shirt was, and you'd never guess it but it was Lucy's old boyfriend, who's apparently a complete tosser and basically a total waste of oxygen.

I did the only thing I could do in the circumstances. I deleted the message. I saw no reason why Ham & Tongue needed to know this. He liked me, after all, and I didn't want any shit talk from Piers getting in the way of our burgeoning friendship. Then I restored the automatic screen lock to its default setting, placed the phone on the bedside table and sidled out.

Having completed my mission, I went back to my room, lay down on the bed and was flat out myself within seconds. I didn't even notice if Dorothy was still there or not.

Chapter 23

I woke up late on Sunday morning. I looked out of my porthole window and I observed that there was a lot of activity on the deck below. The motor launch from Bristol had arrived and the week's supply of provisions was being hauled up, crate by crate. I noticed Gunther and Dirk sauntering around, looking menacing, along with Tiger de Montfort, who seemed to be supervising operations. If Dorothy was right, the crates were indeed full of ordinary provisions, although not all of them would go back to Bristol empty. As well as the crates, there was a tattered canvas holdall, which Tiger de Montfort grabbed a little too eagerly as it arrived and took over to the round building.

I packed my bag ready for departure and dumped it with the rest of them by the front desk. Then I made my way to the restaurant for breakfast, to find that the rest of the Todger Squad were already tucking into their cornflakes.

'Morning, lads,' I said. There was a chorus of grunts by way of reply. 'Well, it's been good to meet you all,' I added. No one bothered to acknowledge this. I began to whistle a chirpy tune.

'Will you shut the fuck up?' said Ham & Tongue.

I stopped whistling and put up both hands. 'Hey, man, chill,' I said. 'No need to be like that.'

'Yeah, well, Hammo's right,' said Gobshite. 'Just shut it.'

'OK, OK,' I said. I went to get some cereal. When I came back, I took my seat next to Gobshite. I nudged him in the ribs.

'What now?' he said, wearily.

'Well,' I said. 'Did you?'

'Did I what?'

'Did you get off with her? You know, that little croupier girl?'

'No, he fucking didn't,' interrupted Ham & Tongue, with barely suppressed anger.

I raised an eyebrow at Gobshite.

'Sorry,' I said to Ham & Tongue. 'Touched a nerve, did I?'

'Oh, shut it,' he said.

'Anyway,' said Gobshite with a mischievous grin, 'who says I didn't?'

There was a chorus of 'Ooohs' from round the table.

'Well, I do for one,' said Ham & Tongue.

'And how exactly do you know, Mr Omniscient?' said Gobshite, leaning back in his chair. 'Unless you've had your eye glued to her keyhole, which, I may say old chap, is just a little bit creepy.'

'Wouldn't be the first time,' said The Jizz Bandit with a casual smirk.

'And what the fuck do you mean?' said Ham & Tongue.

'I'm saying nothing,' said The Jizz Bandit, 'but I think we all know of what I speak.'

'Oh, for fuck's sake, that never happened, you twat. And if it did, it wasn't like that. And it was just the one time. Once.'

The Jizz Bandit put two fingers together and brought his hand down as if firing a gun at Ham & Tongue. Then he made a 'poof!' noise and pretended to be recoiling from it. 'Gotcha!' he said. Gobshite was grinning from ear to ear.

'What time are we leaving?' said Pisspot suddenly, as if he'd just woken up.

Ham & Tongue looked at his watch. 'About half an hour's time,' he said.

'Is the bar open?' said Pisspot, looking round.

'I don't think so. Most of the staff seemed to have buggered off.'

'Bollocks.'

Dorothy had explained to me that Sunday was usually the day when everyone got the chance to nip into Bristol, so there was usually a mad scramble to get ready in time to get a place on the ten o'clock boat.

The charges were all in place. It was time to light the fuse.

'Time for a quick group photo, then?' I said. 'Give us your phones,' I said to Gobshite and Ham & Tongue. They handed them over to me, and I got ready to take the first picture with Gobshite's camera. The Todger Squad arranged themselves in a practised manner, making a variety of obscene gestures at each other and gurning until their faces split open. I was almost going to miss them.

I took a few pictures, varying the angles so that it looked as if I was taking more care over this than I actually was. Then I made a great play of scrolling through Gobshite's photo stream as if looking for the best shot.

'Eh up,' I said. 'What's this?'

'What's what?' said Gobshite, grabbing at the phone.

'Patience,' I said, pulling it away and out of his reach.

'Oi. Give that back.'

'Well,' I said. 'What DO we have here?' Keeping a firm grip on Gobshite's phone, I showed everyone the picture that Dorothy had skilfully assembled. It showed her and Gobshite apparently sharing a tender moment together. The picture was cut off at shoulder level, but it was clearly intended to give the impression that neither participant was wearing anything.

'Phwoar,' said The Jizz Bandit. 'Nice one.'

'You bloody dark horse,' said Badger Pubes.

'Cor,' said Tampon.

Gobshite looked completely bewildered for a moment, unsure what position he should take. 'Well,' he said eventually, leaning back in his chair again and spreading his arms, 'what can I say?'

'Give me that,' said Ham & Tongue to me, smouldering with fury. I handed the phone to him.

'Lads,' said Furball.

'You keep out of this,' said Ham & Tongue, waving the phone around as if debating whether or not to smash it to pieces on the table.

'Give it back,' said Gobshite. 'Just 'cos you lost out this time.' He paused for a moment. 'Again,' he added.

'You bastard,' said Ham & Tongue, hurling the phone at him. It bounced once on the table and then flew off onto the floor, breaking into a number of pieces as it did so. Gobshite bent down to gather everything together, while the others looked accusingly at Ham & Tongue.

'You shouldn't have done that,' said The Jizz Bandit.

'Shut it,' said Ham & Tongue.

'Lads,' said Furball.

Gobshite sat down again and gave a deep sigh. 'You stupid tit,' he said to Ham & Tongue.

'Guys?' I said.

'Oh, what the fuck do you want now?' said Ham & Tongue.

'Another picture? With your camera this time?'

'Oh, for fuck's sake,' said Gobshite.

'Well, we won't have your picture if your bloody phone's broken, will we?' said Badger Pubes.

'He's got a point,' said The Jizz Bandit.

'Oh, all right,' said Gobshite. 'Just get on with the fucking thing.'

This time, the expressions on the faces of the participants in the photograph were significantly less exuberant. In fact, I fully expected Ham & Tongue's eyes to have burned a hole in the lens.

I went through the same theatrical display of checking Ham & Tongue's photo stream, until I found the one I wanted.

'Ooh,' I said to Ham & Tongue. 'Better not show them that one, had I?'

'Which one?' he said, sounding slightly worried.

'I think you know the one I mean,' I said.

'I have no idea what you're talking about.'

I acted confused for a moment, as if I couldn't work out why he wasn't understanding me. 'Well, this one of course,' I said, showing it to the assembled party. It was a similar picture to the previous one, except this time,

Dorothy had chosen a picture of Ham & Tongue as one half of the couple. As for the other half, I'd had significant reservations about this, but Dorothy had insisted, saying that if she was going to expose herself for the good of our operation, then it was only right that I should do the same. There was, after all, no reason why this should seem at all wrong or unusual in this day and age, was there?

'What the fuck?' said Ham & Tongue, unexpectedly blushing.

'Mate,' I said. 'It's OK. There's nothing wrong with it at all.'

The others, however, were beside themselves.

'Fucking hell,' said Gobshite. 'Well, THAT explains a lot.'

The Jizz Bandit, Badger Pubes, Pisspot and Tampon all burst into uproarious laughter, and a whole slew of homophobic insults followed.

'But it's not real,' protested Ham & Tongue. 'It's a fake!'

'Yeah, yeah,' said Gobshite. 'Looks pretty real to me.'

'All right,' said Ham & Tongue. 'I've had enough of this, you little shit.' He thrust the table away from him, pushing Gobshite and Tampon over. Then he stood up and strode over to me, with his jaw set at an aggressive angle and preparing his fist to strike. I threw his phone at him to confuse him and then ducked out of the way. He made a vain attempt to catch it, but he failed to unclench his hand in time and merely succeeded in knocking it back over his shoulder, where it bounced off Tampon's cheek and collided with The Jizz Bandit's head before smashing onto the floor, whereupon The Jizz Bandit stepped up to Tampon and punched him in the chest.

Meanwhile, Gobshite had picked himself off the floor and was laying into Ham & Tongue, egged on by Badger Pubes and Pisspot.

'Lads,' said Furball, before being knocked to the floor by Pisspot.

'Been waiting to do that all weekend,' remarked Pisspot.

The skirmish between The Jizz Bandit and Tampon had now escalated to the point whereby chairs were now being thrown about. In the course of this, the breakfast table was tipped over, smashing whatever crockery was still sitting on it. Right on cue, the breakfast chef emerged from the kitchen, gasped in alarm and retreated.

Excellent. This was progressing exactly as Dorothy had anticipated. It was time to make an exit before the security team showed up. While everyone was now involved in knocking six bells out of each other, I nipped away to the exit and headed down to the lower deck. As I walked away down the corridor, I heard running feet heading up towards the restaurant.

Dorothy was waiting at the end, by the fire exit.

'Nice work,' she said, dangling a set of keys in front of me.

'Worked like a charm,' I said. 'It's not far short of a full-scale riot up there. So, you managed to get hold of them?'

'Yup,' she said, handing the keys over to me. 'Everyone left the office as soon as the alarm went off, leaving it open for me to sneak in. I've got this for you too.'

She handed me a thick document.

'What's this?'

'It's the instruction manual.'

I flipped through it. It had clearly been translated from the original Chinese via a rare dialect of Venusian.

'I'm not going to be able to make sense of any of this,' I said.

'Well, you shouldn't need it, if you remember everything I told you. You *will* remember everything, won't you?'

'Yeah, sure. Definitely. Yeah, definitely.' I was one hundred per cent sure about this.

'OK, then.' She reached up to kiss me. 'Go. Do your worst. Wish me luck.'

'Good luck,' I said. 'Take care.'

I turned and pushed open the fire exit door. The alarm immediately began to sound.

'Shit!' I said, putting my hands over my ears.

'It's OK,' said Dorothy, leaning in close to my ear. 'This is good. I was expecting this. Look – it says, "This door is alarmed".'

'I thought… oh, never mind.' I was about to make a joke about the door not looking that alarmed really, but thought better of it. Jokes rarely work when you have to shout them. 'So why is it a good thing?' I said instead.

'It's obvious,' said Dorothy. 'The more chaos and confusion there is, the better it is for us. Right. I've got to go.'

Dorothy disappeared back down the corridor, while I took the fire escape up to the main deck, taking care not to look down at the sea churning beneath me. I quickly found the wheelhouse and fumbled with the keys until I found the right one to let me in. I locked the door again from the inside, sat down in the chair and stared at the instrumentation in front of me.

The control panel was a substantial section of industrial grey metal that stretched all the way across the room. It was embedded with somewhere in the region of three and a half million dials and about as many lights, buttons and switches, labelled with impenetrable abbreviations, such as FLG URF, IG. BLX and FEK WMP. It was, frankly, terrifying.

In the middle of it all there was a computer screen and a slide-out keyboard, and this is what Dorothy had told me to concentrate on. On the right hand side of the screen there was a large red button, inviting me to press it. I took the button up on its invitation and the screen lit up and began running through some kind of start-up sequence. Some of the lights on the panel began to flicker as well, and the needles on one or two of the dials twitched. Significantly, there was one just to the left of the computer screen (DSL LEV) that looked as if it might be indicating that there was about half a tank of fuel left. I glanced over my shoulder at the window in the door. I was still OK. No one had rumbled me yet.

The screen eventually came up with a dialogue box welcoming me to the Wave Weaver Mk IIb and asking me to log on. I entered the username and password that Dorothy had given me. It let me in and then unexpectedly informed me that the password had just expired, so would I like to enter a new one. This was something of a bonus, as Dorothy had told me to change it if I could somehow. I chose the word 'TulpencoinBastards', adjusting it to 'Tulpenc01nBastards' when it complained that I needed a combination of alphabetic and numeric characters.

The next screen announced itself as the 'Course Selection Wizard' and asked me to choose a type of course from a drop-down menu. Well, this wasn't going to be too hard after all. Those dials, lights, buttons and switches must just have been a holdover from when they did all this by hand. Dorothy had told me to go for a circular course, basically so that the rig would simply wobble round and round for a while, keeping everyone confused and distracted while we did what we had to do.

'Circle' wasn't, however, an option. The nearest thing I could find to it was 'Quadrant', so I went for that. Then it asked me for a radius, so I entered 500 metres, as Dorothy had suggested, initially heading due West at a speed of 5 knots. I pressed OK to confirm, and then… nothing happened. I was back at the course selection screen again.

What?

There must have been something wrong with the course I'd specified. I thought hard about what Dorothy had said, but, no, it was definitely 500 metres. Maybe that had been too tight? Maybe it had simply rejected the course because it wasn't feasible? I selected 'Quadrant' again and hesitated over the radius. Maybe if I doubled it to 1000 metres? But that was a whole kilometre! How about one and a half times 500? So I put in 750 metres and pressed OK to confirm.

Exactly the same thing happened.

I was now sweating a little. I was doing something really stupid here, but I couldn't for the life of me work out what. Come on, Winscombe. Think!

Maybe the course was still too tight. So, what should I choose next? I decided to be systematic. It's what Dorothy would have done. So the next attempt would be one and a half times 750. Fortunately, there was a calculator lying around, and I used to work out the next radius had to be 1125 metres.

This still didn't work.

I tried a few more times, with 1687.5, 2531.25, 3796.875 and several others, but none of them seemed to have any effect on the computer.

Clearly the Course Selection Wizard was all out of spells, which is why there were three and a half million dials, lights, buttons and switches still on the control panel. The only way I'd ever get this thing going was by pressing the right combination of them. Or to put it another way, I was never going to get this thing going.

Wearily, I selected 'Quit' from the course selection menu, whereupon it informed me that the course was complete and the rig was ready to go.

Hang on.

Heart in mouth, I pressed OK to confirm, but once again, absolutely nothing happened. My heart sank again.

I had failed.

At this very moment, Dorothy was walking into the Seigneur's quarters without any cover. Chances were, the fight in the restaurant would have been subdued by now and there would be no further distractions to take its place. In all likelihood, Dorothy would already be in the Seigneur's hands.

I thumped the control panel, partly in frustration, partly in the vain hope that it might persuade the thing to spark into action. But nothing happened. The dials didn't move in the slightest. A green light somewhere over to the right hand side flickered briefly and then went out again. The rig was as good as dead.

I had to go. Somehow, I had to find Dorothy and warn her before it was too late. So I stood up, unlocked the door to the wheelhouse, slipped out onto the main deck and locked it again.

I was wondering which way to go, when I heard a sound like shots being fired. Shit. Was that in the restaurant or where Dorothy had been heading? I really hoped it was the former and that they were just warning shots fired over the heads of the Todger Squad to bring their little skirmish to an end. Having already seen Gunther and Dirk in action, I didn't feel I could trust either of them not to shoot to kill on this occasion and, in any case, I wasn't entirely sure what the position was on state-sponsored murder with respect to the Autonomous Bailiwick of Channellia's bylaws. It was entirely possible that we'd all, unknowingly, signed some kind of waiver before we came on board.

I skirted round the restaurant block, fervently hoping that the disturbance in there was going to carry on for long enough to give me time to get to Dorothy. Then the fire alarm stopped, which was great from the point of view of the health of my ears, but was also another worrying indication that the authorities here were beginning to re-assert control.

This was underlined further when I reached the front of the block and I heard the sound of several pairs of feet coming out of the restaurant area, accompanied by shouts of 'Keep moving!' and 'No stopping!' and occasional mumbles of 'What about my rights?'

I flattened myself against the side wall and watched out of the corner of my eye as all seven members of the Todger Squad, most of them sporting a Technicolor patchwork of cuts and bruises as well as a significant amount of tomato ketchup and brown sauce, trooped disconsolately down the gangway, followed by Gunther, who was waving his gun about in the manner of someone who couldn't believe his luck that he'd somehow got a job that allowed him to wave a loaded gun around. There was a tiny window of opportunity for me opening, whereby I could slip away into the shadows to my left while he dealt with them.

Unfortunately, I hadn't reckoned on him being as quick and efficient as he turned out to be. I started to jog across the deck towards the round house, but I'd only got half way before I heard steps running after me. I glanced over my shoulder and saw Gunther there, gun still unsheathed, heading in the same direction as me. My tiny window of opportunity had banged shut before I'd even had the chance to peer out of it.

I stared at Gunther like a rabbit trapped in the head-lights, and he stared back at me like a set of high-intensity Xenon headlights illuminating a terrified rabbit.

'Who the fuck are you?' he said, with a very slight accent.

'I've come to help you,' I said, improvising wildly. 'This place is under attack and you need to take urgent action.'

'You come with me,' he said.

Chapter 24

The good news was that I was now precisely where Dorothy had intended to sneak into while everyone else was distracted by the chaos that I had engineered. The bad news was that I hadn't quite anticipated it being full of people who, when they found out what I was intent on doing, would quite likely decide to kill me. The canvas holdall I was after was only a few feet away from where I was sitting in the middle of the room, but right now there seemed to be absolutely no chance of me getting out of here alive with it in my possession.

We were in the observation deck on top of the round house. The interior was furnished in varnished oak and polished brass, with windows running all the way round with bookcases above and below the frames. Access to the room was achieved by a spiral staircase leading up from the floor below. The focus of the room was a large desk, on which sat an old school red telephone. This was clearly the Seigneur's seat of power.

'Please excuse my tooled-up friend standing so close to you,' said the Seigneur, staring out towards the North Atlantic with his back to me, 'but I find that *si vis pacem para bellum* is a most helpful maxim. If you want peace, prepare for war.'

I looked up at Gunther. I had to agree that he seemed to be exceptionally well prepared for war. Apart from his gun, he had a nightstick dangling from his belt and a knife of some sort in a sheath attached to his right ankle.

'Right,' I said. 'Right.'

Kevin Wilberts, attired in a plain white T-shirt and a pair of distressed jeans, lounged awkwardly in a chair in the corner, alternately scratching his crotch and picking at his teeth, while Tiger de Montfort, wearing a scruffy blue pullover and beige chinos, paced up and down, casting the occasional anxious glance in the Seigneur's direction.

'Boss,' he began.

'Easy, Tiger,' said the Seigneur. '*Festina lente.*'

'It's just, if, as this guy says, we're under attack, we need to take prompt action.'

'I see no attack, Tiger. Do you?'

'This place is a fucking fortress,' said Kevin Wilberts, yawning. 'We're impregnable.'

'Indeed we are, my good friend,' said the Seigneur. 'Indeed we are. So, I'm wondering what on earth to make of our new acquaintance's startling assertion.' He turned and looked straight at me. He was wearing an immaculately cut three-piece suit, with a jaunty red handkerchief adorning the breast pocket. 'Hmm?'

'Well, for one thing,' I said. 'You might like to ask this man here—' I gestured towards Gunther '—about the seven violent men he currently has locked up in a cell.'

Gunther looked nonplussed. 'I take them to staff showers,' he said. 'Help them to calm down a little before they leave.'

'Ha!' cried the Seigneur. 'Capital, Gunther! Capital! In any case, if my own observations are correct, they're hardly violent, just a bunch of young scamps with no more vices than youthful exuberance, high spirits and a strong desire to *carpe diem*. Fine young men, every one, and no threat whatsoever.' He turned back to the window. 'No, the one that interests me out of that particular party is you, my friend. What's your *vera causa*?'

'I'm sorry?' I said.

'Your true cause. You're with them and yet you are not with them. I sense that you barely even know them.'

'You're making some bold assertions there.'

'But I'm right, am I not?' he said, turning round once more and staring me straight in the eye. 'We've met before,' he added suddenly. 'I don't know where, but I have a strong sense of *déjà vu*.' He paused. 'Who are you working for?'

'No one,' I protested.

'You're lying.' He turned to Kevin Wilberts. 'Isn't he?'

'Well, I'm bored with him,' said Wilberts. 'Can't we just kill him?'

'Strewth, mate,' said de Montfort. 'Do we have to?'

'I don't know,' said the Seigneur. He turned back to me, his bright blue eyes piercing twin holes in my retinas. 'Do *you* think we should kill you?' he said. 'The law of Channellia is quite clear on the execution of spies.'

'I'm not a spy,' I said.

'So you say. But if you're not spying on me, what on earth are you doing here?' He cupped his chin in his hand

and appeared deep in thought. 'Unless, of course, you came here for love. Ah, yes!' He clapped his hands. '*Amor vincit omnia!*'

'What do you mean?' I said, beginning to panic now.

'Dirk!' he shouted over my shoulder. 'My good man! Splendid! Do come and join us!'

I turned round, dreading what I might see. But there it was. Dirk was standing at the top of the stairs with one hand holding Dorothy's arm. Our pathetic little two-person rebellion was over before it had even started.

'I have to say,' the Seigneur was saying, 'that you two are the most unlikely saboteurs I have ever encountered. What on earth did you imagine you could achieve? More importantly, why? I find it all rather sad.' He paused and looked up at the ceiling before carrying on. 'The problem, as I see it,' he said, 'is that there is an excess of envy in the world today. I know I have many enemies, certainly more than I deserve. But my aims are entirely noble, are they not? I have built myself my own kingdom here. I am no longer a burden to the economy. Surely Channellia should be held up as an example of what could be done if everyone had my vision? The ultimate triumph of individualism! The state would wither away, leaving every man unshackled to do as they wished. *Libertas perfundet omnia luce.* Freedom will flood all things with light.'

'I'm not sure everyone can afford to do that,' said Dorothy. 'How will the poor and the sick be helped in your vision of the future, for example?'

'Ah, yes. You people always bring up the poor and the sick, don't you? Well, as Our Lord puts it, the poor will always be with us. But so will charity. I am not an evil man. I am not saying for a minute that we should abandon our consciences.' He paused and looked hard at Dorothy. 'The future is already here. We have the philosophical foundations—' here he gestured towards Kevin Wilberts, who acknowledged him with a lazy wave '—we have the monetary system—' here he pointed at Tiger de Montfort '—and of course, I provide the political leadership. Channellia is the shape of the world to come.'

'But the whole thing is based on a scam,' said Dorothy.

'What do you mean?' said the Seigneur, narrowing his eyes.

'The whole lot. Your whole operation is financed by crime.'

'That's a very serious allegation, young lady. But, tell me, how do you define crime?'

'What?'

'It's a serious question. Who makes the rules? If I were to suddenly decide that sprawling in a chair was a capital offence, I could have Mr Wilberts here shot without a moment's hesitation.'

Kevin Wilberts sat up immediately and began straightening his hair.

'But that's absurd!' I said.

'Is it?' said the Seigneur. 'Many of the laws on the mainland are no less absurd, my friend. You are perhaps confusing the concept of *malum prohibitum* with *malum in se*. Just because something is against some law or other, it does not necessarily mean it is inherently wrong. Likewise, if something is wrong, it doesn't mean that it is against the law.'

'So, are you saying,' said Dorothy, 'that, within your jurisdiction, things like murder, theft and drug-dealing are somehow no longer crimes?'

Tiger de Montfort stood up. 'OK, I've heard enough. You're right, mate. Let's just kill 'em.'

The Seigneur held up a hand to stall him. 'Murder?' he said. 'Theft? Drug-dealing? This is all terribly exotic, young lady. I have no knowledge of these things. But if they were occurring, I would perhaps consider reclassifying them as legitimate acts of war.'

'War?' said Dorothy.

'It would not be unreasonable to consider my relationship with the mainland as being in a state of undeclared war, even if for the moment it is largely waged by my accountants and their tax-gatherers. As far as I am concerned, with regard to the mainland, anything goes. Bear in mind that when the East India Company was selling opium to your ancestors back in the nineteenth century, it was entirely legal as far as the British government was concerned.'

'You bastard,' said Dorothy.

'I'd watch yourself,' said the Seigneur, moving closer to her, with his voice dropping to an icy whisper. 'We could make this quite difficult for you—'

The Seigneur was cut short by an ear-splitting klaxon that suddenly erupted from the other end of the rig. He frowned and turned his head towards the main building. Tiger de Montfort was also peering out into the distance, and he was soon joined by Kevin Wilberts.

'What's going on?' said the Seigneur.

'Dunno,' said de Montfort. 'Never heard that one before.'

'Think we'd better get moving,' said Wilberts, heading towards the staircase.

The Signeur held up a commanding hand. 'Wait one moment,' he said in a steely voice. 'No one leaves until I say so.' He softened slightly, adding, 'Gunther, be a good chap, will you, and go and find out what the hell's going on out there? I think Dirk can probably handle this on his own.'

Gunther grunted and left the room. Out of the window, I noticed seven young men with damp hair, dressed only in towels around their midriffs, hurtling out of the stairway from the lower decks towards where the motor launch was moored. Somewhere in the bowels of the rig, an engine began to hum. I risked a glance at Dorothy and a brief moment of understanding passed between us. Amid the panic, no one else in the room seemed to notice it.

'Now,' said the Seigneur. 'Where was I before I was so rudely interrupted?'

'The Opium Wars,' said Dorothy. 'You were explaining how exporting opium to China was a good thing.'

Nicely done, I thought to myself. If she could keep him on topic, she might just spin this out for long enough.

'Oh, I'm bored with that,' said the Seigneur. 'In fact, I'm rather bored with you two altogether.' He paused for a moment. Kevin Wilberts and Tiger de Montfort had now both turned away from the window and were looking at him expectantly. 'Kevin, Tiger,' he said, addressing them, 'can you think of any reason why we shouldn't execute these two spies? Because I honestly can't.'

'Nope,' said Kevin Wilberts.

'Nah, just do it,' said Tiger de Montfort.

'Well,' said the Seigneur, 'that would seem to conclude the proceedings. Do you have anything you'd like to say before the sentence is carried out?'

'Wait,' said Dorothy.

'That's it?' said the Seigneur. "Just "wait"? What for, pray?'

'This,' she said, grabbing my hand.

The humming noise had been growing steadily for the last couple of minutes, but now it was superseded by a horrendous metallic scraping noise, followed by a dreadful ear-splitting, gut-wrenching straining as if some robotic beast from the depths had just woken up from a century of slumber and was struggling to surface.

Then the entire rig lurched downwards and everything in the room tipped towards the window. Books flew off the shelves and ornaments fell onto the floor and smashed. Dirk slipped over on the polished floor, losing his grip on his gun, which slid away towards the corner of the room. Dorothy leapt onto him and grabbed his knife before he could gather his wits together. The Seigneur, meanwhile, had collapsed against the wall underneath the window with a bewildered look on his face.

'The bag!' I shouted to Dorothy, but it was too late. Kevin Wilberts had managed to grab hold of the canvas holdall as it went past him and both he and the bag were now on the floor, trying to crawl back to the middle of the room. Tiger de Montfort was out cold, having been hit by a low-flying first edition hardback of *The Fountainhead*.

The noise from the rig had briefly died down but now it intensified again as the engines gathered themselves for the next step. With a ghastly, portentous clanking as if the final minute of earth's history was being counted out, the rig wheezed back upwards, sending everything in the Seigneur's quarters back towards the rear of the room. Dirk's gun slid past me out through the door into the corridor, while on the other side of the room, Dorothy was tussling with Kevin Wilberts for the canvas bag. I forced my way over there, avoiding the lumbering form of Dirk, who was trying to stand up and failing very badly.

Now the Seigneur had seen what was happening with the bag and he began to crawl over to where we were all scrapping. When he arrived, he appeared to make a decision that Kevin Wilberts was not to be trusted with it, because he grabbed one of the handles from him and began pulling the bag towards himself. It was now quick work for Dorothy to use Dirk's knife to cut through both handles with four deft slashes, while I took hold of the bag itself.

'Let's go,' said Dorothy, scrabbling to get to her feet and trying to get away from Wilberts, who now had a firm grip on her ankle. She kicked out several times, but he wouldn't let go. Guessing what was about to happen next, however, I threw the bag down the staircase into the room below and took a firm hold of the banister.

'Dorothy!' I shouted, holding out my hand to her. She looked confused for a moment and then realised herself what was about to take place. Sure enough, the rig groaned into life once more and everything in the room, apart from the two of us, tumbled back towards the window. It only took a single kick from Dorothy to make Wilberts let go this time, and we were both free at last.

Chapter 25

The rig was now beginning to pick up speed, and it continued to pitch, roll and yaw as we staggered down the spiral staircase, then through the round house and down to the deck.

'I thought I hadn't managed to get it going,' I shouted to Dorothy. 'I was panicking back there.'

'Nah,' she said. 'It just takes a while to warm up. That's what the manual said, anyway. I should probably have mentioned it. Didn't expect it to be quite so unstable, but I guess they haven't bothered maintaining the hydraulics. Serves them right.'

'What if they just try to put the brakes on?'

'First, they've got to find someone who knows how to drive it, and I've stolen the only manual on board. Second, they've got to make their way to the wheelhouse, third, I assume you managed to change the password, and fourth, even if they do hit the brakes, it'll take a long time to come to a halt.'

She stopped for a moment, staring out to sea.

'Tom,' she said. 'What course did you actually set?'

'Well, that's the weird thing,' I said. 'It didn't seem to let me.' I explained what had happened when I'd tried to use the Course Selection Wizard. As I did so, I became aware that Dorothy was looking at me strangely.

'What's wrong?' I said when I'd finished.

'Tom, I'm almost speechless,' she said. 'Somehow, you've managed to send this rig into what is pretty much a Fibonacci spiral.'

'I did what?' I said. I suddenly felt exceptionally proud of myself. 'Wow.'

'Well, that's what you've done. Every time you entered a new quadrant, it wasn't failing to work. It was adding it to the course you'd previously set. So each quadrant was one and a half times the radius of the previous one. I mean, for a proper Fibonacci spiral, you'd need to be looking at a series of multipliers. You'd start with 3/2 or 1.5, sure, but then you'd need to go to 5/3 or 1.67, 8/5 or 1.6, 13/8 or 1.63, 21/13 or 1.62 and so on. Still, not a bad effort.'

'Gosh.' I was still glowing.

'Unfortunately, what it also means is that this rig is going to be heading for the edge of the continental shelf sometime soon, so we need to get off it pretty damn quick.'

'Ah.'

'Yep. Ah.'

The reception area was empty when we finally got there.

'Where is everyone?' I said.

'Down there!' shouted Dorothy. 'Look, the boat's leaving!'

I peered down towards the water, holding on to the rail at the side, and I could see the little motor launch chugging away from the rig. On board were the half-naked seven other members of the Todger Squad, huddled together for warmth, plus most of the staff. I was quite relieved that they'd managed to get away OK.

'Is Gunther with them?' I said.

'Don't think so.'

'Bugger. Better keep an eye out for him, then. Now what?'

'There's a couple of dinghies moored down below. All we need to do is get down there.'

'Right,' I said. 'Run that past me again.'

'There are a couple of dinghies—'

'They're at sea level, right?'

'Yes.'

'Just bobbing up and down on the water.'

'Yes.'

'Nowhere near the harness?'

'No. They're actually in the centre of the rig.'

'Excellent.'

We both looked at each other.

'We're fucked, aren't we?' I said.

'Basically, yes.'

'Unless you fancy shinning down one of the middle legs, of course.'

'The hydraulic legs? The ones that are basically an array of stupidly large pistons? Tom, that may be one of the worst ideas you've ever had.'

'I thought it might be. Shit.'

My deliberations were interrupted by the sound of a gunshot. I instinctively ducked and then looked around to see where it had come from.

'It's Gunther,' said Dorothy, who had also ducked down. 'We're sitting targets here, come on.'

There was a temporary lull in the movement of the rig and we took advantage of it to scramble back towards the main entrance of the hotel section. We crouched down behind the reception desk and I noticed something sitting there.

'Ha, look,' I said. 'My bag.' It was where I'd left it earlier. I suddenly had an idea. I opened the bag up and took out the bottle of champagne.

'Bit early to celebrate, isn't it, Tom?' said Dorothy. I ignored her and removed the wire cage from around the cork. Then I peered over the top of the desk to see Gunther walking slowly towards us across the main deck, gun in one hand and the other braced for whatever might happen. I got back down again and began working the cork loose.

I counted one… two… three… then I crawled round the edge of the desk and fired the cork at the advancing Gunther. It hit him full in the face, and as he staggered back, the rig began to move again, tipping the deck away from where we were hiding. Dorothy and I stood up now, holding on to the desk to steady ourselves, and watched as Gunther scrabbled about, desperately trying to regain his footing as he slid towards the listing edge of the rig, which was nearing forty-five degrees to the horizontal. Then he hit the rail and spun over into the sea.

'Holy shit,' I said.

'Come on,' said Dorothy. 'Dirk'll be on our case next if we don't keep moving.'

I looked at the bottle of champagne that I was still holding and took a swig. I looked around for somewhere to put it down, but there wasn't a horizontal surface in sight, so I took it with me instead. I tucked the canvas holdall under my arm, grabbed my other bag and set off after Dorothy, who was edging her way around the side of the building. We were halfway round when I saw something that gave me an idea.

'Over there,' I said to Dorothy, pointing to the bungee apparatus.

'Two problems,' said Dorothy. 'First of all, won't we just bounce back up?'

'Not if we both go down together.'

'And you're absolutely sure about this?'

'Not exactly. It's more like informed speculation. Provided we both let go at exactly the same time, nothing at all can go wrong.'

'This is excellent. Can I offer up my second problem for your analysis?'

'Go ahead.'

'Knowing what I know about the location of the dinghies, I don't recall either of them being moored directly under the jump.'

'This is true,' I said. 'But come with me.'

The deck was now levelling off again, so we gingerly made our way towards the bungee station. I looked over the edge. There was indeed no dinghy directly underneath the jump. In fact, if I leant over the edge I could confirm that both the dinghies were exactly where Dorothy had said they were – slap, bang in the middle of the area underneath the rig.

'OK, now hear me out,' I said, 'because this is slightly wild.'

'Go on.'

'If we time it right, we can launch ourselves outwards when the deck is at its maximum seaward tilt, then when the deck rights itself, we'll end up swinging back underneath, in between the legs, so that, with a tiny bit of luck, we can manoeuvre ourselves to exactly where the dinghy is.'

'When you say "tiny", you actually mean "massive", don't you?'

'Possibly. But what's your alternative?'

'I haven't got one.'

'Let's go with this one, then. If it fails, we can always do something else. Provided we can climb back up again, which we probably won't be able to do, now I come to think of it.'

'You know what,' said Dorothy, 'I think this is actually worse than your idea of shinning down one of the legs.'

'Yeah, you're probably right. But here comes our moment.'

The deck was tilting away from us again. I decided to force the issue.

'Right, I'm going,' I said. 'Are you with me?'

'I'm really not sure about this,' said Dorothy.

'Trust me,' I said.

'Give me that bottle.'

I handed her the bottle of champagne. Dorothy took a swig, paused for a moment, then took another swig and handed it back to me. I did the same and then tossed it over the side. Right. I was ready.

I gripped the canvas holdall between my legs, slung my other bag over my shoulder and grasped the bungee cord. Dorothy gripped me round the waist and I pushed us both off into oblivion. As we reached the apogee of the bungee, we skimmed the surface of the water and for a moment I panicked in case my visual assessment of our combined weight had been completely wrong. But then it jerked back a little at the same time as the deck tipped back the other way and we found ourselves flying down through the legs towards one of the dinghies. By leaning from side to side, I managed to adjust our trajectory until we were absolutely bang on course. It was, of course, at this point that everything went completely pear-shaped.

First of all, as we neared the dinghy, my knees lost their grip on the canvas bag and it began to slip away from me. I took one hand off the bungee and reached down to grab it, at which point the bag on my shoulder helpfully slid off so that it was dangling from my elbow. The only thing I could do now was let go of both and hope that they landed in the dinghy. Amazingly, they did. However, the resulting reduction in weight now meant that the bungee began to pull us back upwards again.

In my panic, I shouted to Dorothy, 'you've got to let go!'

'I can't,' she said. Her hands were now firmly locked into position around my waist.

By now, we were definitely moving away from our landing spot, on a diagonal trajectory back towards the open sea. I failed to notice that we were also heading straight for one of the legs. When we hit it, I involuntarily loosened my grip on the bungee cord and at that point Dorothy let go of me too. Once I realised what had happened, I managed to grab the very end of the cord and wrap it around my wrist just before I slid off and I continued on my journey out, bouncing against the legs as I went, like the worst ever Spiderman tribute act in history.

Meanwhile, Dorothy had landed in the water and was splashing about trying to stabilise herself. I watched helplessly as the water boiled around her and the rig began the next part of its manoeuvre. Then something miraculous happened. The rig began to move away from Dorothy, but as it did so, a cable leading away landward from the central leg began to surface and become taut. Channellia's umbilical connection to the outside world was about to be cut, but before it was, it gave Dorothy something to grab onto and pull herself towards the dinghy.

However, just as fate was busy offering her this olive branch with one hand, it was happily preparing to set fire to it with the other, because a hatch opened above her and the figure of Dirk appeared, gun in hand. He took aim just as Dorothy reached the little boat, but just as he was about to fire, the cable snapped in two, recoiling wildly upwards and slashing him across the face before knocking him into the water. The Tulpenbot network had, at last, gone dark, taking Dirk with it.

I was now bouncing up and down on the end of the bungee, sometimes well out of the water and sometimes horribly close to it, depending on the attitude of the rig. By the time Dorothy got the outboard motor going, I was beginning to flag, and when she eventually positioned the dinghy underneath me, I landed rather heavily and all but launched her out of the boat again.

'Tom,' she said, as she steered the boat away from the wildly circling rig, 'if you ever say the words "trust me" to me again, remind me not to, OK?'

With Dorothy still in the driving seat, we headed straight for the nearest point on the shore, which was Burnham-on-Sea. We had no idea how much petrol there was in the outboard motor for one thing, and we were feeling too traumatised to undertake anything other than the shortest sea journey for another. Dorothy was also in danger of hypothermia. I'd offered her some of the clothes from my bag, but for some reason she'd balked at wearing my Todger Squad rugby shirt.

From time to time, I looked back at the Autonomous Bailiwick of Channellia, which had stabilised slightly now that it had been in motion for a while, but was still continuing to wobble on its mad Fibonacci orbit into the unknown. I swore I could still make out the lone figure of the Seigneur in his observation deck, standing firm, staring out into the distance. I wondered how long it could carry on until it either ran out of fuel or it fell into the sea when its legs tipped over the edge of the continental shelf.

We continued on in silence until we got close to Burnham-on-Sea. The tide was in, so it would have been quite straightforward to motor in and tie up. However, we could now see that a crowd was beginning to gather on the seafront, binoculars at the ready, pointing either at us or over our heads at the doomed rig.

'Don't fancy having to deal with that lot,' said Dorothy.

'No,' I said. 'Too many questions to deal with.'

'Could do with a map.'

'I was thinking that myself. Have you got a signal yet?'

'Don't know,' said Dorothy, pulling out her phone. 'The thing's waterlogged.'

'Well, if you're looking for a replacement,' I said, pulling out my Happy Wednesday Gold Star 3000, 'I can certainly recommend this one.'

'Tom, don't.'

'Sorry, I—'

'Just don't, OK? Unless you're about to tell me that it's magically acquired the ability to access Google Maps, don't mention that phone to me again.'

'Right.'

There was a long silence between us as we came closer to the shore.

'OK,' said Dorothy, 'I'm going to head south for a while. See if there's some kind of inlet.'

Dorothy pulled the tiller towards her and we changed course southwards. Out to sea, there was noise like a muffled crack of thunder as the rig finally tipped over and the Autonomous Bailiwick of Channellia disappeared beneath the waves to become a curio to be explored by future trainee scuba divers.

'So that's it, then,' I said.

'Yup,' said Dorothy. 'That is most definitely it.'

There wasn't much more to say. A little way beyond the town, an inlet opened up. Dorothy looked at me and shrugged. I shrugged back and she pushed the tiller away from her to turn inland. After a few twists and turns, we found ourselves chugging along a narrow river with flat marshlands on either side of us. Half a mile further on, houses began to spring up on one side and then we passed first under a road bridge and then under a railway bridge.

'Right,' said Dorothy. 'That'll do. We'll ditch the boat and catch a train.'

'Is there a station around here, though?' I said.

'If not, we'll just walk along the track until we get to one.'

A short way beyond the bridge, there was a mooring point on the side where the houses were and Dorothy steered us towards it. A brisk walk through a housing estate took us to a main road that led back to a bridge over the railway by Highbridge and Burnham station. A quarter of an hour later, we were on a train to Bristol.

'What now?' I said.

'We take what cash we need to get the company going again and find some suitable cause to donate whatever's left over to. Then we'll tip the wink to the police about what they might find if they pay a visit to the wreck of Channellia.'

'Seems fair.'

My phone went off. It wasn't a number I recognised at all, but I answered it anyway.

'Ah, Mr Beam,' said a familiar female voice. 'How are you? I've been hearing all *manner* of stories.'

'Hello, Matheson,' I said.

'Call me Helen, sweetheart. Look, we need to talk. Where are you?'

Chapter 26

'Who is that?' hissed Dorothy.

'Sorry, one moment,' I said to Matheson. 'It's Matheson,' I whispered to Dorothy.

'Who's Matheson?' said Dorothy.

'She's… oh, I'll explain later,' I said.

'Is this a bad time?' said Matheson. 'I can call you later if it's more convenient.'

'No, it's fine,' I said.

'Where are you?' she said again.

'On a train into Bristol. Just left Highbridge and… what was it…? Burnham.'

'Perfect. Get off at Weston. Go to the sea front. There's a row of perfectly darling little beach huts there. Wait in the second powder blue one from the far end and I'll meet you there in half an hour or so.'

'OK. Hang on,' I said. 'Which is the far end?'

The line had gone dead.

'All right, Tom,' said Dorothy. 'Who's Matheson?'

'She's some sort of… well, I think she probably works for Special Branch or MI5 or something.'

'But you're not sure.'

'Well, no. But I'm pretty certain she does, because she definitely acts like she does.'

'In what way does she do this?'

'Hey, chill, D. You're acting as if you don't believe me.'

'No, Tom. I'm acting as if I believe that you don't really believe yourself. Tell me again, how *does* she act like she works for Special Branch or MI5 or something?'

'Well, for example, she shoots people.'

'I'm not getting the right vibe quite yet, Tom. Who has she shot?'

'Oh, the bloke who was trying to abduct Benjamin Unsworth.'

'What?'

'Oh, long story. Basically, Benjamin's still alive. Only he got poisoned and then someone tried to abduct him from the hospital. But I helped Matheson get him out of there instead.'

'So, basically, *Matheson* abducted him, right? With your help?'

'No!' I said, 'you're twisting my words. He was definitely a bad guy, the one she shot. Because *he* was trying to shoot *us*.'

'Fine. So it's basically a case of my enemy's enemy being my friend, yes?'

'Ye-es. Why are you looking at me like that?'

'And is Benjamin OK now?' said Dorothy.

'I don't know.'

'You don't know. But you definitely helped her take him away from the hospital.'

'Well, yes. But then she chloroformed me. Yes, I know that sounds odd, but... you're giving me that look again, Dorothy.'

'What else do you know about her, Tom?'

'Well, she had someone on the inside of the Tulpencoin operation.'

'And what happened to him?'

'He got killed.'

There was a long silence.

'He got killed,' repeated Dorothy.

'You're twisting my words again.'

'In what way?'

'Oh, you know what you're doing. Look, I think we can trust her. She's definitely on our side.'

'Tell me more about her, Tom. She sounded terribly glamorous. Is she as sexy as she sounds?'

'What are you... oh, I can't be doing with this, Dorothy. I do believe you're jealous.'

'No, Tom. Just careful.'

We still weren't talking to each other when we arrived at Weston. The beach huts were around twenty minutes away and we quickly located the second powder blue one from the end. It was locked.

'Well, what do we do now?' said Dorothy.

'We wait for her,' I said.

She looked from left to right. 'Not many people around this lunchtime, Tom. Good place to kill someone.'

'She won't do that.'

'How do you know?'

'Oh, I just do.'

Dorothy wandered down towards the beach.

'What are you doing?' I said.

'Making sandcastles.'

But it didn't look quite like that.

Helen Matheson turned up half an hour later. She was wearing a simple but elegant black dress, a red bolero jacket and Vantablack sunglasses. A neat leather bag was slung casually over one shoulder.

'Mr Beam, darling,' she said, 'how lovely to see you again!' She took off her sunglasses and held out her hand for me to shake.

I remembered just in time that I was Jim Beam as far as she was concerned. 'It wasn't so lovely last time,' I said, pulling my hand away. I felt I ought to make some show of standing up for myself, if only for Dorothy's benefit. 'You chloroformed me.'

Matheson looked guilty. 'Mr Beam, I am so, so sorry,' she said, putting her hands together as if in prayer. 'I made a terrible mistake. I underappreciated your abilities. I now know you have so much more to offer.' She clapped her hands, then turned and looked at Dorothy, who was close to gagging at this point. 'And you are…?'

'A friend,' said Dorothy.

'With no name?' said Matheson.

'For now, no.'

'Ah.' Matheson paused for a moment, nonplussed. 'Well,' she said, eventually, 'shall we go in?' She took out a key from her bag and opened up the hut. Inside, there was just enough room for the three of us to sit down amid the clutter of lilos, deck chairs and beach balls.

'So then,' said Matheson. 'I understand that you have had an interesting weekend.'

'You could say that,' I said.

'I believe I just did,' said Matheson, with a supercilious smile. 'So, tell me, sweetheart. What was your intention? Was it just about sinking that ridiculous Channellia contraption, or were you after something else?' As she said this, I couldn't stop myself glancing down at the canvas holdall. She looked down at it as well.

'Sorry?' I said, feeling the heat rise in my cheeks. 'I'm not sure I understand what you're saying.'

'Come on,' said Dorothy, standing up. 'I don't think this is getting us anywhere.'

'Sit down, please,' said Matheson. Dorothy sat down very quickly and when I looked back at Matheson, I understood why. She was now holding a gun, and it was pointing at Dorothy.

'Now, Mr Beam, would I be right in saying that the shabby canvas holdall underneath your seat contains a large sum of cash that was used to pay the Seigneur of the preposterous, tinpot Autonomous Bailiwick of Channellia for a large consignment of crack cocaine? I appreciate that I've been a little behind you in my investigations, but fortunately you've been there to do the heavy lifting. Incidentally, I'd like to put it on record that I really do appreciate this.' She tilted her head on one side and gave a sad little smile. 'However, the time has come for the grown-ups to take back control of the operation and reassert the project's aims and objectives.'

'Which are?' said Dorothy.

'To restore at least some of the money that has been stolen from my client.'

'I'm sorry?' I said, suddenly very confused. 'But your client is the British government, isn't it? I mean, you are basically the British government, aren't you?'

Now it was Matheson's turn to look confused. 'Good heavens, no. What on earth made you think that?'

'Well, all the licence to kill stuff,' I said. 'Shooting that guy in the hospital. Talking about your people fixing Benjamin Unsworth. How is he, by the way?'

'He is being dealt with, although it may be a while before we can make use of him as an active asset.'

'But you talked about a client. I don't understand this at all.'

'Sweetheart, let me explain,' she said. 'You are half right. The people I report to used to be a government agency, but then they got privatised. So now it's all about providing return on investment and all that dreadfully boring fiscal stuff. Which means we end up having to take on work for other clients as well.'

'Who?'

'I can't tell you. Obviously.'

'Well, what sort of people do you work for?'

'Our charter does not permit us to act in a discriminatory manner.'

'What does that mean?' I said.

'Basically, it means we're not that fussy. It was something of a culture shock to the organisation at first, but now I am finding it quite bracing.'

'Would you take on the Seigneur of Channellia, for example?'

'If he's still alive,' said Matheson, glancing out to sea, 'it's entirely possible.'

'But he's evil.'

'Define "evil".'

'He's a criminal.'

'Define "criminal".'

'Oh please,' said Dorothy. 'We've had this conversation once already today. Just tell us what you want.'

Matheson shrugged. 'The money, I guess. Pass me the bag, please.'

I was about to hand the holdall over, when Dorothy interrupted. 'Wait a moment,' she said. 'This isn't fair. Why can't we just take what they owe us and you can have the rest?'

'How much are you proposing, my dear?' said Matheson.

Dorothy gave a figure, which seemed remarkably low to me.

Matheson shook her head. 'No dice, sugar,' she said. 'Fairness doesn't come into it when only one of us is holding a gun. My client, or rather my client's late husband, had a substantial amount of money looted from him in the period leading up to his premature demise, and I have been instructed to recover whatever I can by whatever means. Whatever's in that bag is unlikely to even begin to cover the missing amount.' She waved the gun at me and then at the bag. 'Pass it to me, please.'

I pushed it over to her, and she reached down, undid the zip and peered into it. Satisfied, she re-zipped the holdall and tucked it under her arm. Then she stood up, still pointing the gun at us and began to walk out of the hut.

'Well,' she said. 'A transaction most satisfactorily concluded. I look forward to meeting again some time, Mr Beam.'

'So you're not going to kill us?' I said.

'Why should I do that?' she said. 'I'm not some kind of psychopath, you know. Murder's a damn messy business, and one tries to avoid it wherever possible. Ta-ra, my lovelies.'

With that, she blew us a kiss and strode off back in the direction of Weston-super-Mare.

'I wonder how long it'll be before she finds out,' I said, once she was out of sight.

'With any luck, long enough to get ourselves away from here,' said Dorothy, picking up my bag and checking that the bulk of the cash was still there. The holdall contained just half a dozen bundles of notes on top of my Todger Squad rugby shirt, now filled with sand to weigh the bag down. I wasn't that sorry to see the back of it.

'You were right,' I said.

'What? About you being taken in by the first glamorous woman who crossed your path while I was away?'

'No, that's not what I meant. I was talking about her not being trustworthy.'

'Hmm. How trustworthy are you, though, Tom?'

'Oh, that's not fair,' I said, stepping out of the hut.

We began to walk in the opposite direction to Matheson. Out to sea, a small flotilla of boats was heading out to where the Autonomous Bailiwick of Channellia had last been seen.

Chapter 27

μ looked up from her position on the caravan step as I arrived, and glared at me. 'And where do you think you've been?' she seemed to be saying.

'It's ok,' I said, reaching down to scratch her neck. She acquiesced briefly, before she remembered that she was on duty and made a half-hearted attempt to remove the skin from my fingers instead. I withdrew my hand and looked around me. There was no sign of my father.

Eventually, he appeared, staring at his mobile phone and looking worried. He was accompanied by Wally the dog, who bounded up to me with obvious excitement on seeing an opportunity for some hardcore crotch-sniffing.

'OK, that's enough,' I said, pushing him away. I was always concerned that Wally might accidentally bite something off in his enthusiasm. 'Dad', I said. 'Hi!'

My father had stopped outside the caravan and was still studying the screen. 'Sorry, what?' he said after a while, 'I was just—'

'Anything wrong?' I said.

'You bet there is, son. Come inside.'

μ moved aside a millimetre or two to let us pass, and then reasserted her position. Wally bounded up behind us in the hope of joining the discussion, but she hissed at him and he slunk away.

'Well,' said my father, without any further preamble, 'things have gone a bit to shit lately.'

'Why's that?'

He waved his phone at me. 'First of all, I have been bloody suspended from Tinder for supposedly—' here he mimed some air quotes '—lying about my age.'

'Dad, what did you put your age down as?'

'Well, maybe a little bit less than I actually am, but it's how I feel inside that counts, isn't it?' Here he thumped his chest. 'Look at me. I'm a perfect specimen of manhood, am I not? This body may have lived a bit, but it's in perfect working order.' He paused to deal with a prolonged fit of racking coughs, that in any other man would have been taken as *prima facie* evidence of advanced tuberculosis, possibly with a number of interesting complications that might even have been worthy of a paper or two. 'Sorry, son, just need to make myself a ciggie.'

As he set to work with his packet of Rizlas and pouch of rolling tobacco, I took a good look at him. He had the face of a man whose approach to life had been to listen to every single piece of advice regarding his health and well-being and then do the precise opposite. It was as if his body had actually died some time ago, but his mind had somehow kept the show on the road by sheer force of will and bloody-mindedness.

'So what else has gone wrong?' I said.

'It's those bloody Tulpencoins,' he said, putting the roll-up in his mouth and flicking his cheap plastic lighter several times to get it going. He took a long drag and then picked up his phone again. 'Look at this,' he said.

The graph he'd shown me last time had been reflected about a horizontal axis. The value of the Tulpencoin had plummeted.

'Dad, don't worry,' I said.

'But all my bloody money,' he said, waving his arms. 'It's gone.'

'I thought you weren't worried about money,' I said, and then felt bad about it. It was a cheap shot.

'Well, I never wanted to be a breadhead, son.' He leaned back in his chair. 'Y'know,' he said, 'I think I was born at the wrong time. I should have been making my living off the land. Sowing seeds, keeping pigs, bringing in the harvest, that sort of thing.'

'Dad, you'd have been terrible at it. You know that.'

'Yeah, well. I just wish things were a bit simpler. Can't believe I got conned. I'm usually so good at spotting that sort of thing.'

'A lot of people did, Dad. Anyway, I—'

'Thing is,' he said, interrupting me. 'I never wanted my life to be boring like yours. I mean, you'd admit it yourself, son. You're a bit dull. Not your fault, it's the way you're made – I blame your mother. But there it is. You are what you are. Y'see, I wanted to travel the world.'

'Dad, we went to Italy once. You got food poisoning and we all had to come home.'

'It's not so much what you actually do, son, it's more a state of mind.' He tapped his head.

'Right,' I said. 'Right. Look, have you got anything to drink? I think I need one.'

'You want to watch yourself, son. I've told you before about this. But the answer's no, I'm afraid. Shortage of funds.'

'Ah, well,' I said, remembering the reason for my visit again, 'I might be able to help you out.'

'You? That'll be the day, son.'

'No, really, I can.'

'Son, I don't want any charity.'

'Look, I found out there's a compensation scheme for anyone taken in by the Tulpencoin scam, so I went and applied to it on your behalf.' This was the story I'd concocted to avoid having to explain everything to him. If I'd tried to go through half of what had actually happened, he would have spun at least seven different conspiracy theories out of all the available new material by the time we'd finished, and the internet would have gone berserk as soon as I'd left.

'I don't want any handouts,' he said, folding his arms.

'This isn't a handout,' I said. 'It's what you're owed. Look.'

I waved the wad of notes in front of him. He stared at it for a moment, and then took it from me. He counted it out with meticulous precision once, before turning all the notes over and repeating the process.

'It's a fiver short,' he said when he'd finished.

'Oh, for fuck's sake,' I muttered to myself. I took out my wallet and gave him the missing fiver.

'Cheers, son. So, are you going to drop in on one-eyed Kev?'

'Who's one-eyed Kev?'

'You know, the bloke round the corner who told me about investing in this stuff. I've just been to see him and he's right pissed off. Even his bitcoins aren't worth what they used to be. I'm sure he'd be dead keen to hear about compensation. Actually, I'll tell him myself. I think he was feeling a bit guilty about encouraging me, to be honest.'

I put up my hand. 'No, don't worry, I'll tell him,' I said. 'To be honest, it's probably best not to mention it ever again as far as you're concerned. Treat the whole thing as a learning experience.'

'You're probably right, son. Still, it's good to know that someone out there's keeping an eye on all this. There's some right dodgy buggers out there.'

'So, this is where you've been living?' said Dorothy, sniffing the fetid air in the flat.

'I guess it is.'

'Classy.'

'We thought so.'

'What's the tank for?' she said.

'Oh, a ball python. Bertrand. He's gone now.'

'Far?'

'Far enough. Have you spoken to Ali?'

'We've exchanged a few words, yes. Although, to be fair, a lot of them were the same word, along with a couple of variations, so it didn't really amount to much of a conversation.'

'She'll get over it.'

'I hope so. Have you got any rice?' said Dorothy.

'Rice?'

'To dry my phone out.'

'Ah. No.'

'You don't cook?'

'No, it's mostly pizza here.'

'Right. I'll buy some tomorrow, then.'

Dorothy sat down on the edge of the bed.

'Tom,' she said, 'you know that night when it all happened? When you went off to Bristol, did you really think you were going to get the Vavasor papers?'

'Well, yes. I thought I was.'

'Well, that was very sweet of you.'

'Except they turned out to be complete pants.'

'Yeah, well. No surprise there.' She paused. 'You sure it wasn't just because it was Lucy who called you?'

'No! That never crossed my mind.' It hadn't. It really hadn't.

'The reason I ask is that I found something out when I was on Channellia.'

This sounded ominous.

'Go on,' I said.

'Did you know Kevin Wilberts was a hardcore Vavasorologist?'

'I had a feeling he was lurking at the back at that convention Ali and I went to.'

'Yep. Vavasorology is how he got to Fairbanks in the first place.'

'Of course.'

'He was the perfect introduction to the world of Tulpencoin. Mutual interest in mathematics and right-wing philosophy.'

'I'm surprised Fairbanks fell for it,' I said.

'Tom, everyone has a weakness. All you need to do is find the right lever. Come on, you've seen Wilberts in action. He can work a crowd, can't he? Working a greedy bastard like Fairbanks would have been child's play.'

'I guess so.' Having been on the receiving end of Fairbanks's undoubted charisma, I couldn't imagine ever being in a position to manipulate him.

'But going back to Wilberts, it turns out he had – maybe still has – a team searching for the Vavasor papers.'

'You're kidding me.'

'Nope. He had – maybe still has – the money to fund it. So why not?'

'So, what are you saying?'

'What I'm saying is that I might have overheard one or two things.'

'Don't tease, D.'

'Take a look at this.'

Dorothy handed me a sheet of paper on which she'd transcribed various telephone conversations of Wilberts's that she'd overheard when she was working in the casino.

'Oh,' I said, after I'd read them.

'Not only that,' she said, 'but if you take a look on *vavasorology.com*, there's been some unconfirmed sightings of Isaac Vavasor recently in the exact same place.'

'There was something about that at the Vavvies. But what are you saying?'

'What I'm saying is that maybe we should go and take a look ourselves?'

'Right,' I said. 'Right.' I paused for a moment before continuing. 'OK, I have a number of responses to your suggestion. On the positive side, I like the fact that you haven't just decided to go off on your own without telling anyone this time. Please don't take this as indicating my approval of your underlying proposal in any way, but I feel that your use of the word "we" in this context is a definite sign of progress.'

'Thank you. I appreciate that. Anything else?'

'Nope, that's about it for the positive side,' I said. 'On the negative side, however, I feel that we may run into considerable difficulties with Ali.'

'I can't see that as a problem, Tom. With the bundle of cash you have in that bag down there, we can set her up with a super slick new development environment and let her get on with things for a week or two, while you and I chase down the papers once and for all.'

'A week or two?'

'Possibly a bit longer.'

'And Ali is going to be entirely cool with this? You running off and leaving her to "get on with things", as you put it?'

'I think so, if we present it right. You're the one with the PR skills, Tom.'

'Oh, no,' I said, putting my hands up. 'Keep me out of this.'

'But that dev environment is going to be beyond top of the range. She'll be in heaven.'

I looked at Dorothy and frowned at her. 'It's been a long day,' I said. 'Let's talk about it in the morning.'

'OK, but I mean it, Tom. There's a bigger prize out there.'

'It's not over yet, is it?' I said, shaking my head.

'Not by a long chalk,' she said. 'Not at all.'

Through the partition wall, a woman's muffled voice shouted, 'You bastard, Keith! Where have you been?'

'Actually,' I said. 'The first thing we need to do tomorrow is find somewhere else to live.'

Also available

Something doesn't add up about Archie and Pye...

After a disastrous day at work, disillusioned junior PR executive **Tom Winscombe** finds himself sharing a train carriage and a dodgy Merlot with George Burgess, biographer of the Vavasor twins, mathematicians Archimedes and Pythagoras, who both died in curious circumstances a decade ago.

Burgess himself will die tonight in an equally odd manner, leaving Tom with a locked case and a lot of unanswered questions.

Join Tom and a cast of disreputable and downright dangerous characters in this witty thriller set in a murky world of murder, mystery and complex equations, involving internet conspiracy theorists, hedge fund managers, the Belarusian mafia and a cat called μ.

A Mathematical Mystery, Volume One

OUT NOW

Acknowledgements

Thanks as ever to my wonderful family Gail, Mark and Rachel for their support and encouragement. Gail's assessment of *The Truth About Archie and Pye* as being 'much better than she expected' is probably my all-time favourite review. Apologies to Richard Kerridge of Bath Spa University for inexplicably renaming him 'Richard Kerrigan' in the acknowledgements to the early editions of *The Truth About Archie and Pye*. Thanks to the living legend that is David Gerard for giving the crypto-currency and blockchain stuff the once-over; any glaring errors remaining are all mine. David's book, *Attack of the 50 Foot Blockchain* is strongly recommended as the definitive guide to the weird world of crypto-currency. Finally, massive thanks to my editor Abbie Headon and all the team at Farrago, especially my copy-editor Caroline Goldsmith, who definitely went the extra mile this time.

If anyone out there is interested in Fibonacci poetry, there just happens to be one in my collection *Love and Loss and Other Important Stuff* (Silhouette Press, 2017). Oddly enough, it's about nanotechnology and it's called 'Grey Goo'.

About the Author

Jonathan Pinnock is the author of the novel *Mrs Darcy Versus the Aliens* (Proxima, 2011), the short story collections *Dot Dash* (Salt, 2012) and *Dip Flash* (Cultured Llama, 2018), the bio-historico-musicological-memoir thing *Take It Cool* (Two Ravens Press, 2014) and the poetry collection *Love and Loss and Other Important Stuff* (Silhouette Press, 2017). *The Truth about Archie and Pye*, the first novel in his Mathematical Mystery series, was published by Farrago in 2018. Jonathan was born in Bedford and studied Mathematics at Clare College, Cambridge, before going on to pursue a moderately successful career in software development. He also has an MA in Creative Writing from Bath Spa University. He is married with two slightly grown-up children and now lives in Somerset, where he should have moved to a long time ago.

Note from the Publisher

To receive updates on new releases in the Mathematical Mystery series – plus special offers and news of other humorous fiction series to make you smile – sign up now to the Farrago mailing list at farragobooks.com/sign-up.